CHAPEL BAY SECRETS

JULIE SNIDER

MULARD
PRESS

LCCN: 2025917147

Print ISBN: 979-8-9997150-1-2

ebook ISBN: 979-8-9997150-0-5

Cover design by Karen Phillips: https://phillipscovers.com/

Publisher's Cataloging-in-Publication Data

Names: Snider, Julie.

Title: Chapel Bay secrets / Julie Snider.

Description: Gold River, CA : Mulard Press, 2026. |Series : Chapel Bay series ; book 1.

Identifiers: LCCN 2025917147 | ISBN 9798999715012 (pbk.) | ISBN 9798999715005 (ebook)

Subjects: LCSH: Secrecy – Fiction. | Friendship – Fiction. | Identity (Psychology) – Fiction. | Healing – Fiction. | Sexual minorities – Fiction. | California – Fiction. | BISAC: FICTION / LGBTQ+/ Lesbian. | FICTION / Small Town & Rural. | FICTION / Women.

Classification: LCC PS3619.N53 C43 2026 | DDC 813 S—dc23

LC record available at https://lccn.loc.gov/2025917147

❀ Formatted with Vellum

PRAISE FOR CHAPEL BAY SECRETS

When immigration, book bans, and identity collide, healing begins with the courage to connect in Julie Snider's *Chapel Bay Secrets* – a terrific book club pick!
— Sharon J. Wishnow, author of *The Pelican Tide*

"Julie Snider's *Chapel Bay Secrets* blends small-town charm with timely urgency, making it both comforting and thought-provoking . . . The world of Chapel Bay is tangible, with its tea shops, wharf paths, and community events, but it's the undercurrent of conflict that gives the book its strength . . . Snider's prose is clear and engaging, balancing suspenseful twists with heartfelt moments . . . It's a perfect choice for readers who love contemporary fiction rooted in community, history, and the fight to let every voice be heard."
—*Readers' Favorite*

Don't let *Chapel Bay Secrets'* sweet coastal facade fool you--the novel brims with depth and complexity. Snider's protagonists face off with the small minded bigotry that so easily co-exist in a small community, uncover past secrets, embrace their truths, and find that sometimes connection is closer than you think. An uplifting, optimistic novel perfect for these times.
—Jordan Rosenfeld, author of *Fallout* and *The Sound of Story: Developing Voice & Tone in Writing*

"*Chapel Bay Secrets* . . . is a tale of secrets, love, and forgiveness, woven together in ways that show how much, in the end, we are all more alike in the heart than we ever believe at first glance."
—Amanda Royal,
award-winning conservation writer and editor

For my wife, Tina.

To all those who have felt unseen and unheard:
Know that I see you. I hear you. I am you.

Injustice anywhere is a threat to justice everywhere.

—Maya Angelou

1

Brenda Kato's stomach churned. Bile rose in her throat. The street outside her office window, so noisy just moments ago, was as quiet as the library stacks on the other side of her door. Her heart pounded in the vacuum of sound, a pain growing as the pressure rose in her chest. She shook her head and blinked, then scooted her chair far back, away from the vile words on the computer screen.

From: Lovers of Literature

To: Brenda Kato, Chapel Bay Library

Re: Author Events/Inappropriate Books

Date: November 18, 2022

Dear Ms. Kato:

As the person in charge of the Meet the
Author events for the Chapel Bay Library, it is
your responsibility to make certain that
authors and books featured are of a HIGH
MORAL CALIBER. In these uncertain and
morally ambiguous times, our families—
especially the children—are in great need of
protection from corrupt, harmful, Un-American
sentiments. We have noticed that several of
your recently featured selections veer toward
what we can only describe as dangerous. The
threat to our way of life is serious. America is
and always has been a nation of believers. But
many among us are hell-bent on taking the
truth out of our schools and libraries.

We, the Lovers of Literature, are here to guide
you toward a more moderate and sensible set
of offerings to the public. Below, you will find
a list of objectionable titles, authors, and
topics.

THE LIST WAS EXTENSIVE. Topics included LGBTQ themes
and authors, tomes concerning Jewish, Muslim, and atheist
people, books written by and about Black and Brown people in
America and—here it was—Asian American stories, including
those about Japanese incarceration. Stories about people such as
her own mother, Toshi. Put into an internment camp in this state,
California. On the so-called "left coast."

She felt a full-blown panic attack approaching.

Stop.

Breathe.

Counting to twenty as she slowly inhaled, then exhaled, she
pulled herself back from the abyss.

～

THIS BRIGHTLY LIT Tuesday in November had started like most other days in the idyllic town of Chapel Bay. Brenda had eaten breakfast—oatmeal with raisins and one slice of wheat toast—then strolled downhill from her blue bungalow to the town's library. Her street was quiet, especially before nine a.m., and she'd felt a calmness settle into her bones as she walked.

Entering the library, she'd removed her sunglasses. As her eyes adjusted to the muted indoor lighting, she'd gazed across the expanse of grey marble floor toward a round oak table just to the left of the circulation desk. The table displayed new acquisitions, behind which stood a light brown three-panel display board. The words, "It's Autumn: Time to Fall for a New Book" blazed across the board in bright orange script.

As Brenda watched, a mother and her elementary-aged son inspected an LGBTQ-themed chapter book. The boy's dark eyes sparkled; he clutched the volume to his chest. Brenda's heart swelled with pride, and she wiggled the fingers of her left hand in a little wave as the two walked toward the circulation desk. She had waited for this moment, hoped for it, since taking the position of library events and acquisitions coordinator in Chapel Bay. That was three years ago. It felt good to see that the diversity ball was rolling, that her hard work was finally paying off.

Still feeling the afterglow, Brenda had walked the short distance down the hallway to her office. Her Nikes squeaked on the recently polished floor, and she'd made a mental note to ask the custodian to go a little lighter with the wax next time. Opening the door, she glanced at the cluttered but cozy workspace. File folders of research material and partially read books sat on chairs and atop file cabinets, yet the small Turkish rug in the center of the room brought warmth and charm to the relative chaos. Green, round-framed reading glasses planted on her nose, she'd sat down in her swivel desk chair to prepare for the Meet the Author event taking place in two weeks. In short order, she had a ton of details to nail down. At a minimum, emails needed to be sent to hopeful attendees, flyers picked up from the printer and posted, and catering decisions made. Would the usual coffee and cookies suffice, or should she spruce things up with cucumber sandwiches? Would enough volunteers arrive to set up, serve, and clean up?

At 53, Brenda had done her fair share of grunt work. As much as she enjoyed micromanaging, she'd leave last-minute details to the volunteer coordinator. Brenda was the show runner. She would need to be in full babysitting mode on the big night, ensuring the speaker's tie was straight, his water glass full, and that he'd be at the podium promptly at seven p.m., ready to speak. A sudden bout of stage fright had overtaken last month's speaker, and the one before had a coughing fit in the middle of her talk.

Postponing the complexities of planning, Brenda had taken a swig of water from her NPR flask and moved on to the less taxing job of reading emails. Her inbox held the usual array of clutter. Then she'd discovered the email that wiped away her feelings of self-satisfaction, sending her into a dark and lonely place.

The email ended with a threat:

> Be warned that attempts to glorify these 'woke' authors and their books will result in protests and possible other actions.

Possible other actions? Like what? Never mind that the last sentence was not grammatically correct.

Thoughts about a recent news article flooded her mind. *What did it say, again?* Brenda took a sip of water, and the gist of the article came back to her. Several community members in Southern California had protested the local library's LGBTQ display during Pride Month. They defaced the display, checked out every book related to LGBTQ people, and never returned them.

Shit!

Shaking with anger, Brenda closed the email and thought about deleting it. She paused, hand hovering above the trash can symbol. *This needs investigating.* She forwarded it to Justin, the head librarian, with a request that he ask the IT department to do forensic research, hoping to learn the origins of the hate mail. After some deep breathing and a walk around the block, Brenda actually got some work done. But her heart continued its rapid beating.

Hours later, she snapped her laptop shut and stretched her neck.

How is it already after four p.m.? Her neck and back popped, reminding her it was high time to go for her run. As she rose from her chair, pulling her whole body to a vertical position, April, the volunteer coordinator, called out.

"Hey there, Brenda! I got your note about volunteers. I'll call the five folks who've offered to arrive early on Friday for setup. I still need to nail down my cleanup crew."

"Okay, great, thanks. I couldn't do this job without you!"

"Well, looks like you're heading out for the day, so talk later?"

"Ok, see ya tomorrow," Brenda said as she put first one arm and then the other into her wool sweater.

Brenda rose and strolled out of the library. Walking uphill, she passed Chapel Bay's new tea shop and bed-and-breakfast, gables and turrets wearing a new coat of paint. The irony of the town's ambience never failed to bring a smile. The 'good old days' in this coastal tourist town, midway between San Francisco and San Luis Obispo, seemed more real than Brenda's memories of growing up in Sacramento forty years ago. A vibrant, upscale version of the nineteenth century, sanitized for one's protection. When storms took out the electricity and Wi-Fi, tourists fled quaint Chapel Bay and sought twenty-first century conveniences inland.

As she rounded the corner, the moist air hit her face and seeped into her lungs. Picking up her pace a bit, Brenda couldn't wait to get back to her cottage and put on her leggings, running top, and shoes. She needed to get going. Fog could roll in at any time.

As she opened the front door, Brenda was already planning her run. The marathon was twenty-six days away, and next

Sunday's half marathon would be a kind of tune-up. Today, a tempo run—nothing hard. A moderate seven miler would work fine. Two chilled water bottles nestled into her running belt, she headed out the door for her daily dose of freedom. Cap donned, she stopped to select the run mode on her Garmin watch and began her warm-up mile. Two neighbors waved from their front yards, and she nodded, but kept moving with her goal in mind.

Today's run felt especially liberating. The day's tension melted away as muscles warmed and expanded. Thoughts about the hateful email receded. At her turnaround point just beyond the wharf, Brenda stopped for a long drink. She wasn't looking for perfection. Wear and tear were par for the course. Sore knees, plantar fasciitis, the list went on. Brenda's body carried the scars and stars of the spills and thrills she had taken over the many miles she'd covered. Now, here she was. Middle age was behind her and old age was still up around the bend. May as well make the most of this time, as it wouldn't last forever.

It was easy to speed up on the return trip, as there were relatively few pedestrians on the path today. Such a nice change, as the warmer months brought big crowds to Fisherman's Wharf. Other than this weekend's half marathon, November was relatively quiet by the bay.

Only one more mile to go. Brenda looked down at her running watch to check her speed. At that exact moment, a dog appeared directly in her path. *What the hell!*

"Hey, watch out!" shouted Brenda.

On the other end of the lab's leash was an older guy, tall and gaunt, staring off into space, not even looking at his two dogs. Yes, two! Luckily, the other one was far enough off the path to avoid what would have been a truly bad tangle.

The old guy whipped his head around and pulled the wandering pooch out of her way. *Why are some people so oblivious when out with their dogs?*

The man muttered something—maybe an apology—but she'd already gone up the path. Heart pumping, Brenda rounded the final corner. A dark sedan approached her from behind, lingering for a minute before speeding past her. Endorphins from the run weren't powerful enough to counteract the chill that crept up Brenda's spine. The smell of exhaust made her gag, and for a moment she was afraid she might puke. Heart pounding, she looked around. *Who was that? Why were they following me?* Unfortunately, she'd been unable to get a clear view of the driver. All she could see was the profile of a male wearing a red ball cap. *Was that the person who'd sent the creepy email?*

Ugh.

Pausing at the front door of her house, Brenda felt a rush of lightheadedness. She placed her hands on her thighs and lowered her head until the feeling passed. The table lamp in the front room cast a warm glow through the slight mist. She imagined her piano inside the house and had a quick twinge of guilt for neglecting her practicing of late.

As she slipped the key into the lock, Brenda had a quick flashback to a particular evening in 2010, twelve years earlier. She was a new runner then, in a new relationship. She couldn't help but wish Cynthia was waiting on the other side of the door now, just as she had been that evening in their San Francisco apartment. She wondered if Cynthia even thought about her anymore. *I should call her. She always listened when I was scared. But will she answer?*

JOE WEST WAS QUICKLY RUNNING out of patience. "Well, if that isn't just the damnedest thing," he muttered, rifling through papers atop his scratched wooden desk. His slender frame bent over the pile of miscellany, blue eyes searching, restless hands shoving aside bills and letters.

"It was just here yesterday. What the hell?" Joe sighed heavily, then sat down, temporarily abandoning his search for his cell phone. Chapel Bay might be a small town, but you still needed your mobile to function in life. He'd already given twenty minutes to the pursuit of this loved and hated thing. The scrabble and scratch of two sets of toenails on the hardwood floor brought him out of his funk. Kibble and Bones, the two black labs from heaven (or hell, depending on the day), were ready for their daily walk along the ocean.

How could Joe stay pissed when his two best friends were smiling expectantly, urging him to grab their leashes and get a move on? As he attached the leather leashes to each dog's harness, Joe reflected upon what had changed—and what had remained the same—since he started working as a psychologist in 1977. No cell phones to lug around everywhere he went back then. No expectation that he would constantly be available. No worry that some idiot would steal his identity just by cracking some kind of code in cyberspace—who even knew what that was back in the day? This was a rude time for those in their seventies!

Joe and the dogs headed out of the small white cottage and into the slightly overcast afternoon. They meandered down the uneven sidewalk, interrupted by occasional sniff breaks as the dogs checked pee-mail. As the sharp scent of eucalyptus trees washed over them, Joe's shoulders lowered. His nerves stopped jangling. No matter what, this pungent odor always brought him back to himself, gave him a sense of the sacred tucked inside the ordinary. Joe paused while Kibble marked a bush, and he looked up and over the bluff ahead. This was heaven, a respite from technology, ugliness, and general dismay at the way everything was circling the drain since the 2016 election. The smells, sounds of the gulls, wind blowing off the water—all of it.

The trio crossed the road separating the neighborhood from the beachfront and headed for the boardwalk. They'd traversed this path many times, and Joe knew which spots were narrower and required a firmer grasp on the leashes. Kibble and Bones accepted the harness tugs in the spots where the trail made sharp turns. In the wider, less rocky places, they could lollygag a bit, looser leashes draped across their fur. Joe liked to pause in the flat, open spots also. He often stared out at the open water, watching sailboats in the middle distance, observing barking seals and fluttering waterfowl closer to shore. Aimless thoughts and half-formed wishes blew away with the bay breezes as he relaxed into the languid pace of life at the edge of the continent. Usually, the sounds of the gulls pierced through his trance and brought him back to the walk.

On this day, something even better pulled Joe out of his thoughts. A whale breached right up close to one of the small harbor boats carrying tourists! Whoosh—he could almost feel the spray as its tail entered back into the dark water, splashing those aboard. Bones, suddenly impatient, pulled him to the right. Kibble went behind Joe and nearly toppled him as the leash encircled his lower legs.

"Kibble! Bones! Knock it off!"

So much for being suspended in time. The wind whipped at Joe's collar. It was time to get going. He let the dogs lead him, tails wagging. At least they didn't have to worry about their legacies. Could he be more like Kibble and Bones? Could he just trust that each day would reveal its own beauties? Joe sighed, determined to enjoy the rest of the walk. He was getting hungry. Maybe they would stop at the taco stand on the way home. Better than reheating yesterday's soup.

As Joe and the dogs rounded the bend at Friendship Point, he glanced up at the gray and white three-story Victorian house that overlooked the trail. His heart sank. If only he hadn't allowed his feelings for Patricia Star to get the best of him so long ago. Their difference in ages—she had been over ten years his senior—had made no difference to his heart. If only he could take back the words, the embraces, the kisses.

Her house—this house —was forever a reminder of their indiscretions. *Which was worse, that she had been a client, or a married woman? Why did her beauty lure me into a boundary-crossing relationship?* If only he could have stopped after that one lovely afternoon. If only, if only ... regrets and ruminations were today's special, it seemed.

The heavenly scents of spicy meat, cheese, and fresh tortillas struck Joe's nostrils as he and the dogs continued their walk. The taco stand was just ahead. Joe cleared his throat. Time to put past and present miseries out of his mind, let his appetite take over. There was a short line of people waiting to place their food orders, so Joe grabbed one of the free papers from the newsstand to read while he waited.

Opening it to the local events page, he nearly fell over. There, in an announcement for the upcoming Meet the Author event, was a photo of Stuart Franks, a guy he'd grown up with back in Ohio. But the name listed in the announcement was different— Franklin Fargo. *Could Stuart and Franklin be the same person? If so, did he live nearby?*

Stuart had been a talented writer as a young man. He also served time in an institute for the criminally insane in Athens, Ohio. He had thrown knives at his mother as a teen and later attempted to murder two young women who refused to date him. *Is he really cured?*

As a trained psychologist, Joe knew that the odds of overcoming problems such as Stuart's were extremely thin. Joe furrowed his brow and sighed. If Stuart was really coming to speak at the author event, there was no telling what he may be up to. This was most unsettling. *Is Franklin Fargo just a pen name Stuart uses, or is he burying his true identity to escape notice?*

With the thought that Stuart was here, hiding in plain sight, Joe felt a slight chill creep up his spine. Walking back with his bag of food in one hand, two leashes in the other, Joe passed the gray Victorian house once more. He noticed someone—an older woman—standing on the porch. She was holding on to the metal railing and had a rather puzzled look on her face. *Do I know her?*

Something about her eyes, their shape and color, reminded him of Patricia. He remembered Pat had a daughter back when they'd been seeing each other. It had been thirty-some years since he'd seen this daughter, and then it was only in passing. She'd have to be in her sixties by now. *IS it her? Has she lived here all along?* Joe decided it was likely that this lady was Pat's daughter.

How have I not seen her before now? In a town of 15,000, you'd think I would have noticed everyone. Then again, I have neighbors living across the street whom I've never met.

Bones pulled Joe out of his reverie, barking at a terrier that passed on the other side of the bike path.

"Okay, alright, let's get a move on," Joe commanded the two labs. Just then, a runner nearly collided with Bones.

"Hey, watch out there!" shouted the short, middle-aged Asian woman as she skirted the hefty dog.

"Sorry about that!" Joe called after her.

Sheesh. He understood runners deserved some space. But some people ... well, they could be nicer in passing. Runners were so entitled! Joe remembered a few distance runners who'd been clients back in the day. Messes, every one. He picked up the pace, dragging the dawdling dogs back up the path toward home. His walk had set off quite a few triggers.

Approaching his own street, he heard the familiar howl of a leaf blower. The gardener was blowing a carpet of maple leaves into piles. Meanwhile, as if defying his paltry efforts, the trees continued to drop their leaves. They fell one by one, like drops of water into a bucket. No amount of diligent work by any human would ever be enough to drain the bucket. It was as if the trees were taunting the gardener, saying, "You want something to do? We'll give you something to do, you fool. Just try to catch all our litter. Never going to happen!" Joe smiled at the irony of the situation.

As he and the dogs approached the front stoop, Joe wondered whether he was more like the shedding trees or the frustrated gardener. Both, he guessed. He knew how to make a mess of things, that was for certain. Maybe not to the degree that Stuart Franks (aka Franklin Fargo) did.

Closing the door, Joe shook his head. Dinnertime at last.

~

"EVERYTHING IN STORE HALF PRICE, my left foot," muttered Harriet Conley as she pushed open the door of Carla's Classy Thrift and made her way to the sidewalk. Why, Harriet herself had donated six pairs of gently used slacks currently hanging in the shop. Each pair had set her back $110.00, and now each bore a price of $40. Was the proprietor *really* planning on getting $20 for these Ann Taylor classics in a thrift store? *It's not the price, but the audacity!*

The bell on the shop door rang as she opened it. Harriet wondered whether its clang might bring the shop's owner to her senses. Probably not, she decided, noticing that Carla, the proprietress, couldn't even be bothered to look in her direction as she exited the small store. Harriet weaved her way across Barnacle Street and headed for her favorite tea shop. A "big-boned" woman, she was difficult for drivers to miss as she marched from sidewalk to sidewalk.

Once she had reached the other side of the street, she ambled toward the blue clapboard building with its red front door. As she grasped the door handle, it surprised her to see Brenda Kato, the woman who ran the library's speaker series, running toward the wharf. She obviously wouldn't want to be pulled into a conversation just then. Harriet shook her head, lips pursed. *Too bad ... I really would like to speak with her about that dreadful book talk given by the guy who claimed to be Benjamin Franklin reincarnated. God. I'm a better writer than him. That claptrap has been enough to keep me away from the library ever since!*

Harriet looked down at her cane. She mused that her own running days were definitely over. *I'm sixty-three and arthritic. The only 5K I have any connection with is in my bank account,* she thought, a half-smile crossing her wrinkled face.

As she stepped out of the tea shop, Harriet turned to her right to check for cars. There, on the lamppost, was a bright green sign advertising an estate sale. *An estate sale on a Thursday? Interesting.*

She headed up the hill in the direction shown by the sign's neon pink arrow. Once in front of the green and white cottage with 'Sale Today' out front, Harriet realized she knew the woman standing in the driveway. Brown-haired and lean, she'd always reminded Harriet of her mother.

"Hey, Sally! It's been a while since I've seen you. Those roses in the front of the house look magnificent!"

"Oh, thanks. Mom always prided herself on her garden. An interest and talent I unfortunately did not inherit," said Sally, hands on hips.

Harriet glanced around. There in the driveway sat a beautiful Mission-style dining table with eight matching chairs, a Morris chair, and several tables filled with nice costume jewelry. The front door was open, and Sally motioned for Harriet to follow her into the home. Harriet was careful not to trip over the uneven steps as she entered.

"The house still has a ton of furniture, books, and dishes. Not to mention the clothing. I held the sale last weekend and there was so much left over that I thought I'd try a weekday. It's getting a little discouraging," Sally said with a frown.

"You know, friend, I would suggest taking some of the less valuable items and putting them out with a FREE sign at this point. I mean, I know that some in the neighborhood may get their noses out of joint if someone is trying to give things away, but you have every right to do so," said Harriet.

As they were speaking, another lady turned toward them.

"It's not that we have our noses out of joint, as you say; we just care about the neighbors and the neighborhood. We want to maintain our standards around here," said the woman, dressed in a red velour leisure outfit. Her dyed black hair did nothing to hide her age.

"Well, honey, there's such a thing as *too much caring*," replied Harriet. And with that, she turned on her heel, grabbed her cane, and walked toward the door.

"I'll call you tomorrow, Sally. Let me know how much FREE

STUFF you have moved by then!" she said with a gleam in her eye.

There was nothing she hated so much as a self-righteous busybody, and this officious lady personified that title. A good example of a bad example. Well, if she ran into this one again, she surely would be on her guard. No excuse for that kind of behavior!

Harriet ambled down the hilly street toward her Victorian home. As the three-story shingled structure that she'd inherited from her parents came into view, she noticed a loose shutter on the top floor. *I'll have to get Arthur to fix that.* With the next step forward, a coldness settled in her heart. *Arthur died in 2012. I need to call a handyman.* What was the timetable for grieving over a dead husband? Harriet glanced at her Cartier watch and the five-carat diamond ring that had belonged to her mother. *I can hire handymen, pay for catered dinner parties, and buy as much jewelry as I like. But I can't buy love, or make local writers accept me into their fold.*

The sound of a gull squawking brought her back to the present moment, and Harriet unlocked the back door of her well-furnished home. She paused, grasping the porch railing and gazing out toward the bay in the direction from which the gull's cry had come. A man with two dogs had stopped along the path below her house. Tall, wearing a green cap, he had two large dogs in tow. *Are those Labrador Retrievers? Why is he looking up at me? Do I know him?*

Hmm ... probably lost in his own thoughts, as she had been. No big deal. The fog was coming in, and it was time to see about dinner.

Harriet placed her hand on the smooth brass door handle. As she was about to turn it, she saw a woman running toward the familiar-looking man. It was Brenda Kato, whom she'd just seen running on Barnacle Street. Ooh! Brenda almost got caught up in the leashes! He and Brenda exchanged words, though she couldn't tell if they were arguing. *More reasons not to run.* Glad that she could still at least walk, she opened the door and traipsed into her house.

2

D inner was over, and the phone rang, jarring Brenda from her thoughts of Cynthia. She shook herself out of her tandoori chicken stupor, crossed the kitchen, and picked up her iPhone. It was Jonathon, her best friend from San Francisco. *Thank God.*

"Hey honey, did I wake you up? It took ages for you to answer," Jonathon asked.

"Oh JB, I'm so glad you called. No, I'm awake. Just not in a good place is all. It's good to hear your voice."

"What's going on? Last time we talked, you were living the charmed life of a single, middle-aged lesbian with not a care in the world. Do I need to remind you that you live in paradise?"

"Even paradise sucks at times. Today, I got an anonymous email from a nut job, nearly tripped over a poorly trained dog on my run, and just now, I was tempted to call Cynthia. Does that sound like paradise to you?" Brenda switched the phone from her right hand to her left so she could take a sip of wine without spilling it.

"Oh, sweetie. I remember when you and Cindy broke up— wasn't it because she outed the two of you to your mom at your graduation?"

"Something like that. We kept living together for a while, but things were never the same." Brenda trailed off, remembering the descent into relationship hell. *It was a rent-controlled apartment in the city, after all. But she kept telling me to "claim my identity" and be my "true self." But the worst part was that she drove a wedge between me and Mom, and then Mom's cancer returned.*

"Wow, yeah, I remember now. Glad you broke up with that woman. Can you hang on for a sec? My cat is scratching the new armchair, the little shit."

Brenda heard him put the phone down, then shouting in the background. While she waited for him to calm the cat, her thoughts returned to her mother. *Mom was so closed mouth about her early years. She was only seven when her family was taken away to Tule Lake internment camp—the same age I was when I started piano lessons. She spent three years of her childhood there ... I complained about going off to scout camp for a week.*

The phone resonated with Jonathon's dulcet tones once more.

"Are you still there, Brenda? Sorry about that. My new roommate keeps giving Farley catnip, and then all hell breaks loose. I had to throw him into his carrier, and you'd think I was setting his tail on fire for all the yowling and caterwauling he's doing. Anyhow, let me call you back later, OK?" He sounded as frazzled as his cat.

"Sure, I understand. And thanks for the call. I feel better," Brenda said, hanging up. Jonathon had said she lived in "paradise." The small, beautiful coastal town appealed to Brenda's need for safety and solace. After she'd left San Francisco in 2016, the inheritance from her mother's estate had allowed her to buy her small home here in Chapel Bay. She'd heard it referred to as "California's Mayberry," an apt description. Tourists kept the small town afloat during high season, but the artsy atmosphere, ocean views, and walkability made it a pleasant place to settle. *Until today, that is.* At least she hadn't caved in and called her ex.

She'd spent the past six years avoiding intimate relationships. *Attachment causes pain.*

As she put her dinner dishes into the dishwasher, a curious box she'd found in a room of uncatalogued donations at the library appeared in her mind's eye. Like her mother's past, it, too, contained mysteries. She'd brought home one piece of paper from a folder in the box. The typeface looked to be from an old Smith Corona typewriter, the kind her mom used to use.

It was a poem, written by someone called Elsie Star. She read the first half of the poem.

> *Here in these times, and in this place*
> *How can we move on from disgrace?*
> *Our better selves must be allowed*
> *To speak, to move, to lead this crowd.*
> *And yet, it's true, the pain is near*
> *The path is so much less than clear*
> *The eyes, the heart, the mind can fill*
> *With images that cast a chill.*

Being stuck, unsure of her direction—this familiar territory, so long buried, boiled up inside of Brenda. And the disgrace she felt after Cynthia outed the two of them to her mother. *Did Mom feel disgrace when confronted with a lesbian daughter? Did it go back to having a child born out of wedlock? Did Mom feel like having a gay kid was her punishment, her karma?*

As she looked at the poem once more, Brenda bristled at the painful, chilling images conjured up that very morning. The hate-filled email, written by cowards who hid behind a feigned concern for children, was born of pure evil. This was the same sort of thinking that "othered" her mother in the 1940s. Before heading to bed, she carefully tucked the paper back into her book bag. Focusing on her breath, Brenda's thoughts returned to the upcoming author talk. *If I can just get through this event, I can finally rest and refocus.* She drifted off to sleep, but the dream waves were not calm. For the first time, she had nightmares about the father she'd never met.

MORNING BROKE AT LAST. *Today couldn't possibly be as bad as yesterday.* Brenda left her house and strode down the hill, passing the gentrified buildings. She entered the one-story, stone-fronted library, walked through the main room and then headed straight down the hallway to her office. She thrust her right hand into the pouch of her beige canvas book bag. Yes, she *had* remembered to put the poem inside. The memory of last night's dream brought on a wave of dizziness. *Did the hate mail about banning books trigger the dreams about Dad?* The library's computer geeks hadn't been able to trace the origin of the email. They promised to keep trying, but the tone of their email didn't fill her with hope. Nobody seemed to know who the so-called "Lovers of Literature" really were. Brenda felt like a cat at the end of a slender limb. If the branch broke and she fell to the ground, who would catch her?

After shedding her sweater—a green cardigan this time—she placed her shoulder bag on her desk alongside the poem she'd been clutching in her left hand. She sat down, unfolded the faded, typewritten page, and carefully smoothed it so that she could see the entire poem. She read the second half of the poem softly to herself:

Yet here we dwell, like grains of sand
Eroded down from rock to land
So small, so changed, so bent and broken
Hurt by deeds and things unspoken.
The overarching task ahead:
To seek the good and thus be wed
To all who feel the warming sun

And know that truly, all are one
And gratitude, that soothing balm
Can be a way to bring some calm
For goodness past or not yet here
Can touch the soul and dissolve fear

Wow. Brenda was struck by the idea of seeking good amongst broken fragments of one's psyche. Finding Father, the kind-hearted mystery man she imagined him to be. *Until I can know who Dad was, I will never find a sense of calm. I will never trust my heart to a partner, never know true love again.*

Why the new urgency to find him? Why now? Brenda shut her eyes and shook her head from side to side, trying to clear the cobwebs. With a sigh, looked at her computer keyboard, her attention drawn to yesterday's yellow sticky note to-do list she'd stuck beneath the space bar. *Better get Franklin Fargo on the phone.* He answered on the second ring, proof positive that not all writers slept until noon.

Franklin was more effete than she'd expected, requesting a special chair and lamp for the reading. In Brenda's experience, this wasn't the usual sort of request authors made for their readings. She guessed he was just a bit "extra." He became strangely avoidant when asked about his Midwestern background. Maybe he came from a poor family and didn't want to reveal it. *I guess we are all entitled to a few secrets.*

By four-thirty, Brenda was exhausted. She'd staffed the circulation desk from eleven a.m. until one p.m., missing lunch. Starving, she'd scooted a noisy group of toddlers into the children's room, as the "book lady" was out sick. She'd no choice but to read to them. It was a good thing that Maurice Sendak's illustrations were just as lovely as his writing. Hunger forced a growl from Brenda's stomach, and she grabbed a power bar. It was time to go home. No clouds this afternoon; it would be a great day to run by the ocean. Twenty-five minutes later, she was heading out the door of her house, headed for the trail. She took five deep inhales and exhales, did one final hamstring stretch, and began her strides.

The first mile was arduous. She had trouble getting her breathing to settle down. By mile two, though, things had loosened up, and she settled into a relaxed cadence. Brenda liked to count steps when she ran. Counting every fourth step, she made it to 440. One mile. *Ah—this was good.* Brenda looked at her watch, checking on her pace every few minutes. Mile three found her at a ten-minute mile pace, and she sped up just a tad.

Her mind betrayed her, turning to the hate mail she'd received the day before and the strange car that had followed her. *Why me? Why now?* As a kid, she'd stood out as the little Japanese girl in classes of mainly white kids. Now, she was a middle-aged Japanese lesbian with nowhere to hide. The thought that others wanted to ban books about her people, both Asian and LGBTQ—hurt so much.

Run faster. Hide. Escape.

SHIT! Just then, the curb came up and grabbed her foot. Nearly toppling, Brenda righted herself before gravity forced her to the pavement. She took a breath and found herself eye-to-eye with that same old guy from yesterday. Green cap, scuffed leather shoes, blue eyes big as saucers.

"Hey, there! We meet again! Are you okay?" he blurted, attracting the attention of two teens on bikes.

"Oh, thanks. Yes. Got a little distracted. Glad your dogs weren't in my way ..."

Wearing a half grin, the man looked down.

"It seems like that curb could do a lot more damage than

either of these mutts. Better watch where you're going, my friend. You could get seriously hurt!"

"No kidding. Well, I'd better get on with it. Big race on Saturday."

"By the way, I'm Joe. What's your name?"

"Brenda." She tipped her water bottle up and took a long gulp. "I've really gotta go now."

The man stepped back. "I'll cheer for you from the sidelines!"

"Okay, thanks," Brenda replied, with a curt nod.

Great.

Bystanders judged her from their safe perches on the berm of the road.

Don't I already do a good enough job of judging myself?

~

ON THURSDAY, Brenda's right ankle was sore and slightly swollen from catching the curb the previous afternoon. Still, she was determined to stay focused on the upcoming half marathon. By Friday evening, the swollen ankle was back to normal. Her pre-race thoughts were a mixture of a little more joy than fear. The joy, for Brenda, was in anticipating that moment when legs, heart, and lungs all cooperated, and her mind joined along for the ride.

The fear was that somehow those elements wouldn't click into place, would leave her gasping for air and desperate to get to the finish line without dying. In fact, she had run her best time, setting a personal record in the 2018 Chapel Bay Half. She'd missed the one in 2019 because of a pulled hamstring, and Covid knocked out 2020 and 2021. With any luck, she'd rediscover her former fast self this year.

Just before bedtime, the phone rang. Brenda looked at the screen and saw that Jonathon was calling again. *Yay!*

"Hey JB! Thanks for calling back."

"Yes, no screaming cat this time. Honey, why in the world has it been over a year since we've seen each other? I mean, Covid and all, yeah, but *still.* Girl, I need some face time with you!"

"Oh, I feel you. You're the one and only person I can truly relax around. Can you come down for a visit soon? Like maybe next month?"

"Oh, perfect. I need a break from SF. The men I've gone out with here are so pretentious, and I've gotten really tired of being ghosted by Tinder dates. You have NO idea!"

"Sweetie, I do kind of get it. Here in CB, the only lesbians I ever meet are married or are so into themselves that there is no room for anyone else in their universe. Are we too picky?"

"OMG, Bren. It isn't being too picky that got me into and out of three rotten relationships. I just think I need a break. Why don't we get in touch at the end of next week and figure out which weekend works for both of us?"

"Yes, let's. Meanwhile, I'm running the CB Half in the morning, so send me some good energy. Sure wish I had you to train with, like in the old days."

"Baby, I'll picture you running by the ocean with a big smile on your face, crossing that finish line with a flourish. Then the most important part—gorging on delicious pastries!"

"Okey dokey, Mr. Carb. I'd better get to bed now—O'dark thirty comes early."

"Sweet dreams, love. Send me a text of your finish times. I need to be inspired."

"Will do, and thanks for the call."

"Nighty-night, Brenda."

AFTER THEY HUNG UP, Brenda heaved an enormous sigh. Hearing her best friend's voice was the healing balm she'd needed. Fear got pushed a little farther down the running path, and joy got a little closer. This was going to be a great race!

Saturday morning came, and Brenda drove down the hill to

the parking area that abutted the starting line at Fisherman's Wharf. Dawn was just breaking, pink streaks decorating the sky. It was a cloudless morning with a slight wind. Perfect day for a race!

Five minutes passed. It was time to get into the starting corrals. The race organizers had divided nearly four thousand excited runners into three groups, placed according to expected finish times. After the national anthem, the mayor spoke and off went group one. Brenda started up her running watch. The usual "Wait for GPS" message crossed the screen. Two minutes later, Brenda hit "start" and she and her temporary comrades in group two were off and running.

The first three to five miles were always the hardest for Brenda, and she concentrated on not going too fast too soon. The water stops every two miles had never been more welcome. A beautiful blonde woman ran past her, nearly elbowing her as they rounded a curve. *I wonder who that pushy one is?* Next, she noticed a crowd of ten people gathered in a wide area along the side of the road.

Someone called her name. "Hey, Brenda! Good job!"

It was old "blue eyes," the guy with the two labradors, desperately trying to get Brenda's attention. He had a big sign. It read, "You Are All Kenyans to Me." Brenda gave him a nod as she ran past and glanced toward the turnaround point less than a quarter mile ahead of her. Although she would never be as fast as a Kenyan, the thought made her smile.

The second half of the race was nearly all downhill, and the miles went by quickly. By the time she hit the "Mile 11" sign, Brenda had a great feeling about her race time. She looked at her faithful watch and noticed that she was running at a nine-minute mile pace. *If I can keep this up, I may set another personal record!*

Thoughts ran into one another; before she knew it the "Mile 13" sign appeared. A tenth of a mile to go, and the roar of the crowd enveloped her like a warm blanket. *I made it!*

"Brenda Kato just crossed the finish line," said the booming voice.

She gratefully took her medal and bottle of water from the volunteers and looked up at the sky.

"*Thank you, Green Tara.*"

Hmm ... maybe the Tibetan Buddhism she had studied was taking hold.

Just then, the pretty blonde from earlier appeared next to her, ruddy-cheeked from the run.

"Well, people rarely call me 'Green Tara,' but my name IS Tara, and I DO try to follow an eco-friendly path," said the woman, winking suggestively.

"Oh ... um ... you caught me talking to myself ... kinda. Oh— I'm Brenda, it's nice meeting you," Brenda blurted, her feet stumbling in sync with her words.

"Great race, Brenda. Enjoy the rest of your day!" With that, she was gone.

Brenda couldn't shake the feeling that there was something significant about encountering an *actual* Tara while visualizing the great Green Tara, the goddess who had sprung from a lotus blossom. Green Tara, the protectress of navigation, spiritual travel, and a guide toward enlightenment.

What about this human Tara? Was she as mystical as she was beautiful? Brenda sighed, aware of a warmth spreading from her lower belly. *I wish I could have said something more eloquent. Admitting to talking to myself was probably the least dignified thing I've said to anyone, ever ... but it doesn't really matter. I won't be dating anyone, let alone this angelic creature.*

Oh well. Time to check race results. Walking to the results booth, she punched her bib number into the computer.

Overall time: 2:00:17

Pace: 9:10 minute mile

Race Place: 1341/3766

Age Group Place: 32

Gender Place: 477

Two hours, seventeen seconds. She wasn't in danger of getting any prizes or awards, but it looked as if the goal of running a four-hour marathon was still a possibility, maybe even a probability! With that in mind, Brenda walked slowly back to her Camry. *Would this great race time have pleased Mom? Probably not.*

Brenda scooted in behind the steering wheel. *Here I am, still wishing for approval from one who didn't even approve of herself.*

With a sigh, she inserted the key into the ignition and started the engine. *Mom, you'll forever be a mystery to me. Why couldn't you have told me about Dad? What would the harm have been? I asked again and again, and you always cut me off.* Driving off, Brenda realized how remarkable it was that her spiritual longings could morph into a longing for her family. *Maybe it's a case of trying to substitute one type of belonging for another.*

3

Two days before Thanksgiving, Harriet Conley woke with a start, sat up, and rubbed her arms against the chill in the room. But it was more than the cool air, more than the fog outside her window that made the hairs on her arms stand at attention. She felt like she'd forgotten something important, and it unsettled her.

In her dream, she was in a bookstore. An author was signing copies of his book. Harriet blinked. *How is that related to me??* Book talks were fun and all, but if she was honest, they sometimes left her remorseful, and a little envious. It had been ages since she'd felt the urge to write. The short stories she'd published after college were gathering dust inside a folder on a shelf in the study. After Arthur died, she'd stopped going to her book group. She hadn't even crossed the threshold of the local library in over six months. *I blame it on that terrible fake reincarnated Ben Franklin jerk who gave the dumb book talk, but there's something else ...*

She rubbed sleep from her eyes and sat up in bed. *Wait— didn't I see a flyer about a Meet the Author event coming at the end of the week? Was that what spurred my dream?* Harriet rose, dressed, and made her way to the kitchen. She put her drip coffeemaker onto the brew cycle. *Where was the Meet the Author event taking place? Was it at the local bookstore?* No — that wasn't right. Her memory was suddenly less like a steel trap and more like a leaky faucet.

Inhaling the rich aroma of her prized Jamaican Blue coffee, Harriet walked into her sitting room. On the walnut secretary, underneath a magazine, she saw her laptop. She pulled out the black swivel chair—ergonomic, naturally—and with just a little searching, she found Chapel Bay's upcoming literary event. It was only a few days away, sponsored by the library. *Lucky I had that dream!*

Back in the kitchen, Harriet poured coffee into her favorite mug. It was light blue and displayed Yosemite's Half Dome. The cup reminded her of the wonderful trips she and Arthur had taken to Yosemite. *I miss those days.*

As she took another drink of her coffee, Harriet's thoughts returned to the matter at hand. The magic elixir allowed a plan to form in her mind: *Go to the library and find out whether I can help with Friday's event.* The website mentioned that Franklin Fargo was the featured author. *Oh, I know who he is .... Dad did legal work for him in the past. He even came over for dinner once or twice.* Harriet raised her eyebrows, remembering that Franklin had once been quite handsome. The website displayed a recent photo of him, revealing thinning hair and more eye wrinkles than she remembered, but he was still a good-looking fellow! *No harm in looking him up, right?*

Decision made, she grabbed an apricot scone, refilled her mug with coffee, donned her raincoat, and headed out the door. Two minutes later, she found a parking spot in front of the library. As she approached the heavy metal and glass door, a lanky man wearing a hat was opening the door from the other side. He held it for her. The guy looked at her for a second longer than decorum dictated.

"Good morning, milady!"

"Oh, thank you very much!" replied Harriet, glad to be out of the chilly air.

"You're welcome. My pleasure."

She noticed his eyes were a startling shade of blue, almost azure. *Wait ... have we met? Was this the same guy who was walking his dogs on the trail by my home the other day?* Harriet shook off the thought and went to the library's circulation desk. There was work to be done, a plan to be executed.

"Excuse me," she said to the young man at the desk. "I'm interested in speaking to whomever is in charge of this week's Meet the Author event. I think it's Brenda Kato, right?"

Nodding, he picked up the telephone receiver and punched in an extension.

Brenda appeared from the hallway to the left of the desk a few minutes later. Dressed in black pants and an expensive-looking peacock green sweater, she walked toward the desk, a sense of purpose in her long strides. Although she wore a slight smile, her eyes conveyed irritation. Harriet wondered what important library task she'd interrupted.

"Good morning, I'm Brenda," she said, removing her reading glasses. "I understand you have a question." Her tone was flat, matching the business-like look on her face.

"Yes, hi. My name is Harriet Conley. You may not remember me, but we met at one of your Meet the Author talks about a year ago. The one by the man who claimed to be Benjamin Franklin reincarnated? Anyway, I've lived a few blocks from here for years. My passion is books—reading them, writing them, the whole shebang. I heard about your Meet the Author event this coming Friday. This time, you're hosting someone special and I would just love to help!"

"Well, that's wonderful, Ms. ... what did you say your name is?" asked Brenda in a slightly warmer tone.

"Oh, just call me Harriet."

"Okay, then. Harriet, let me put you in touch with our volunteer coordinator. I'm sure she still needs folks to help with serving snacks, setup and cleanup, that kind of thing," Brenda said.

"Is it possible to obtain Mr. Fargo's contact information?

He's an old friend of the family and I would just love to have
some time to chat with him away from the event. I have a spacious
Victorian home, and I know he would enjoy coming over. In fact,
he had dinner there with me and my family many years ago. You
must have his cell number, right?" Harriet asked, left eyebrow
raised in what she hoped was a somewhat authoritative manner.

"Oh, no, I don't think I can give out his private number,
Harriet. I'm sorry, but I need to keep that sort of information
confidential. Perhaps if you help during the event, you can strike
up a conversation with Franklin and make time to get together
that way," replied Brenda.

Harriet pursed her lips. This wasn't going the way she had
hoped. *She's obviously a "rule follower,"* Harriet mused, stifling a
snort. *Well, you can hardly blame her. Poor thing probably has to
answer to a curmudgeon.*

"Oh, I see. Well, could you at least give him MY number?
Here, I'll write it down." Harriet pulled out a pad of yellow Post-
it notes and her green pen.

"Thank you, Harriet. I'll let Mr. Fargo know you came by.
And here comes April, the volunteer coordinator. Would you like
to speak with her about volunteering on Friday?"

"Oh, sure." Harriet thanked Brenda, and walked toward the
tall, slender, red-haired woman who had ducked in from the hallway. The woman asked for her contact information and promised
to get in touch.

I guess serving cheese and crackers is better than nothing. It
wasn't all that Harriet had hoped for, but at least she could start
getting back into the local literary scene. Perhaps even renew her
acquaintance with the dashing Franklin Fargo!

Harriet's head spun with literary possibilities. *Could I write a
novel about people I admire? Perhaps members of this community,
or maybe people from the past who shaped the Chapel Bay of today?*
With a spring in her step, she walked outside. The scent of rain
was in the air. Harriet put her raincoat on and got in the car just
before the raindrops hit the pavement.

A FEW HOURS before Franklin's reading, Joe found himself in his humble abode, taking stock of the situation. He lay down on his bed and sifted through his feelings about the man. He remembered a place two thousand miles away from California's Central Coast, a Midwestern town best known as the birthplace of Civil War General William Tecumseh Sherman. That, and its week-long county fair.

It was a sweltering August afternoon in 1972. Most residents in Lancaster, Ohio, were in backyard swimming pools or sitting in front of box fans, hoping for a summer shower to cool things down. Joe was twenty-five, and he was renting a white shingle house with a large vegetable garden in the backyard. He'd been picking tomatoes and had just come in the back door for a glass of water. The phone rang. It was Gwen, his fiancé. She was crying, and he couldn't make out all of what she was saying. Between sobs, he figured out that someone had upset Gwen and her best friend while they were picnicking in Rising Park.

Minutes later, still covered in sweat, Joe arrived at Gwen's Lancaster apartment. He'd held her in his arms, and she finally calmed down enough to give him the whole story. Stuart Franks, a guy familiar to Joe and Gwen from high school, had appeared at the park while they were eating. He'd walked up behind the two girls and put a hand on Gwen's shoulder. She'd jumped; Franks had laughed at her reaction. He told her he'd never gotten over her rejection of him when they were teenagers. He told her he knew where she lived and would come by one day with an offer she couldn't refuse.

Gwen's friend had pushed Stuart to get his hand off her shoulder. Angered by this, he said he would come for her, too, if both women didn't start giving him the respect he deserved. Gwen threw her glass of lemonade in his face and, as he was wiping his face, another man saw what was happening. The guy confronted Stuart, giving the two time to run to Gwen's new orange Chevy Nova and speed away.

Moving ahead a few months in his mind, Joe wondered if Gwen had called off their wedding because of the situation with Stuart. She never again felt safe in her home and was nervous every time she was out in public. In fact, only a few months later, a court found Stuart guilty of attempted murder. Joe was less clear on the details of the incident, but Stuart obviously posed a danger to people other than Joe's bride-to-be.

Joe wished that he and Gwen had taken their relationship further, getting married and maybe having kids. He ended up marrying another woman in 1974, but they divorced a year later. Would things have lasted if he and Gwen had tied the knot? He would never know, but one thing was certain. Stuart Franks was responsible for turning Gwen from a trusting, cheerful person into a frightened, bitter one. *Is it any wonder that when I saw his picture in the newspaper and read that he was giving a talk in town, my blood pressure rose?*

Still, Joe was curious about Stuart, whom he was fairly sure was the same man as the author Franklin. He'd known Stuart even before the guy had terrified his girlfriend. They'd grown up on neighboring farms in Southeastern Ohio. Neither of their families ever had much money. A few years after Joe moved from Ohio to California, he heard something about Stuart from a mutual acquaintance. The person said an aunt had passed away and left a sizable inheritance. Years later, he'd apparently taken his writing to a new level and made it big in the world of books.

Shaking his head to clear it of the somber thoughts, Joe rose, took a shower, and headed out to the community center for Franklin Fargo's author event. *What do I have to lose?* As he left for the early evening talk, another thought crossed his mind: *I mustn't let seeing Patricia Star's daughter twice this week bother me so much. I'll just put that whole messy part of my life back in the little box where it belongs.*

ONCE NINE O'CLOCK ROLLED AROUND, nearly everyone had vacated the community center, across the street from the library. The volunteers, including Harriet, were clearing the leftover food and drink, and Brenda packed up her shoulder bag. As she put her half-finished plastic cup of punch on the refreshment table, she felt her neck and shoulders loosen. Franklin's reading that Friday evening was a success. The small but appreciative audience applauded at all the right times. There seemed to be a buzz of excitement concerning the upcoming release of his book. Hey, his stuff wasn't to Brenda's taste, but variety was the spice, right? She reached for her coat, smiled appreciatively at Franklin—who had turned out to be less demanding in person than over the phone—and nearly collided with a man beside her.

"Whoa, sorry!" said the man, placing his hand on her back to avoid the collision. Before she turned, she could smell his strong cologne, a mixture of sandalwood and citrus. Facing him, she saw he was tall, with eyes that were a rather startling shade of blue. In a flash, it came to her. *Oh crap, it's the dog guy …*

"We literally keep running into one another! Great job at Sunday's Half, by the way!"

Oh, Lord, will this man ever go away? He's always IN the way!

Brenda smiled, glad he couldn't read her thoughts. "Oh, right, I recognize you. So glad you could make it to the event tonight, Joe. I hope you enjoyed it."

"I did! Franklin and I go way back, and we're going out for a nightcap now that he's finished his reading," Joe said.

"Alright! Enjoy yourselves. I guess I'll see you later—it seems inevitable, considering how often we bump into one another."

Brenda noticed a slender, well-dressed older blonde woman light up like a candle when Joe moved past her on his way to the door. *Joe has a secret admirer.* Brenda overheard Harriet call out to the woman and learned that her name was Sally. Next, she saw Harriet rushing to Franklin to make contact.

Mom would have hated her—she's a woman with no sense of boundaries.

~

BACK IN THE cocoon of her cozy cottage, Brenda poured herself a glass of merlot and sat down at her piano. Fingers found familiar territory on the keyboard and moved nimbly up and down a three-octave scale. A noise outside her cottage—perhaps a skunk rustling through the leaves—interrupted her flow. With a sharp intake of breath, Brenda lifted her hands from the keyboard. *Today marks exactly ten years since Mom passed. No wonder my subconscious is in overdrive.*

Brenda no longer had the urge to play the piano. Instead, she picked up her crystal glass— half empty of wine by now—and walked to the built-in bookshelf on the wall perpendicular to the spinet piano. A long-neglected photo album, brown cover worn with age, called to her. She took it and the glass of wine to the sofa across the room. She turned pages until she came to a scene from the small home she and her mother had shared in Sacramento.

In the photo, she and her best friend Lisa sat at the small round dining room table covered with a white tablecloth. There was a birthday cake between them. Brenda's cheeks were puckered, and she was leaning toward the brightly burning birthday candles. A sugary number twelve outlined in blue sat atop the white frosting. Behind Brenda was a china cabinet, and in the glass doors she could see her mother's reflection as she took the photo. *Oh, Toshi ... you always had that camera at the ready!*

Also in the reflection was a photo of a Japanese man that had hung on their dining room wall. Mom always said he was her cousin, but now Brenda wondered: *Was he really her cousin? Could that have been my dad?*

Closing the photo album, Brenda knew she must not give up on the search for her father. Ten years ago, she lost the chance to get the truth from her mother's own lips. But now, her heart was seeking the truth. A truth she could only hope to find now. So much time had passed since she'd been born out of wedlock, yet she clung to that hope.

Hoping for the truth, something so long denied her. *Was Mom afraid that telling the truth about Dad would put us in some kind of danger? Did someone instill the habit of keeping quiet during her time in the camps? Or was it a case of shame ... shame at becoming pregnant before tying the marital knot?*

Thinking of shame brought Brenda's focus back to the present. She fought hard against the shame her mother had carried, yet being gay and Asian made her a target in today's world. With the attacks on both communities becoming ever more pervasive, she wondered—not for the first time—whether the so-called Lovers of Literature were coming after her specifically because of her identity.

As she pulled her nightgown over her head, Brenda was sad that, even here, in California's Mayberry, hatred found a way in. Yet if the anonymous email writer, the hate monger who was too cowardly to come forward ... if they thought they were going to scare her into submission, get her to go along with the book-banning crowd, they had another thing coming!

Not wanting that to be her last thought before sleep, she turned on the local jazz station and sunk into happier feelings, courtesy of Ella Fitzgerald.

4

"Who's there? Kibble? Bones? HEY!" Joe bolted upright in his bed, sure that he'd heard a knock at the door. He looked at the alarm clock on the bedside table. It was three o'clock in the morning. *Who would be at the door at this hour?*

Joe put on slippers and shuffled into the hallway, then turned right toward the front door. The dogs followed on his heels, now pretending they had heard the sound, too. *Some guard dogs these two were!* The outside light was on. He parted the window curtain to the left of the front door and felt his heart pound against his chest. There, sitting on his doorstep, was Franklin. *What the hell?* He turned the door lock to the left and eased the door open.

"Franklin! I thought we said good night three hours ago. What's going on?" Joe whispered, not wanting to alert the neighbors. Whiskey, mixed with men's cologne, wafted past him.

"Joe, th-thanks for coming to the door! After I dropped you off, I turned around. I ... I wanted to get home. When I got to the turnoff, at the valley, a deer ... it darted in front of my car. Whoosh!" Franklin waved his hand in front of his face. "I swerved, missin' the animal, but my damned car went off the road. By the time I could get a tow truck to show up, two hours had gone by. It was frickin' cold! I called an Uber and, well, here I am. I hope it's okay if I spend the night ... I'm really shaken up. I don't want to be alone."

Swallowing his apprehension, Joe let the still drunken rascal into his house.

"Um, sure, Franklin. I can make up the bed in the spare room. C'mon out of the cold."

Franklin pulled his stout body up from the stoop, nearly tripping over the step as he grabbed the handle of the open door. He stumbled in, and in the dimly lit room, Joe could see that the accident had taken a toll. Fancy hat askew, Franklin was missing one black leather driving glove, and chunks of mud clung to the top of his once-shiny black leather wingtips.

While the dogs sniffed his pants, Franklin removed his muddy shoes, hat, one remaining glove, and cashmere coat. He followed Joe through the living room and into the hallway. As they passed the primary suite and turned into the guest room, Joe flicked on the overhead light.

"Have a seat in the chair," Joe said, rubbing his stubbly chin. This was clearly going to be a night of little sleep.

Within minutes, Joe made up the bed. With a curt goodnight, he left the room. He mentally replayed their conversation at the bar. Recalling that the guy asked Joe to not call him by his birth name of Stuart, Franklin had laughed off the idea that he was trying to hide his identity.

"It's my *nom de plume* buddy, the name I came up with years ago when I got serious about my writing. I'm just used to it, and everyone calls me Franklin now," he replied.

When Joe had expressed surprise over Franklin's success in the literary field, Franklin said, "You need to get out to the bookstore more often, pal! But since my books are mainly popular with the ladies and those who love a good mystery, I can understand it if you maybe haven't cracked the covers of my lovely tomes."

Later in the evening, after they'd downed a couple shots of whiskey, Franklin had been the one to mention his years in confinement. According to him, his youthful crimes resulted from abuse by his mother. They'd been 'misunderstandings,' in his words. Joe wondered whether his former fiancé, Gwen, misunderstood what had happened to her. *Doubtful.*

"Nope, I'm all good now, buddy. Spending time in that hellhole they call a mental hospital in Athens, Ohio, was all I needed to see things clearly," he said. "And those assholes who thought they were better than me? Ha! They should see me now! How many of those hicks have my kind of money? My kind of fame?"

As they had left the bar, Franklin amplified this sentiment, saying, "Getting rich has been nice, but it's only the beginning of my revenge ... certain people need to watch their backs. The time for playing Franklin Fargo for a fool has ended!"

And there it is, Joe thought.

Shaking his head, Joe stumbled back to bed. He'd thought seeing this dude's name in the paper the week before, announcing the reading, was a bad omen. He'd shrugged it off as an overreaction; given it no more space in his head. Now, he wondered ... *WAS* there cause for concern? And if the guy had really changed, what was up with the veiled threats?

LATER THAT MORNING, the smell of coffee and fried eggs wafted through Joe's bungalow.

"Franklin, are you up yet? I have eggs, toast and coffee ready, so come and get it," Joe said in a slightly raised voice.

"Yes, okay, here I come." Walking out to the small, green-tiled kitchen, Franklin nearly collided with Bones, who had posted herself just outside his door. The dog gave him a glare and snorted as he squeezed past.

Joe was at the stove, adorned now in a gray sweatsuit covered by a long chef's apron. Franklin sighed and collapsed onto an old slatted wooden chair.

"It was a complete surprise seeing you at the reading last evening and then getting to have drinks after the event. I wasn't aware you still lived in the area, Joe. Thought maybe you would have retired elsewhere." Franklin pulled the chair closer to the walnut dining table.

Joe looked straight at him. "I've been here for forty years, living in my modest little abode. I didn't know you called this area home until I saw the announcement advertising your event. Last night, when you described your lavish estate in the hills, it made me realize that the income from your books, however much it may be, is not what allows you to live like the Rockefellers. Your Aunt Clara really did you a solid when she made you the sole heir of her fortune."

At the mention of his Aunt Clara, Franklin coughed.

"Yes, I heard about that from someone back in Ohio," Joe said.

Joe offered a reflexive smile, then tilted his head in a gesture of fake admiration.

"Well, good morning to you, too! You act like I'm doing actual harm to the planet, just because I prefer to enjoy the simple luxuries which anyone in my position would want. Is this jealousy, Joe? I think it is! Why else would you be attacking me like this, especially after the night I had?"

Franklin crossed his arms. Joe wasn't sure whether this was an offensive or defensive move. This asshole was getting on his last good nerve.

"The night *you* had, Franklin? The more you drank, the more you talked about your sordid past. It was one lie after another. Do you remember telling me that the knife-throwing incidents were total fabrications made up by your mother to get you out of the house? Saying that the charges of attempted murder of the two young women were 'gross over exaggerations'? It was when you said that the time spent in the mental hospital in Athens, Ohio, was more like a long vacation that I was positive you were truly full of it. Remember, I'm a retired psychologist. I've seen more than my share of people inside places like that. It's no Club Med, that's for sure!"

Joe's face was as red as the ketchup bottle on the table. He sat down, dishing himself up eggs and bacon. He passed the platter of eggs to his guest. A minute passed. Franklin stared across the table at Joe, making no moves to get breakfast on his plate.

"Here, eat something, Franklin," he said, now speaking at a normal level.

"I'm very sorry to have upset you so much, Joe. I only viewed coming to the Chapel Bay area as a fresh start, a way to reinvent myself," Franklin said, now serving himself some eggs. He pierced two slices of bacon from another plate. Grabbing a ketchup bottle, he squeezed a little too hard, and it emitted a loud splurt as the stuff oozed over his eggs. Franklin avoided eye contact with Joe, making a big show of blending the ketchup with the eggs while keeping the bacon away from the mess on his plate.

"Fair enough. I just wonder what you meant when you said that getting rich was only the beginning of your revenge." Joe put his fork down. He realized he was baiting Franklin but figured this was possibly the only chance he would have to see how disturbed the man actually was. Joe's face twitched, and he tried to cover his anxiety by rising to grab napkins from the kitchen counter.

This caused Franklin to stop playing with his eggs. He lifted his head, raised his left eyebrow, and drew in a sharp breath. His exhale was loud, pent-up anger seeping through his fleshy lips.

"I didn't want to have to mention it, Joe, but I have dirt on many people, including you. Now that you seem so obsessed with my past, I feel I must tell you I know about your affair with Patricia Star. I found out about it when I was sleeping with her shortly after the two of you broke up. You should always ask for your love letters to be returned when you end an affair, dummy! I found a rich one in a drawer of her bedside table one morning after we'd thoroughly enjoyed ourselves between the sheets." Franklin ended his statement by slapping the table with his hand.

"I only mention this now because I'm sure you don't want the good people of Chapel Bay to know that a man who has treated some of them in the past, a respected psychologist, breached his professional code of conduct. Oh ... and does Harriet, Pat's daughter, know? After Pat and I broke it off, Pat paid me not to reveal our affair to her husband or daughter. But we never discussed your little imbroglio. Just saying."

Hands shaking, Joe cleared his throat. This was not the bad omen he had imagined. It was so much worse than that! This was a nightmare come to pass! *So much for putting my remorse over the affair with Pat back into its tidy little box.*

He stood, noisily scooting his chair across the tile floor as he rose.

"I have to get ready for a rehearsal of Bach's Christmas Oratorio. Set the bottom lock on the door when you leave."

"Can I send you a copy of the new book, Joe?"

Is this guy for real?

"Suit yourself."

Joe stormed out of the kitchen.

Franklin called after him. "I know you won't ever mention my past again, now that you know what I know about you!"

Joe yelled from the hallway. "Please leave my home. I can't spend any more time with you now ... or ever!"

Franklin picked up his muddy shoes from the mat, gingerly set the lock, and pulled the front door shut. He walked down the street for a coffee, as he had had none at Joe's. There, inside Mallory's Magic Brew, sat Harriet Conley. Smiling up at him, she patted the seat next to her. Franklin sat down with a sigh.

WIND GUSTS WHIPPED FALLEN leaves from neat curbside piles onto the street, and Brenda shivered as she walked up the hill to the weekly Tibetan Buddhist meditation service. Wrapping her dark blue woolen scarf around her neck more tightly, Brenda flashed back to the Pure Land Buddhist services offered by the

Sacramento Buddhist Church. Her mother insisted she attend Sunday School, with its short Buddhist lessons, songs, and games. By the time she reached puberty, Brenda lost interest in these little activities, rites, and rituals. She rebelled and stopped attending the church.

As a Sansei, or third generation Japanese American, this all seemed like forced assimilation, like trying to make Japanese people worship in ways similar to what her Protestant friends did in their Lutheran, Presbyterian, and Methodist churches. It seemed fake. It hadn't even been 100 years since The Immigration Act of 1924—commonly known as the Oriental Exclusion Act— had specified that "aliens ineligible for citizenship," code for Asians, couldn't enter the United States.

Despite the baggage she carried from her youth, Brenda had found herself hungry for spiritual sustenance. Two years ago, a friend told her about the little Tibetan Buddhist temple in Chapel Bay and the kind man who ran it. So, she'd shown up at the yellow Dharma Center one Saturday morning. Although the practices were foreign at first—her mother's church did not offer meditation, for instance—a feeling of comfort came upon her once she learned how to settle onto the floor cushion.

It was a fresh approach, a way of connecting her aching heart with a larger sense of meaning. For a while, Brenda wondered whether she was the only lesbian who attended Dharma services. People didn't always disclose the secrets of their hearts. She'd kept her own heart under wraps as tightly as her scarf hugged her neck.

Now Brenda realized she had acted from a place of fear when hiding her sexuality. *The internees, Mom included, must have had terrible fear as well. No wonder they tried to be like the white people in as many ways as they could, including with religion,* she reasoned. The lure of assimilation became clear. She understood that her fear of being "seen" as gay was in some ways a lot like Toshi's fear of being considered "too Japanese."

Meditation service over, Brenda found herself at the intersection of Garden Street and Barnacle, the town's main drag.

Hunger, and possibly a need for caffeine, beckoned. Mallory's Magic Brew to the rescue. Latte and bagel ordered, she turned from the counter and grabbed a seat at an empty table. Laughter exploded from the table across the room. Turning to see who was having such a jovial time, it surprised her to see Franklin Fargo and that busybody volunteer, Harriet. *I guess they DO know one another.*

Mallory called her order out, and when Brenda crossed the floor to grab her nosh, Harriet made eye contact.

"Oh, Brenda! I thought that was you! Want to join me and Franklin?" Harriet bleated, cutting through the café chatter.

Oh, brother. Brenda's shoulders tensed, creeping up toward her ears. *Did the effects of meditation have to wear off THIS quickly?*

"Oh, that's okay. I wouldn't want to intrude upon your conversation. Thanks, though," Brenda replied, hoping her tone of voice did not betray her inner angst.

"Oh, but you wouldn't be intruding at all!" Harriet said, sweetening her tone.

"Harriet let's let her enjoy her morning meal in peace. She probably needs some alone time," Franklin intoned.

For once, Brenda was grateful for Franklin's snobbish attitude.

"Yes, I think I'll hang out alone for now," Brenda responded, offering a nod and a smile.

"Okay, well, it's your choice then." Harriet turned back to Franklin and their conversation continued. Finishing her latté and bagel, Brenda did her best to ignore the two. Briefly wondering what Harriet and Franklin might have in common, she stood, donned her gray parka and blue scarf, and walked out of the coffee shop. The sugar and caffeine combo revived her, and she could actually smile as she walked the three blocks home to her cottage.

5

Ten minutes later, Brenda's front door sighed its way shut. Finished with Franklin's talk, she could now devote more attention to the California International Marathon. Two weeks from tomorrow—a Sunday—she would line up at zero-dark thirty along with ten thousand others and anxiously await the start of the race. The course would begin across the street from the infamous yards of Folsom Prison, would take her twenty-six miles, and end blocks from the capitol in Sacramento. The email threat was still weighing on her mind, and that on top of the ten-year anniversary of her mother's death could force anyone to run fast and far.

Perched on her living room sofa, she closed her eyes and imagined the moment right after the air horn blasted, signaling the start of the race. The chill in the air—predicted temperature was thirty-one degrees—the smacking sounds of feet slapping the ground as people crossed the start line, the soapy smells of clean bodies as they bumped and edged past her. Sweat would change those sweet, soapy smells to pungent perspiration once the first six miles were in the rearview mirror.

Brenda opened her eyes and looked down. Under her feet

were oak floorboards milled from trees that possibly once stood just miles from where she sat. She flexed her toes and felt the support of the earth underneath her, the platform upon which daily life played out, the giant stage that hosted acts good and bad. She repeated the Metta phrases from her Buddhist training.

> May I be safe
> May I be well
> May I know peace
> May I know joy

She sent these wishes out to her friend Jonathon, to coworkers at the library, to people in the community, and finally to all beings. Brenda's sangha frowned upon selective compassion. With effort, she included Harriet, Joe, and Franklin in her prayer. Devotions complete, she placed her hands together and touched her lips and then her forehead. She stood and rotated her neck several times. After stretching quads, hamstrings, and hip flexors, Brenda grabbed her hat, water belt, phone, and keys and headed outside. The early afternoon sun was making an appearance, and shafts of light struck the grass, spreading out like angel wings. The wind had dialed itself back a notch, and the temperature was neither too hot nor too cold. Nature was full of reminders of why running was such a welcome change, a glorious escape from everyday life as she strode down the block. The sight of blue, white, and green cottages and the briny scent of the ocean brought her fully into her body.

As she came to the end of the first three miles, Brenda congratulated herself on not going out too fast. Like all marathoners, she knew nerves could force her to push too hard at the beginning of a race, spelling trouble later on. Best to practice patience now, during these last training runs. As if acknowledging her wise moderation, a flock of gulls shrieked overhead. Just beyond the tide pools, Brandt's cormorants strutted atop protruding granite rocks, clearly disinterested in humans and their mile times. Turning away from the flock, she reciprocated their ennui. Patience ... not Brenda's strong suit. A trait well worth honing, though, and not only with her running. At least the physicality of running gave consistent, obvious feedback. There were causes, and there were effects. Go out too hard, burn out before the end. *Why can't the rest of my life be so simple and obvious? How can I ever know when I should reach for lovers or friends, and when to hold back?*

Frowning, she had a realization. *I always hold back as a default mechanism.* She thought about Tara, the pretty runner she'd seen at the half marathon. *I hope I see her again, and don't act like a crazy person the next time.*

At mile five, Brenda paused for a swig of water and gazed across the expanse of sun-splashed water. Boats out on the bay with their multicolored sails moving in concert with the western gusts of wind; small, drab fishing boats; white cruise boats full of tourists hoping to see humpback whales, sea lions, otters—all formed a lovely matrix of life atop the waves. Fully warmed up, she was impervious to the wind coming in off the water. She took a deep, cleansing breath. *Life is good!*

Brenda saw she'd been running for 47 minutes. Satisfied with her pace, she stretched her neck and shoulders, drank in the fresh air, and headed back the way she had come. By mile seven, she felt a bit winded and slowed her pace to a ten-and-a-half-minute mile. Several dark clouds appeared over the foothills ringing the bay. It seemed a good idea to do mental games for a distraction. Counting steps, an old favorite, could get her to mile eight if she went by fours. As she approached the end of the count, and glad of it, male shouts interrupted her step counting. They came from behind, and she could tell they were gaining on her.

The last thing she heard was, "Oh, shoot, dude! You really gonna run into that lady?"

"Haha! Ten bucks says she jumps out of the way just in time!"

THE BICYCLE PLOWED INTO HER, throwing Brenda down with a sudden jolt. The impact slammed her right cheek into the ground, grinding it into the gravel. Black asphalt, the mineral smells of pebbles and earth. Red hot bolts of pain. So much pain.

"Hey, it's Brenda, right? Hey, are you okay?" A deep male voice cut through the sounds of the blood pounding in her ears.

"Oh, honey! What a tumble you took! Can you turn over?" A woman's quivering voice.

"Don't touch her! Call 911! Those young men hit her and didn't even stop to help her up. No telling what her injuries could be." The man's voice.

The conversation continued for a moment, then one set of footsteps receded. Of all the shitty things to happen on a run, this had to rank right up at the top. Painful, embarrassing, disruptive. *Ugh!*

"Don't worry, Brenda. Harriet went to get help. The EMTs are on their way. You must be really hurting."

Well, duh. He knows my name? And Harriet? THE Harriet? Local busybody and eager volunteer about town? Oh. My. God. Saved from her meddling at the coffee shop once today, only to fall prey to Harriet on the running path. *What a shit show!*

The siren, which had started a moment ago, came closer and stopped. Now, the sounds of doors opening and closing, voices of two young men, booted feet walking toward her on the pavement. The EMT began addressing Brenda.

"Ma'am, can you hear me?"

"Mumm. Hurts."

"Yeah, I'm sure. Sounds like you took quite a hit. Mind if I try to turn you over?"

While the EMTs turned her and checked for broken bones, a terrifying thought came to mind. *Oh God ... was I just the victim of a hate crime? Were those two guys part of the Lovers of Literature group? Am I being stalked?* Cold sweat trickled down her back and pooled in the waistband of her running pants.

"Can you sit up, Brenda?" *Oh, now we're on a first-name basis. Great.*

Brenda wrenched herself into a seated position. Small stones fell from her forehead and landed in her lap. *I'm gonna puke.* As she focused her eyes, more horror revealed itself. *What in God's name is my least favorite dog owner doing here? What was his name? Joe?* Yes, she remembered now. Joe, the wearer-of-too-strong cologne, the Friend of Franklin Fargo. *Wow. Just Wow.*

"How's it going? Are you feeling any dizziness? Nausea?" The EMT was talking again.

All she could do was nod. She lowered her head to stop the nausea. *Hopefully, the questions will stop soon. Talk about losing face!*

"Let me help you up. We're gonna take a little ride." This coming from the second EMT. In short order, the uniformed men helped her up. Each took up a position alongside her.

As if this was not bad enough, the way-too-helpful Harriet came trudging across the path toward her, one gray eyebrow arched, hands extended toward Brenda in a helping gesture. *Please don't touch me .... Please don't touch me ....*

"Oh, honey! So glad to see you standing up! The EMTs said they're taking you to the hospital. Joe, can you ride with me? I don't want her to go there alone."

"Sure, sure. I didn't realize you knew my name! But yeah, let's do that," Joe said.

Escorted toward the back of the ambulance, Brenda realized that the injured had little control over their fate once the rescuing sort came along. As the doors closed, she flashed back to the attack. *Will I ever feel safe in my community?*

~

TWENTY MINUTES LATER, Joe and Harriet arrived at Chapel
Bay Community Hospital. Joe wasn't accustomed to finding
himself in these kinds of situations, and certainly not with the
daughter of the woman with whom he'd committed adultery. As
the two entered the front doors, a security guard instructed them
to put on masks and sanitize their hands. "Hospital protocol," he
reminded them. They complied, then walked toward the young
woman who stood behind the admissions desk.

"Excuse me, but we're here to check on a person who was just
admitted to the emergency room," Harriet said, her bracelet
clanging against the desk as she perched both wrists on its black
plastic surface.

"Ma'am, you *REALIZE* that the hospital doesn't allow visi-
tors to the ER because of Covid restrictions," the desk clerk said,
not even trying to conceal her irritation.

Harriet continued her appeal. Eventually, she left her name
and contact information (but not without directing a glare
toward the attendant). As the pair made their way back toward
Harriet's sedan, Joe spoke up for the first time since they'd started
the journey to the hospital.

"You know, I worked here at the hospital before I retired. It
seems they've gussied the place up a little since my departure."

Harriet made eye contact with him across the hood of the car.
"Oh really? So you were a doctor? How nice!"

"No, well, not an M.D., that is. A psychologist. Head doctor,"
Joe said, smirking a bit.

"Well, head doc, it seems we may have to wait for a little while.
Shall we go find a coffee shop and hang out? I don't know about
you, but my nerves could use some settling."

"Yes, okay. Whatever you'd like to get, my treat." Joe smiled,
feigning acceptance of this unexpected situation. He wondered
whether Harriet was flirting with him, very much hoping that was
not the case.

"Sounds great," Harriet responded, getting behind the wheel.

She leaned uncomfortably close to Joe while buckling her seat belt.

They drove several blocks to a café. After ordering, they took their drinks to the table furthest from the counter. Gazing absently out the front window, Joe addressed something that had been on his mind since just after Brenda's accident.

"So, I'm just wondering—you called me by name back there on the trail. How did you say you knew it?"

Joe nervously fidgeted with his napkin, not sure he really wanted to know the answer. *What if she really knows about me and Patricia? What if Franklin has already told her about us? Or is she interested in me romantically? Did she ask around and find out who I was?* He hoped none of that was true.

"Oh—funny story! I don't know if you saw me or not, but it seems we both were at the author event last Friday evening—the one Brenda put on? Anyway, as I was helping put the refreshments out on the table in the back of the room, I heard Franklin call out to you. Looks like we're both acquaintances of his. Also, I saw you recently when you were on your way out of the library, and I was on my way in. But I didn't yet know your name, of course."

Harriet smiled, taking a sip of her drink while Joe absorbed the information.

"Oh, right! I remember seeing you at the reading now that I think of it. Yes, Franklin and I grew up together in the Midwest a lifetime ago. It's interesting that both of us came to live out here on the Left Coast, amongst folks that neither of us would have known if we'd stayed back in Ohio."

Joe pointedly omitted the part about how much Harriet resembled her mother, Patricia. *Best to keep that under wraps.*

"Well, that's very interesting, Joe. I met Franklin when he came to our home here in Chapel Bay many years ago. I must have been in my early twenties then. He had dinner with me and my folks. He was a client of my dad's San Francisco law firm. That must've been just before he received the big inheritance from his aunt. Dad told me about that. Anyhow, it was cool to see him again after so many years. I rather like his books."

"Right. He seems to have kept himself busy with the writing, although goodness knows that he doesn't need to do it for the money. Of course, I AM glad that he's shared his gifts with his devoted readers."

Joe hoped that this little spark of positivity would allow Harriet to understand he wasn't some shallow cad, seeing people through only one lens. He needed a little buffer here, an insurance policy in case Franklin leaked the information about his affair with Pat. He had to be careful not to lead her into thinking he wanted a romantic relationship, however. *How can I find out how much she knows about her mom's extracurricular activities, if anything?*

Just then, Harriet's phone buzzed. It was the hospital, saying they could come pick Brenda up. They rose from the table. Joe was glad to have an excuse to stop musing over Patricia Star, the possibility that he was being blackmailed, and the questions he had about other ways in which Franklin's warped plans might unfold in Chapel Bay.

As they drove away, the sky suddenly became much darker. A bolt of lightning sliced through the sky in the near distance; the roar of thunder that followed caused Joe to inhale sharply.

"Gee whiz! That sounded close, Harriet. It's a good thing that the hospital is just up the street."

Joe noticed that the only lights in the area were coming from the hospital itself. All the homes were dark, and even the street-lights had gone out. What a mess! It was only five o'clock, but the short days of winter meant that dusk was already upon them. The storm had snuffed out any remaining ambient sunlight. Without a generator, the hospital itself would have been completely dark as well.

"Crap, well I guess we can go around to the emergency room entrance and see if we can retrieve Brenda. I'm sure she is more than ready to be set loose from the confines of modern triage,"

Harriet said in a modulated tone, different from her usual devil-may-care blare.

She's worried.

"Okay, well, get as close as you can. I'll jump out and find her."

Joe didn't even wait until the car stopped to release his seat belt. He'd been feeling anxious before the storm hit, and his anxiety was topping the charts now.

"Ok, yeah. I'll meet you at the ER entrance."

Joe zipped up his coat, glad he had remembered to wear the black, water repellent jacket he picked up at the thrift store and ran through the pelting rain. His new leather shoes were getting ruined as he landed in puddle after puddle. Once safely at the emergency room door, Joe opened it and ducked his drenched self into a small alcove just off the entrance. Coming out of the downpour was quite a relief, and the bright, glaring lights of the emergency room felt like beacons of hope.

Noisily sloshing past several rows of plastic chairs occupied by frazzled, sad-looking people, Joe reached a man in light blue scrubs seated behind a plexiglass partition. The employee pointed him toward a seat two feet back from the window. Unwilling to move, Joe lingered next to the scratched opaque barrier separating him from the attendant. The man pursed his lips in annoyance.

"How long do ya figure I'll need to wait for Ms. Kato?"

"Just give me a couple minutes," came the weary response. "She's being discharged."

Resigned, Joe turned away from the clerk and plopped into a plastic chair. His coat dripped water in a semicircle around his feet, and little rivulets migrated away from him and merged with puddles other people's coats had formed. While he waited, he pulled out his phone and checked the local weather and power outage conditions.

No comfort here. Widespread outages throughout the area. Rain expected to continue through the night and into tomorrow. Possible flooding in low-lying areas.

It took another ten minutes for Brenda to appear through the doors that separated the waiting area from the emergency room itself. A bandage crossed one cheek, but otherwise she looked nearly normal, other than a slight limp. Upon seeing Joe, she offered a slight smile.

"Hey, look at you! All patched up and ready to roll!" Joe called out.

6

Every muscle in Brenda's torso cried out as she tried, unsuccessfully, not to limp. Her inner 'mean girl' called out in concert with her muscles. *He thinks I'm someone he ought to comfort; he's put me into the category of "people who need his help," the poor, afflicted members of society. The Great White Man comes to rescue the Poor Asian, the straight guy reaches out a hand to lift the downtrodden Asian Dyke.*

They arrived at the car. Behind the wheel, Brenda saw Ms. Busybody smiling like the Cheshire Cat. *A day for the record books.* Sore body eased gingerly into the heated back seat, the rich scent of burnished leather wafted in the air. *Born on third base, thinking she hit a home run.* Oh, well. It beat having to call an Uber.

Harriet drove them through the parking lot Brenda winced as the car plunged into darkness.

"The latest update on the storm shows continued rain, high winds, and possible flooding of underpasses in Chapel Bay," the announcer crackled across the radio. "Power is out in many sections of town, with no sign of when it will be restored. Jim, the manager of the local hardware store, says that they've nearly run out of flashlights and have just a few ponchos and pairs of boots left. Please, everyone, be careful."

Harriet shut off the radio. Her tone was brisk and authoritative. "Listen, you two. I called my neighbor while I was waiting for you to come out of the emergency room, and she says that we still have power on my street. I'm taking us all back there to dry out. I can heat us up some dinner and find you a set of clothes, Brenda."

Brenda couldn't find coherent words for a response. She had neither the strength to refuse nor the graciousness to accept Harriet's kind gesture. She merely grunted, closing her eyes and sank back into what, even in her injured state, she could only describe as one of the most luxurious and comfortable car seats her body had ever experienced. *Can't go home. Head pounding. How did this happen?*

In the silence, Joe cleared his throat. "Harriet, that is darned sweet of you. I have no idea whether my home has power, but I need to get back to my dogs. How about dropping me off at my place, at least so I can check on the pups, feed them, let them out?"

"That's fine. You can bring them over to my house. I used to own poodles; I kind of miss the canines. Can you find my place?"

Joe nodded.

"Great. Tell me where to drop you, Joe."

"Ash Street, three blocks up the hill from Barnacle."

Brenda suddenly realized what was about to happen. She was going to share space with two large dogs! While still in grad school, a therapist diagnosed her with cynophobia. According to Lynn, the therapist, this condition—a fear of dogs— usually came on because of some trauma involving dogs. That stood to reason. As a toddler, she'd been bitten by a German Shepherd.

Harriet interrupted her thoughts about dogs. "Brenda, honey, I didn't even ask you! Do you have a significant other I need to call? Or a roommate?"

Unable to speak clearly, Brenda was relieved when Joe called out.

"Here we are, Harriet. 416 Ash. Just pull up to the curb. Oh, wow! No lights on around here at all! Just let me out, and I'll grab Kibble and Bones and meet you back at your place. And thanks!"

"Okay, it's just you and me, kid. We'll be back at my place in three minutes. You'll see—getting some food in you will perk you right up and I can get you some Tylenol, too." Harriet smiled at her backseat passenger.

"Um." Brenda had once more lost the power of words.

"Yes, I know you're hurting. Almost there."

HARRIET TURNED the Volvo around and kept her eyes on the pitch-black road as she rounded the corner toward home. After pulling into her driveway, she got out to help Brenda into the house. When she was sure Harriet's back was turned, Brenda squeezed her eyes shut. *This sucks.* Slowly, gently, Harriet walked her up four steps—*why must there be steps?*—and around the corner to the front door. As she entered the foyer, made bright by the grand chandelier hanging from the ceiling, Brenda's pupils contracted, and her eyes burned. Her anxieties returned with a vengeance. Feeling completely out of control of the situation—because she was—she limped down the carpeted hallway behind Harriet and into the kitchen.

The kitchen was a cook's dream. A Wolf range with its characteristic red knobs, a Sub-Zero fridge, gorgeous marble counters, a large center island overhung with what appeared to be the best available cookware ... it was dizzying. For a moment, Brenda allowed herself to let go of her worries and float in an imagined world filled with sumptuous feasts prepared in just such a kitchen.

The moment passed; she grabbed hold of the back of a bar stool, the steel frame cold to her touch. She was weak, tired, and confused. *I want to be out of here, back home, away from the strange allure of this place. I want to be left alone.*

"Please, Brenda, have a seat. You look really pale. Let me heat us up some lasagna and bread. Are you vegetarian? Oh, don't try to talk …. I'll heat both the meat and veggie lasagna and you can choose."

Still dazed from the fall and the sudden onslaught of emotions, Brenda was relieved not to answer Harriet's questions. Harriet walked toward the double refrigerator, opened it, and withdrew two large, covered pans. As she was turning on the oven, there was a knock at the front door.

"That must be Joe. I'll be right back."

Harriet left the kitchen and walked back down the long hallway to the door. As the door was opening, Brenda could make out Joe's voice and the sounds of dogs shaking water from their coats. *Here we go!* Her pulse quickened at the thought of dealing with Joe's dogs once more. Only her extreme fatigue kept her from bolting out the back door right that minute.

"Yes, they were really glad to see me," Joe was saying. "My two mongrels like to make a big noise when they hear thunder, but inside, they're frightened little pups. Thanks for letting me bring them over, Harriet."

The troupe had made its way into the kitchen, and Brenda drew her legs up close to her body. *Oh my God.* Tears welled up in her eyes. She felt panic and physical pain all at the same time. She closed her eyes and clenched her teeth. *Damn this cynophobia! Damn those teens on bikes!*

Joe noticed her discomfort, nodded, and herded the dogs into an adjacent room. He closed the adjoining door.

"I'm just getting ready to put these lasagnas into the oven. I don't know about you two, but I could do some real damage to a plate of food right about now!" Harriet smiled as she placed the foil-covered pans into the oven.

"There we go. In about twenty minutes, dinner will be served. Now, as I was asking you earlier, Brenda, is there anyone you'd like me to call? Any family or friends who need to know where you are?"

Through her tears, Brenda smiled weakly and shook her head. Harriet was too absorbed in her role as cook and provider of shelter to realize Brenda still couldn't muster the ability to speak. Brenda hoped the inquisition was over for the moment.

"Ok, well, come with me. Let's get you cleaned up and into dry clothes. I'll show you where the guest bathroom is, and I have some sweats that ought to fit you."

ONCE BRENDA WAS in the shower, Harriet placed underwear, sweatshirt, and sweatpants on the small antique walnut table outside the bathroom. She stood for a moment, enjoying the sweet smells of soap mixed with the alluring aroma of lasagna. Closing her eyes, she hugged herself. A sense of ease overtook her, an unexpected wave of happiness bubbling to the surface. It was wonderful, this energy of other people in her large, empty home. Harriet paused another minute, enjoying the deliciousness of it all.

Thoughts crowded Harriet's brain as she took the steps down to the first floor. *What would Mother have thought about my guests? She likely would have raised an eyebrow, tilted her head to the left, and used her brown eyes to burn a hole right through me. Well, guess what, Mother? I'm doing it MY way now, and there's nothing you can do about it. Not one damned thing!*

"Hey, that Italian food smells pretty good," Joe said from the kitchen, interrupting Harriet's inner monologue. "With all the stress of the accident and then the storm, I'd forgotten all about dinner. But I'm starving!"

While they waited, Harriet took a salad out of the fridge and placed a loaf of garlic bread in the oven to warm. She turned and saw Joe sitting at the small table in her breakfast nook. He looked tired and sad. This may be a good time to get to know him better; she could definitely use another friend. They hadn't finished their earlier conversation in the coffee shop, and she had more questions.

"So—how long have you lived in Chapel Bay, Joe? Do you attend many of the author events around town?"

Joe furrowed his brows and gave a half-hearted smile.

"Oh, I've been here a good while. Moved here from Ohio when I got the job at the hospital—let's see, that would've been forty years ago or so. But no, I've not been active in groups or clubs. Mostly keep to myself."

Harriet rose to look in the oven. The main courses were ready to come out. The air in the kitchen—already filled with aromas of cheese, tomato, and spices—became even denser, headier, and more intoxicating once the garlic bread emerged moments later. It was as if they'd been walking through the woods, enjoying the fall foliage, and suddenly came upon a secret, sunlit sanctuary. Harriet forgot about the day's travails and allowed herself to be drawn into a state close to delirium.

"Wow, I don't think I've been this mesmerized by the prospects of a meal in a long time. If that tastes even half as good as it smells, I may go into a food coma," Joe remarked, expressing her exact thoughts.

"Haha. Well, not to brag, but cooking is kind of a hobby of mine. I usually don't have something like this at the ready, but you folks came along at just the right time," Harriet said, aware that her pride came through in her tone of voice.

At that moment, they heard Brenda's uneven footsteps as she hobbled downstairs.

"Brenda! C'mon over and grab a seat," Harriet called out.

Brenda complied. It was a time for eating, not talking. Once they'd had their fill, silence settled over the group. A clattering sound interrupted the quiet. It came from outside the kitchen door. The lights flickered off and on, and rain pelted the windows. A car alarm went off, and the dogs scratched at the door separating them from Papa Joe.

"Lord, that's a big gust." Harriet ran a hand through her short gray hair. "I don't think I want to drive either of you anywhere during this storm. I honestly wouldn't feel right about sending you to your homes, with the risk of falling tree limbs and such. My shutters are already whining in the wind, and who knows how long it will rage."

"Ok, I'd better go hang out with the labs," Joe said. "I noticed that you have a sofa in the study. Is there a blanket I can use?"

"Oh, sure. It's a sleeper sofa, and I'll get you a set of sheets and a couple of warm blankets," Harriet offered. It was the least she could do, under the circumstances.

"Brenda, I already made the guest bed up. Do you think you'll need anything else?" Harriet asked.

BRENDA NEEDED A LOT ELSE. She needed to escape from this uncomfortable closeness with two strangers. She needed to find her sense of independence again. It had been eroding ever since she'd met these two, with their cloying and annoying intrusiveness. Her new vulnerability made her aware, like never before, that she didn't belong in Chapel Bay. She needed to be somewhere less small townish, where she could find more Japanese Americans, more lesbians, more of her people. *I need to find my family.*

"No, I'm good, thanks," she said, answering Harriet. There was no use trying to explain something she barely understood herself.

As she walked back through the kitchen and down the hallway, Brenda had a sense of being outside of her body. She imagined she was watching herself take one step at a time, almost in slow motion. Up the stairs it walked, onto the landing, down the hallway to the second door on the right.

"How did I get here?" She asked aloud, as though her other self would answer. Other self remained silent.

Brenda closed the door and flipped on the overhead light. She walked toward the queen-sized bed and pulled back the floral print bedspread. Plopping her body down on the soft green cotton sheets, she turned toward the bedside table. Here, inside a gold frame, was a picture of what must have been a teenage Harriet with a tall, attractive dark-haired woman in her mid-thirties on one side and a shorter man with curly brown hair on the other. Her parents, most likely. They were in summer clothes—shorts and T-shirts—and all three were grinning. *What would it have been like to grow up with two parents?*

Brenda shook her head to clear it of this fantasy world, then rose to turn off the overhead. Her hip joints protested this change in position, grating like unoiled hinges on an old door. Brushing teeth sounded like a good idea, but that required too much work. She turned off the light and headed back to bed.

Sleep came quickly, but not gently. Within minutes, Brenda fell into the sort of dream she hated. Shifting in time and form, she was suddenly her mother, age seven, in the Tule Lake internment camp. As Toshi, she was attending a Young Buddhist Association meeting, holding a small book or pamphlet about the life of the Buddha.

Looking around the meeting room—a small, drafty place made of rough boards—she was suddenly all alone. Sounds of people crying out filtered through the chinks between the boards. She looked down at her hands. The pamphlet had become a bloody handkerchief. Suddenly, she was no longer Toshi, but a seven-year-old Brenda. She ran from the room, crying, "Get me out of here! I want to see Dad!"

Jerking awake, heart pounding, breath coming in gasps, she said, "Where am I? How did I get here?" Her gaze came to rest on the harsh, red numbers on the digital clock next to her. Three a.m.

After a minute or two, it came back to her. She was in Harriet's guest room. A storm had blown in. Two men riding bikes had knocked her down. The hospital visit, the strange setting, being held captive by well-meaning people—it was no wonder that her subconscious had churned up visions of the internment camp her mother had endured for three years during World War II.

This dream—another of her recurring nightmares—was a stone in her shoe, reminding her that Japanese Americans had been unwanted in this country for many years. In a rare moment of openness, Mom had revealed that her grandfather, Toshi's dad, was in a seperate stockade within the Tule Lake camp compound. Surrounded by a twelve-foot-high beaverboard wall, the guards had forced him and several hundred other men in six barracks to live in tents. No visits, no medical care, no mail.

Brenda didn't know how long grandfather suffered this inhumane treatment. She wasn't even sure what he had done to merit such treatment. Truthfully, nothing about the camp was the least bit humane. It was a prisoner-of-war camp. This was incarceration, not internment.

The rain and wind pounded against the bedroom window. Through the wooden shutters, she could see the upper limbs of a pine tree flailing. She glanced at Harriet's family photo once more. From deep inside, a sense of despair boiled up, weighing her down. She tried to take a deep breath, but only quick, shallow gasps emerged from her lungs. Brenda felt herself flailing, uprooted, disconnected from all sense of belonging. *Will I ever know my origin story?* Before she had another thought, sleep pulled her into its embrace.

7

S unday morning arrived. The storm was finally over. Shards of daylight cut through the window blinds, and Brenda's eyes popped open at the painful intrusion. Once more unsure of her surroundings, fear grasped her reptilian brain. Her heart skipped a beat. This wasn't her queen-sized bed. These walls weren't the light blue of her bedroom walls. *Oh, right. I'm at Harriet Conley's house. I'm a hostage. Shit.*

So many thoughts and memories flooded her as the result of Saturday's mayhem. She closed her eyes again. Pain radiated through her body and came to rest in her very soul. The physical discomfort unloaded another, deeper ache. Evil twins troubled her mind, two time periods linked by prejudice and hatred. Two arrows shot from the same quiver.

It is February 1943. The U.S. government orders all internees in Japanese American concentration camps to fill out a thirty-question form. It includes questions about family history, relatives living in Japan, and any foreign travel. Two questions—No. 27 and No. 28 — became the match that lit a fuse, a mark of "disloyalty" in the eyes of the War Relocation Authority.

It is February 2016. She sits across the table from the agent at the title company, already tired from signing her name to so many documents. The bright side: Her very own little home awaits her! Chapel Bay is going to be HER home now. *It's about time! I'm forty-seven years old. American Dream, here I come ...*

"Brenda, we're almost finished. Just a few more pages to sign," says the redheaded agent with twinkling blue eyes.

"Oh, great. This is a lot. Hey, wait a sec. I'm looking over the deed here. What is this part about 'only persons belonging to the Caucasian race' allowed to buy the property?"

"Oh, that's just something from a hundred years ago. It isn't enforced. In fact, I'm pretty sure I heard something about legislation coming through that'll require that language to be removed." The title agent says, looking sheepish.

"Why is this still happening? It's 2016! Is this only something particular to Chapel Bay?" Asks Brenda, brows furrowed.

"Oh, no, I'm afraid not. I've worked in Fresno, Sacramento, and Salinas before coming here. The older property records in lots of neighborhoods in those places read the same way. It's a real shame ."

Oh, God. The "model minority." That's what they call us, thinks Brenda. *Be nice, quiet, studious. Don't complain, don't make waves. You will be successful and won't need any help to achieve success. And how does this work? If it ever did work, it isn't working now.*

Oh, what's that? You say you aren't "that kind" of Asian? How did that work for the Chinese Americans during World War II? The ones who wore buttons saying, "I'm Chinese," hoping not to get beaten up, considered Japanese?

Three quiet knocks brought Brenda out of her reverie and back to the present. Harriet let her know breakfast was ready. Brenda was happy for the interruption. Half an hour later, Harriet drove her back to her cottage.

Once inside her house, Brenda called Jonathon. He could usually pull her out of her doldrums. Sure enough, hearing his voice did her a world of good. They agreed to meet up at the California International Marathon and would share a hotel room in downtown Sacramento for the marathon weekend.

Feeling much more like herself, Brenda made a cup of tea and pulled out a mystery novel she'd just purchased. After the upsetting Saturday she'd just endured, she definitely deserved some down time.

DAYLIGHT WANED, and it was time to get ready for the big performance of Bach's Christmas Oratorio this Sunday evening. Joe fumbled around his bedroom, frustration brewing. *Where in the hell were his pants?* Not in the closet. Not on the bed. Not over the desk chair. While he searched, that dumb Christmas song thrummed through his head: "Four calling birds, three French hens, two turtle doves ..." AHA! ... "And my tux pants hanging on the hall tree!"

Once he'd fed the dogs and donned his shiny black shoes, Joe headed out the door and made his way to the car. He hoped that all the practice time put in would pay off tonight as he sang with the chorus. Pulling into the parking lot of Chapel Bay Presbyterian, Joe saw the spaces were filling up. *Glad I'm early.* Two double-bass players pulled their SUVs into spots closest to the back door of the church. One of the two, a tall, dark-haired woman, greeted him as she was extracting her instrument from the back of her vehicle.

"Joe! The chorus sounds terrific! I haven't performed this piece since 2010, over in Carmel. You guys are just as good—better, even—than the Carmel Bach Choir," she said, turning toward him with a smile.

"Why thank you. It's good to have you over in our neck of the woods again. What's it been ... three years? And the orchestra is in great shape. Hey—any chance you'd like to have lunch sometime over the holidays? It must be a little lonely around the house now that Jacob has gotten married and moved out," Joe said, walking alongside the bass player.

Joe opened the back door of the church for his friend. He flashed back to a long lunch they'd shared just after her divorce several years ago. *Could there be a chance of more nice times together?* He really wanted to find a pleasant woman, somebody to wine and dine.

"Oh, that's so kind of you, Joe. Let me check and get back to you, okay? The kids are arriving next week, and I haven't done a thing to get the house ready yet," she replied.

"Right, that makes sense. I'll wait to hear from you," Joe replied. This clearly wouldn't go anywhere.

As he went down the steps to the green room, Joe felt a thickness in his throat and blinked away tears. Was he too old to get back into the dating game? Retired string players lost their calluses, wind players lost their embouchures, and old baritones just fell out of pitch. His singing voice still held up, but evidently his ability to attract women had fallen quite flat.

The three-hour performance earned a long and loud applause. Walking out of the hall, Joe's thoughts turned to his personal life once more. *Which parts of my life would bear up under public scrutiny? When all's said and done, could they make a mosaic of my best compositions?* A hand on his arm startled him, and he flinched.

"Oh! Oh, hello, Harriet! It looks like we've both recovered from that awful storm," Joe said, turning toward her.

"Joe! Yes, that was really something. But what a wonderful performance! I didn't know you sang! My friend and I were just blown away by the beauty of that piece. Congratulations!" Harriet enthused, talking a mile a minute, per usual.

"Thank you! You have a lovely holiday, Harriet," Joe replied, smiling as he unlocked his gray, late-model Honda Civic.

Harriet nodded, smiled back, and headed toward her own car, nearly careening into the oboist as she walked forward while turning her head to the side.

Now there's a woman who is making a unique contribution to the world. Oh well, she's harmless, and it takes all kinds. That's what his Grandpapa Wells always said.

Seeing Harriet again brought on a torrent of unwelcome thoughts. He sat in the driver's seat and let the thoughts tumble forth. In the many years since Joe and Harriet's mother were intimate, he never dreamt he would find himself inside that same house. A collision on the trail, together with a bad storm, had forced him to confront old feelings he'd wanted to put out of his heart. In some ways, time hadn't altered the grand home. The gabled roof and finials still looked the same. A rich, wonderful smell of old books still permeated the study. The hardwood floors still gleamed. The kitchen, though, now wore bright yellow where it once sported pale green. There were beautiful new appliances, too. Although thirty years had passed since the indiscretion, the sense of guilt was as fresh as if the love affair had happened yesterday. Added to that, the threat posed by Franklin made him nervous as a cat.

Apparently, it was time for the "head doctor" to deal with this mess. *Medice, cura te ipsum:* Physician, heal thyself. Joe always thought that was a fine piece of sarcasm, but the quaint expression suddenly took on a fresh meaning. Taken together with Franklin's threat of blackmail, his nerves were a jangled mess. He reflected on his last conversation with Harriet. Harriet had mentioned Franklin again, and it made Joe queasy picturing the two of them getting chummy. He guessed she was lonely, but still … he wanted to warn Harriet off of Franklin without seeming to be too much of a jerk. He'd settled on telling her that Franklin wasn't who he appeared to be. Harriet seemed to think this meant that Franklin was writing under an assumed name, which was true but wasn't the whole truth.

When she asked why that mattered, Joe responded by saying, "Oh, you know. Sometimes writers live in a fantasy world and have trouble separating truth from fiction in their own lives. Just be careful; I wouldn't want you to get burned by getting too close to his flame …"

At that, Harriet had blushed. *Was she attracted to Franklin?* Joe could hardly bear the thought.

Now that Joe had flushed Franklin's little blackmail plan out of the proverbial bushes, he needed to learn how much Harriet knew about the affair. While putting his car in gear, he thought, *it'll take a much more delicate approach than the one I used on Franklin, that's for sure.* All he could do, he realized, was to accrue brownie points with Harriet in whatever way possible, just in case she found out—or was told—about him and Pat. That, and pray.

Looking at the steeple of the Presbyterian Church in his rearview mirror, he wondered if he even remembered how to pray.

8

The next week and a half flew by. By the Wednesday before Marathon Sunday, Brenda felt ready to race. She'd been training, not overdoing it, and her sore muscles and bruises had healed. The good-sized scar on her chin would always serve as a reminder that life could dish up some real unpleasantries. Walking to work, she smiled at the idea of overcoming life's difficulties.

"I'm tougher than people think I am," she muttered under her breath, hoping that was true.

By the end of the day, she was off for a quick run before teaching her only piano student at seven. The run went well, and after a shower and a light dinner, Brenda drove across town to teach young Michaela Muramoto.

"Oh, hi, Brenda, c'mon in," said Michaela's mom, Jenny, smiling as she opened the front door.

"Thanks! Is the little prodigy at the piano?" Brenda asked, taking off her coat.

"You know she is! And she actually practiced her études this week. I enjoy seeing the progress she's making, thanks to your instruction, Brenda."

Jenny wore the unmistakable look of the doting parent, and

her enthusiasm was contagious. Brenda sat down in a straight-back chair next to the piano bench, and the lesson began. Forty-five minutes later, Brenda patted Michaela on the shoulder. "Good work on the Mozart sonata, sweetie. Keep working on the parts which make you cross one hand over the other, and don't forget to start slowly, with the metronome."

The ten-year-old grinned and waved goodbye before jetting off to do homework in her room. Brenda heard her bedroom door close with a click. She grabbed her coat and bag from the blue armchair chair across the room. Walking back through the living room toward the front door, she couldn't help but overhear a conversation between Jenny and Scott, Michaela's parents. They were in another part of the house. The kitchen door muffled their voices, but she caught parts of the exchange.

"What do you THINK I said, Jenn? The child is only ten, for Christ's sakes. She hasn't even met any gay people. How in the world could she know what her own sexuality is at this point? I told her we would discuss this in a few years, once she has a chance to really understand herself better," Scott said, his voice cracking with emotion.

"You're overreacting, honey. Kids today grow up faster than we did. There's so much more information in books, on TV, on the internet. Let's just see if she brings it up again. And I can always talk with my sister. Her best friend is a lesbian ...."

Scott cut her off. "Don't you think it's enough that she's bira-cial, Jennifer? It's not like we live in Berkeley, where every other kid is being raised by queer or trans parents."

Hoping that her footsteps were not as loud as her heartbeat, Brenda walked out the door. So many thoughts filled her head. *Poor kiddo. She's got nobody to talk to who really understands.* Brenda was angry that people still treated LGBTQ family members like damaged goods.

Once she was back in her Camry, Brenda searched the internet for the nearest Parents and Friends of Lesbians and Gays (PFLAG) office. *I may call them in the morning.* There was no way she wanted Michaela to suffer like she had suffered. *Would Jenny Muramoto be open to attending a meeting? She seems so proud of Michaela.*

Brenda caught herself. She realized she had overheard a private conversation between Scott and Jenny. She couldn't act on this information. "I hope Michaela knows she can talk with me," she said aloud. Then she had a second realization. *I'm not even "out" to most people around here, and definitely not to that family. How would she know to come to me?*

LINED up with seven thousand of her "best friends," Brenda shivered in the pre-dawn drizzle near the famous Folsom prison. The California International Marathon was about to begin. *Should I have peed again? Is my water bottle secure? Can I reach packets of Goo in my running belt?* She stretched her quads once more, and just then: "Ten, nine, eight, seven, six, five, four, three, two, one. GO!"

The air horn blasted through the damp air, and fourteen thousand feet thundered across the wet pavement. When it was Brenda's turn to cross the rubberized starting mat, she remembered to start her watch. There was no other way to keep track of her pace as she pounded through the 26.2 miles.

Just past mile five, she rounded a corner behind a group of talkative women. Sipping Gatorade handed to her by a volunteer at an aid station, she threw her cup to the pavement. An approaching siren blared from a side street to her left. The women in front of her slowed and moved toward the right, giving a downed runner and his friend some room as the ambulance pulled up. Mortality raised its ugly head: *I hope that guy's okay. Will I make it to the finish line alive?*

By mile ten, Brenda popped her second energy block into her mouth as she wove her way through the narrow streets of Old Town Whispering Oaks. Another aid stop, another band, and lots of people with signs cheering on family and friends. Half-wishing that she had a posse, too, Brenda distracted herself by going over her bucket list of things she wanted to do before she died—other than this race, of course. Hang gliding from cliffs near the ocean, hearing a live performance of Mahler's ninth symphony, learning to cook French food, going on a month-long meditation retreat, learning to speak Japanese (this one triggered slight guilt), starting a literacy program for needy kids. And the most important thing: finding her dad. So many questions: *Was Dad from Sacramento? Did he ever walk the streets I'm running? Did he stand up to the bullies who called Japanese names and incarcerated them in the 1940s? Would he have stood up to today's anti-Asian hate mongers?* As much as she wanted to understand her full family history, she carried fears about what she might discover. *What if Dad was not the kind, hard-working man Mom wanted to believe he had been? After all, what kind of man abandons his pregnant girlfriend? Or maybe he didn't know she was pregnant....*

The distracting thoughts helped time pass quickly, and the halfway point caught Brenda by surprise. Checking her watch, she was very pleased to note that she'd run thirteen miles in under two hours. Shoes heavy and wet, she smiled through the yuck factor. A sip of water, a packet of Goo, and it was time for part two!

At mile eighteen, she noticed slight fatigue and some cramping in her right calf, but the endorphins were in full swing; ignoring a little discomfort wasn't a big deal. Mile twenty—known as The Wall—found more than a few runners stopped as they "bonked." Glycogen stores were gone, and their legs just wouldn't carry them further.

"Oh, God, Oh, God." Brenda panted, climbing the slight ascent—which felt like a straight-up stair step climb—across a bridge spanning the American River. Passing Sacramento State, heading into East Sac proper; this was the final frontier. The last four miles went by in a total blur. One irritating sign pissed her off, however. It read "You're Almost There." *Didn't that fool know that made runners want to quit?* Two miles to go was NOT "almost there." *Imbecile!*

And then one mile to go! Would she do it? Was this really almost over? Suddenly, thoughts of chocolate flooded her brain. Dove chocolate. Melting in her mouth. She tasted its creamy richness, felt the sweet liquid on her tongue, the imagined buttery sensation nearly making her trip over her own feet.

Oh. Oh. Oh. She did it! The finish line loomed ahead—one side for women, the other for men. Soaked to the bone, she crossed the timing strip. Looking up, she saw the sweetest numbers ever to be displayed on a timing clock.

Time: 3:58:15

Pace: 9:06 min/mi

"Brenda Kato, Chapel Bay, California," came the announcement.

Tears streamed down her face, adding to the slick of sweat and rainwater. She didn't even see the smiling volunteer on her right. The young woman took her hand and placed the circular ribbon around an outstretched arm. Someone to her left gave her a bottle of water. Arms encircled her, and a familiar minty scent broke through her temporary delusion. Jonathon's bright brown eyes met hers. He was holding an umbrella and pulled her underneath its protective cover.

"Honey, you did it! I'm so proud of you! We are gonna celebrate tonight, girlfriend," he said, lips curving up over his impressively white teeth.

"It was exhausting, JB. I can't even feel my legs anymore. And I may throw up ..." Brenda's voice wavered as she leaned to the left.

"I've got you, babe. Hey, let's have you go over to the photo booth. You've got to have a picture to go with your medal," Jonathon said, directing her to the area behind the giant speakers.

Dazed, she allowed him to escort her to the black-curtained booth. There was a line of five or six runners in front of her, sweating, crying, and staggering from side to side. Brenda took in a giant breath—the first she was aware of drawing since crossing the finish line. Exhaling, she jumped when someone tapped on her shoulder from behind.

"Hey, there, lady. I didn't know you were running the CIM this year! Looks like you did a fantastic job," said the slender blonde woman.

Brenda stared at her wordlessly.

"Don't you remember me? We ran into each other at the finish line of the Chapel Bay Half. You were mumbling something about 'Green Tara,' and I told you Tara was my name," she said, green eyes twinkling.

"Oh, yeah! Wow—never thought I'd run into you here! Good job, you!" Despite her fatigue, Brenda was suddenly a bundle of nerves. She forgot, for the moment, that she needed to keep her heart closed to romance.

"Oh! Looks like it's your turn! What's your name again?" asked Tara. She wasn't gasping for air or sweating; *how could she have just finished a twenty-six-mile run?*

"Oh ... uh ... it's Brenda. Nice to see you again," Brenda tried for a smile, but was unsure of what her face was doing. It felt as numb as the rest of her body.

As she emerged from the photo booth, Jonathon rescued her from the social paralysis that had descended upon her. "I found a great Thai restaurant near the Hyatt where we're staying, if you're up for that."

"I could eat. Pad Thai sounds like the cure for whatever is wrong with me after that slog."

"Honey, that's a big can of worms you're opening there! Let's just say that it's whatever was already wrong with you, plus a ton of aches and pains, which you won't feel until later tonight."

Jonathon, always the clown. As she and Jonathon walked back to the hotel among hundreds of others, the unsteadiness of her gait matched her untethered emotions. What could explain the eerie feeling, the sense of déjà vu, that crept up from the damp pavement into her tired body? This wasn't the first time Brenda had strolled these streets near the capitol building, but today, in her exhaustion, it was if the ghost of her father was waving at her from a portal in time.

She shivered, then turned her mind to more immediate concerns. Lacing arms with Jonathon, she took in a deep, cleansing breath. The lure of clean jeans and a hot meal propelled her forward, ghosts be damned.

~

SHOWERED AND CHANGED, Brenda and Jonathon walked two blocks to Best Thai Restaurant. Once inside the restaurant, fragrant with smells of curry, basil, and turmeric, Brenda and Jonathon sat at a small table next to a window. Over green curry and pad Thai, they discussed the race, Jonathon's newest boy toy, and how much they each regretted certain youthful indiscretions. Brenda acknowledged she'd once been the love-'em-and-leave-'em type, and Jonathon chortled, confessing that he wished he'd left a few of his long-term paramours sooner rather than waiting until there'd been nothing left to salvage from the relationships.

After eating, Brenda excused herself to go to the ladies' room. Washing her hands, she looked at her face in the mirror.

"Hey, old lady, good work today!" she said aloud.

It really WAS a good job, and it felt great to have crossed off one of her bucket list items. As she arrived back at the table, Jonathon picked up the boxes of leftovers and rose from his chair.

"Honey, you look like a drowned rat. I paid the bill while you were in the bathroom. Wanna go back to the hotel?"

"You sure haven't lost your ability to compliment a lady, JB," Brenda replied, rolling her eyes dramatically. "I hope you remember to be more polite when you're out with a guy!"

"Sweetie, none of the guys I date run twenty-six miles and then fall soaking wet into my arms," Jonathon said, grinning.

"No, but I'm sure they are just as exhausted and drenched

when they collapse in your embrace after a wild night, Romeo," Brenda cracked back.

"Well, true that."

"JB? Can we go for a drive?"

"Sure, babe. Your wish is my command."

The rain had let up, and the smells of automobile exhaust were gone, leaving the air fresh and sweet. Reflected light shimmered back at them from the puddles on the pavement, little wisps of evaporating water rising and meeting them as they entered the parking structure across the street from the Hyatt Regency.

"Where to, milady?" asked Jonathon.

"I'd like to drive through the neighborhood where I grew up, if you don't mind," Brenda replied.

"Oh, that's right! I'd forgotten that this is your hometown. You don't mention it very often," Jonathon said, pulling the car out of the parking space and driving down the ramp.

"Not all the memories are ones I want to relive. But I was mostly happy here in Sac. I'll tell you how to get to my old neighborhood, Tahoe Park, and show you the house Mom and I lived in when I was a teenager."

They drove through downtown, then through leafy Midtown, and the business district gave way to apartment buildings, Victorians, and older homes built in the 1930s and '40s. Folsom Boulevard carried them through East Sacramento, a wealthy enclave containing a mixture of large and small brick homes. As they approached 65th Street, Brenda told Jonathon to turn right.

"Keep driving and turn right again at the third light."

Once they made the turn, Brenda grew quiet. Coming to a stop sign, she pointed to the left and Jonathon turned as instructed.

The homes in the neighborhood were mostly small, two-bedroom affairs with wood or aluminum siding and one-car garages. Trees lined the streets here, too, but unlike in Midtown and East Sacramento, the streets were narrower, the trees closer together. Children's bikes leaned up against porches, and the cars in the driveways were Honda Civics, Toyota Priuses, and a few older model Chevy sedans and pickup trucks.

Brenda placed her hand on Jonathon's arm and asked him to make a right turn onto 19th Avenue. "One more block and we're there."

Jonathon pulled up outside the home she pointed to. Brenda closed her eyes and took several deep breaths. Opening them once more, tears brimmed from her eyes and spilled onto her cheeks.

"What's wrong? Is this too much for you? Should we go?" he asked, brow furrowed.

"Shh. I just need a couple of minutes." Brenda looked down at her hands, the hands of a pianist. Her long, tapered fingers played a silent scale on her thighs.

They sat in the car for nearly ten minutes. Then, someone living in the home opened the front door. It was an African American man, in his mid- to- late thirties, about five-foot ten. His recently trimmed beard gave him a friendly appearance. Head tilted to one side, he walked toward the white Subaru.

"Hi! Can I help you with something?" the man asked.

Brenda rolled down her window. "Oh, no, sorry. I used to live here with my mom. We must look like we're staking out the neighborhood," she said, trying to sound as cheerful as possible.

"Oh, Mrs. Kato was your mom?"

"Yes, that's right. I lived here too until I went to college in San Francisco. It all seems such a long time ago," Brenda said.

The kind man offered to allow Brenda to come in, but Brenda refused the offer. She was embarrassed to have been caught staring at the home.

"Okay, then. Enjoy the rest of your day, and safe travels," the man replied, lightly tapping the roof of the car and walking back toward the house.

Coming here probably wasn't such a good idea. Fully

embracing her stalker-self, she wiped the remaining tears from her eyes.

Jonathon turned in his seat so that he could face Brenda. His kind, brown eyes showered her with love. "Any other requests, my queen?"

"None. I have zero energy—physical or emotional. Just take us back to the Hyatt, please."

"You've got it, sugar."

On the short ride back, Brenda briefly wondered how she could ever locate members of her family, the relatives whom she'd never met and who maybe didn't even know she existed. But did she really want to unearth ancient family history, opening a Pandora's box of potentially toxic secrets?

Feeling bittersweet over all that had taken place that day, she closed her eyes while Jonathon drove. Almost immediately, she drifted off.

Darkness all around. A Bento Box, packed with steamed rice, sashimi, sweet potato cakes, and shibazuke loaded into a small brown backpack. Walking slowly up a steep hill; it's so very cold. The wind whips through the towering pines. Twigs and leaves flutter noiselessly to the ground. Cresting the hill, the sharp briny smell of the sea mixes with the scent of evergreens. The wind stops, and through the trees, a full moon is now visible.

The car stopped abruptly. Brenda shuddered and opened her eyes, unsure of who or where she was for a moment. The dreamscape was so real, every detail lingering like an airplane's vapor trail. *Were the images drawn from stories Mom told me? Maybe even stories passed down from a previous generation, before everyone came across to America?*

Better to keep the optimism and shelve the desire to learn about things she could never truly understand, let alone control. *I can't live in my past, let alone that of someone else. Besides, what if I dig deeper and wish that I'd left it all alone?*

"Hey, girl, you look like you've seen a ghost," Jonathon said, sandwiching the Subaru between two SUVs in the Hyatt parking structure. "Memory lane is okay, but don't you think maybe it's time to release some of that baggage you're carrying?"

"Yeah, probably. But it's not that simple. There might be a reason my dreams keep nudging me to dig a little deeper, to find more about my father and that side of the family. I can't explain it, it's just ..."

"It's just a feeling?"

"One of the strongest feelings I've ever had."

9

It was the beginning of the first full week of December. Sitting on a bench at Friendship Point, Harriet was awestruck by the atmosphere surrounding her, covering her. The day was young; fingers of fog turned the air gray. The mist approached and receded, never asking permission as it stole in, out, and around the edges of life and landscape. Nothing escaped the moisture. Thick and uniform, descending like a blanket over surfaces even and uneven, gas turning to liquid in an instant. In an hour, this dance would end. The curtain of fog would lift, leaving a layer of damp film on trees, grass, and sidewalks.

Harriet considered how strange it was that she enjoyed observing change, yet detested change when it affected her personally. Her aging body, her bouts of forgetfulness, the loneliness that dwelled within ever since her beloved Arthur had died. These changes she could do without.

The voices of women beginning their outdoor yoga class startled Harriet out of her reverie. Frowning, she rose from the bench. *Why must they trumpet their agility?* Yoga was supposed to be a non-intrusive, meditative activity. She got out of the way before Downward Dog turned into Howling Hyena.

Leaning on her bedazzled cane, Harriet silently cursed her arthritic hips and knees. She started back up the walking path toward her house. A mental image of her famous frittata and breakfast potatoes took her mind off the aches and pains.

As the frittata cooked in the old faithful iron skillet she'd inherited from her parents, scents of Swiss cheese and veggies mingled with the potatoes already cooked, waiting on another burner. The doorbell ding-donged. *Rats!* After pulling the pan from the hot burner, a frazzled and hungry Harriet shuffled down the hallway to the front door. Opening the door, she saw a green plastic bag sitting on the stoop. *What could this be?* She gingerly leaned over and lifted it, forgetting to bend her knees first. Her back popped in protest. *Damn it!*

The shape and heft of the package told Harriet it contained a hardback book. Harriet was seven-tenths curious and three-tenths annoyed. Books were wonderful, yet mystery gifts discombobulated her. She remembered the last one she'd gotten. It was a houseplant, a "thank-you" from a neighbor whom she'd driven to a medical appointment. The plant had died. It turned out plants needed water. Thank goodness books didn't need tending to.

As she sat to eat her now-cold frittata and potatoes, Harriet opened the bag. *Well! Here it is.* Franklin's latest creation, "Two Sides, One Coin." The inscription read: "To Harriet, with appreciation. Hope you enjoy it!" *Okay, well, that's sweet.* Franklin must have been delivering some books to the local bookstore, and it was thoughtful of him to drop one on her doorstep.

Chewing on a forkful of egg, she recalled Joe mentioning something about Franklin last weekend. *What had he said about Fargo? That he wasn't who she thought he was?* She figured he meant Franklin wrote under a pen name. *Was there more to it than that?* Joe followed up his comment with something about authors confusing fact with fiction, and his whole body had tensed, his face becoming pinched.

Harriet had enjoyed her coffee date with Franklin the day after his reading. He'd seemed perfectly nice, just as she'd remembered him back when her parents were both still alive. Kinda cute. *What bone did Joe have to pick with Franklin? Should I try to help them reconcile?* Harriet shelved that notion, determined to come back to it later.

Shaking her head, Harriet realized she'd gone down quite the rabbit hole. But one actionable idea came to her: *Maybe it's time for me to return to my writing, dust off those skills, and invite the muse into this empty house.* She'd allowed herself to be sidelined after Arthur died, thinking that it made no difference what she did or didn't do since her true love was gone. Back then, there wasn't a subject that inspired her in the slightest. But now, things felt different. She was in the last third of her life, and she felt she had things to say. Important things.

Harriet smiled as she remembered Aunt Elsie, always scribbling away in her room upstairs. Elsie was certainly a woman unafraid to explore her passions. Writing seemed to be on the top of Elsie's list. Harriet smiled to herself. *I want to be a force of nature, like Elsie.* As a little girl, she'd found one of Elsie's poems tucked into a novel in the living room. The poem had made little sense to her, but now she wished she'd copied it down. It was a shame that Elsie's work had disappeared when she passed away. Mom had made sure Dad removed all her stuff from the house. In young Harriet's opinion, it was a harsh way to deal with someone's prize belongings.

Harriet rose from the table, empty plate in hand. Yes, she would start writing again, and it didn't matter whether she made any headway in today's crazy publishing world. This was a journey just for her, honoring her own gifts—meager as they may be. "Keep those flames a-burning." She could still hear her favorite Stanford English professor's voice in her head.

In the study, she searched for some kindling for her literary fire, small thought twigs and detritus from her forest of accumulated anecdotes. Journeys began with a single step, one and then another and another, opening new vistas, revealing unexplored territory. She was ready for the trip.

SIPPING HER MINT TEA, Harriet glanced down at her pages of notes. Smatterings of ideas about trips she and Arthur had taken, observations from hikes, but nothing that set her heart afire. She glanced up, toward the bay windows facing the back of the house. The panoramic view allowed her to see the walking path next to the bay. A return to writing was more challenging than she'd thought it would be. It felt like a lonely path, different from the one outside her window, with the frequent throngs of walkers, runners, and bicyclists. The loneliness of writing was especially ironic, since it was loneliness itself that she was trying to avoid. Very few people knew how easily she could fall into darkness and depression. As she continued gazing out the window, she looked past the people walking and the children playing. She saw gulls diving for lunch in the bay waters. She felt a kinship with the scavenging birds, mentally diving through the years, gathering material from long ago.

What about writing a memoir? Drifting into a reverie, she remembered long-ago times .... *I'm at Girl Scout camp, and the other girls and I are learning to tie knots ... first the square knot, then the half hitch ... and later that year, my class visits Carmel Mission .... Why are the Padres making the Indians do their farming?*

Her phone rang, and she nearly leapt out of her chair. Sally's name appeared across the screen.

"Oh, hey, Sally! How've you been?"

"Well, have you heard the latest? Remember that grouchy old lady from my estate sale, the one who thinks she's better than all the rest of us?" Sally said, breathlessly.

"Oh, how could I ever forget Miss Bossy Cow! She acted like

you would be the ruination of the neighborhood if you gave anything away for free," Harriet replied.

"Yes, that's the one. Well, guess what? It turns out that her daughter is the wife of that Italian playboy who was just convicted of banking fraud! NOW who's sullying the neighborhood?" Sally giggled, her glee coming through loud and clear.

"You don't say? A real—how shall we put it—*imbroglio,* huh? And right there on your own block. Who'd have seen that coming?" Harriet asked. She changed topics and asked Sally whether she'd like to meet for lunch soon.

"Oh, that sounds great. I can taste the chowder now! What about the day after tomorrow, say eleven thirty?" Sally asked.

They agreed on a spot on the wharf and rang off.

Hum. A scandal featuring an Italian banker. Maybe Sally's idle gossip could lead somewhere, after all. Harriet recalled a trip she and her parents had taken to Italy. *I was eight years old ... it was my first time on an airplane ...*

Grabbing her notepad, she jotted down the recollections as they flooded her mind. Once in Rome, her dad had rented a green Fiat. After they had seen the major Roman attractions, they drove all over Southern Italy, visiting small villages. The food, the ruins, the fashions, the language—it was all so wonderful. In fact, it was on that trip that Harriet first put pen to paper in a serious way.

Perhaps using fragments of family history, fictionalizing a bit, would work. *After all, Mother's family is Italian—why not set part of the book in Italy?* In fact, it might justify taking a nice trip to Italy to gather more information for the book.

She pictured sitting by the sea, eating scrumptious *fruits de Mer*, drinking wine, listening while a handsome Italian regaled her with colorful tales from his past. *La dolce vita, and why not?*

Another call interrupted her reverie. The word "unknown" appeared, but she answered anyway.

"Hello? Who's this?" Harriet asked.

"Harriet, is that you? It's your cousin Angela, calling from Ventura," came the reply. The woman's voice sounded a bit on the wobbly side, but after a moment, Harriet realized that this was, in fact, a long-lost cousin.

"Oh, hello, cuz! It's been donkey's years since we've spoken, let alone seen one another!" Harriet replied.

They chatted for a few minutes, and Angela invited Harriet to spend the Christmas holiday in Ventura with her.

Well, that's a relief. Now, she wouldn't have to pretend to be too busy to attend well-meaning neighbors' Christmas dinner invitations. Frankly, being older and single was exhausting.

THE FIRST WEDNESDAY in December descended upon Chapel Bay like a gentle caress. It was one of those perfectly sunny and calm days, the kind that lured people to Chapel Bay despite the high cost of living. Visibility was ten miles in every direction, waves were gently lapping at the rocks along the shore, and whales were spouting in front of appreciative onlookers at Friendship Point.

Up the hill and on the other side of Barnacle Street, Joe was driving to the grocery store. Catching sight of a woman tending roses in a front yard several doors down from his own, he realized he'd seen her before. He eased his foot off the gas pedal, and the Honda slowed. *Where do I know her from? She looks awfully familiar!*

While Joe was pondering this question, a truck cornered too quickly and nearly sideswiped his car. Terrified, he pulled over to the curb and took ten deep breaths before continuing to the store. *I need to really stay focused. Wouldn't want to lose my license.*

Heart rate back to normal, Joe parked, looked left and right, and crossed the store parking lot. Sighing, he pushed his squeaky grocery cart around the aisles—*why do I always seem to get the noisy one?*—and finished his shopping before entering the checkout line. While scrolling on his phone, he felt someone tap him on the shoulder. Turning, he smiled as he saw one of the other singers in his choir. It was a busty blonde alto named Cassy, standing behind him.

"Joe, I thought that was you! Fancy meeting you here on a sunny Wednesday in paradise," Cassy said, smiling broadly.

Joe nodded, smiling back. As he began placing his items on the little conveyor belt, the woman continued talking.

"Joe, I had a little brainstorm the other day that involved you. I just retired from the school district—I was a guidance counselor for over twenty years. You were in the mental health field, too, right?" she asked.

"That's right. I worked as a staff psychologist at the hospital until I retired. Why do you ask?" Joe said, pulling out his debit card to pay for the groceries.

"It turns out that there's a need for trained people such as us to help in the schools, now that the kids have returned to in-person instruction. Would you be at all interested in volunteering, say one day a week, to help the youth with some issues they're having?" she asked, putting her own groceries on the conveyor.

"Oh, wow. I've never even thought about something like that. Isn't it tough to get clearance to work with kids these days?" Joe asked.

"Not really. I'm sure your fingerprints have been in the system for ages, and it wouldn't be hard for you to get the paperwork filled out. Do you have a police record?" she said, winking at him.

"It's as long as your arm. I'm the guy who has been stealing library books left and right, not to mention neglecting to pick up his dog's poop on the path," Joe said, smirking.

"Haha—love it. Say, if you aren't doing anything later, would you like to meet over coffee and discuss this idea further? No pressure," Cassy added, wheeling her own cart alongside Joe's as they meandered out of the store.

"Oh, I would enjoy that," Joe said as he and his cart squeaked their way through the double doors and onto the sidewalk.

"Actually, today would be good for me. My husband is out golfing with the gang, so I'm free as a bird. How about meeting down at the wharf early this afternoon? It shouldn't be too crowded, now that we are in between official tourist seasons," she said.

"It's a date! One o'clock, that coffee place next to the boat launch?" Joe asked, loading his groceries into the car.

"Awesome. I'll see you there!" Cassy waved and moved her cart behind her gray sedan.

Driving away, Joe noticed he had headed the car in the wrong direction and was getting further from, not closer to, home. *I really need to focus on where I'm going,* he thought for the second time that morning.

HARRIET SHOWED up at the fish house a little after eleven o'clock in the morning. Within minutes, a tall female waiter showed her to an outside table overlooking the water. Waves lapped the dock in a regular rhythm, hitting the decking just inches from where she sat. After ordering water and a glass of Chablis, she sat back in her chair and kicked off her light blue Skechers. The combination of waves, warm sun, and slight breeze was intoxicating, and she felt her eyes close.

With a clank of glassware on the table, the drink order arrived. Harriet opened her eyes. Sally was right behind the server, grinning from ear to ear.

"Here I am! Good! May I have a glass of whatever she's having?" Sally asked the server. The young woman nodded and gave a thumbs up. When she returned with Sally's Chablis, both women ordered the catch of the day: rockfish seared in garlic. After lunch, the two friends strolled along the wharf. As seagulls cried and dove for bits of sourdough bread discarded by tourists, they passed the candy and ice cream shops, the cheap T-shirt outlets, and the vendors selling jewelry. At last, they arrived at the end of the pier.

Harriet glanced to her left and noticed Joe West sitting at an outdoor table. He was conversing with a woman she didn't recognize. *That lady has a chest on her! Is that the appeal?* Whatever they were discussing seemed serious, as Joe kept nodding his head while the hefty blonde woman in the black jacket held court.

"There's my new friend Joe," Harriet said to Sally, nodding toward the table where Joe and his companion sat talking.

"Oh, I think I know him. He usually shows up at the gift exchange some of us have on Christmas afternoon. Actually, I think he lives around the corner from me. Doesn't he have a couple of Labrador retrievers?" Sally asked, furrowing her brow.

"That's right. In fact, he and his pups spent the night at my place when that big storm came last month," Harriet said.

"You scoundrel! Any excuse to pick up an attractive man! I just knew you'd been hiding things from me!" Sally said accusingly.

Harriet felt her cheeks redden. "It wasn't like that, Sally. Didn't I tell you about the woman who got plowed into by bikes on the path behind my house? I ended up calling the emergency squad and Joe and I went to the hospital to retrieve the woman from the ER after she got bandaged and released."

"Oh, wait a minute; you DID mention that at the city council meeting a few days later. I wasn't aware that was the guy who took shelter with you and that library woman during the storm. What's her name, again?" Sally asked.

"Brenda Kato. She runs the Meet the Author events for them. Anyhow, to return to your accusation, Joe is definitely not my type. And it looks like he's otherwise engaged at the moment, besides. I'm looking for someone tall, dark, and handsome with his own money," Harriet said. Franklin Fargo came to mind, but Sally didn't need to hear that.

"Well, beware of Italian bankers is all I have to say! That type didn't turn out so well for that woman's daughter," Sally said.

"Yes, I shall. Your advice is always so helpful. Oh, by the way, if you're not doing anything on New Year's Eve, I thought I'd have a few people in for drinks and snacks," Harriet added.

"Sounds nice, Harriet. Text me with the details and let me know what I can bring."

Once behind the wheel of her Volvo, Harriet had a brain-storm. *Why don't I invite Franklin and Joe to the party, too? Maybe a jovial atmosphere will help them put their friendship right again.*

Feeling very pleased with her clever idea, she drove home to put her plan into action.

10

W alking into work, everything seemed brighter, more vibrant than before Brenda ran the marathon. She soaked in the rays of sunshine glinting off the ocean, the smiles on the faces of passersby, and the sounds of gulls overhead. The only mar on the surface of this perfect scene was her slight annoyance at the sight of a scruffy-looking man of indeterminate age standing in front of the Baptist church. He was holding some kind of religious sign. She couldn't make out the whole phrase; it was about Jesus wanting something or other.

"Hey, friend! Jesus needs a different font!" she called out.

The man turned toward her, shrugged and scratched his head, but didn't answer. Brenda gave a wave and a shrug of her own and resumed her walk. *He probably thought I was talking about the baptismal font,* she considered, smiling at her private joke. *I wonder whether he has a home here, or just comes to irritate the Chapel Bay residents?*

Once ensconced in her cozy office, Brenda relaxed in her swivel chair and watched beams of light streaming through the windowpane, illuminating dust motes. *Stillness does not actually exist,* she thought. *Everything is always in motion.* Just as she was perusing the cascade of emails that had landed since the end of last week, there was a quiet rat-a-tat-tat on her door.

Turning from her computer, she could see Justin, the head librarian, through the glass. He looked slightly less bedraggled than he had the last time their paths had crossed. Squelching her irritation at this interruption, she opened the door. Justin explained budget cuts would mean trimming food and beverage costs for the Meet the Author program. On the bright side, their library was this year's "Best Small Library in California," a big honor, indeed.

Justin slouched out the door and back down the hallway; Brenda glanced at her desktop. Sitting there, atop sundry other items, was the yellowing folder that contained the poems by Elsie Star. She pulled out a sheet of onionskin paper and eyed several haikus. Themes of nature, human frailty, and the wonder of found objects appeared from the five-seven-five stanzas. One poem in particular captured her attention.

> ***Rain stops at sunrise***
> ***Blue Goose, quietly feasting***
> ***Coyote watches***

The images invoked were at once peaceful and restive. Nature provides water and food, but the gathering of essentials can be a harsh endeavor.

Brenda thought about her mother and grandparents, about their lives in the camps. She'd read poems published by survivors of Camp Tulelake. Each poem evoked a sense of longing, sometimes fused with irony or even appreciation for beauty. No matter what, it seemed, people decorated their lives with art, language, and hopefulness. The healing power of art struck her anew.

Meanwhile, she needed to work on finding inexpensive eats for the upcoming book events. Next week was Christmas, and nobody ever answered emails between Christmas and the new year. *Why not walk up to Mallory's Magic Brew and see whether Mallory can give the library a discount on some coffee and muffins?*

Barring all else, it was a good excuse for a walk.

SEVERAL DAYS after coffee with Cassy, Joe's thoughts returned to the possibility of doing counseling work with children. He remembered his frustrations when working with adults in the community, but also the joys. He possessed plenty of experience working with adults' problems, doubts, and insecurities. Working with kids may require some extra patience, a gentler touch, but he could muster that up if required.

Joe picked up his phone. What was the worst that could happen? That they really wouldn't need his help? He punched in the number. The Chapel Bay Unified School District's director in charge of counseling services sounded bubbly over the phone. She invited Joe to complete a volunteer application. Giving himself a mental pat on the back, Joe sensed that he'd done something potentially worthwhile.

After completing the short application and submitting it, Joe remembered that he still needed to buy a Christmas gift for next week's community gift exchange. He had no family in California, and major holidays came with a tinge of sadness. The same group of friends and neighbors had been spending Christmas afternoon together for years now, and Joe was grateful to have a place to go.

Joe glanced down at his Rolex, the only luxury item he'd ever purchased for himself. He had a couple of hours before dog-walking time. Should he brave the mall or just shop in the small stores in downtown Chapel Bay? Simple choice—go small, skip the mall. He donned his good wool coat—a blue gray that brought out the color in his eyes—and drove his Honda three blocks to the town's business district.

He lucked out and found a parking space right in front of the little gift shop on Barnacle Street. Seatbelt unbuckled, he was poised to exit the sedan when a sudden pain seared through his stomach. It was the same feeling he always got just before bad news came his way. His stomach was like a crystal ball for seeing future trouble. He took a moment, glanced through his windshield at the sidewalk in front of his car. *Was that really Franklin Fargo, the literary imposter, with the wealthiest widow in town? What the hell?* The stomach-o-meter had once again had told Joe the truth.

Joe watched as the love birds got into Franklin's gazillion dollar red Ferrari, never once looking his direction. Triggered by the near encounter with his nemesis, Joe wanted to disappear, evaporate, and crumble into tiny bits. For decades, Joe had tucked away his guilt and remorse over the affair with Pat. Stuart's—er Franklin's—sudden intrusion in his life had stirred up the old recriminations. It was worse than that. He was being held hostage by the constant worry that Franklin would expose him as a violator of professional and personal ethics.

Shaking with anger, Joe made himself inhale and exhale slowly until he reached ten. After they drove away, he sat in his car for another five minutes, focusing on his breathing and allowing his heart to return to a more normal pace. Once he thought he could walk without tripping, he exited the car and headed toward the gift shop.

Back on the sidewalk, gift-wrapped candle in hand, Joe knew he needed a little break before heading home. Mallory's Magic Brew at the end of the block made a mean peppermint latte. As he stood in line at the counter, he heard a familiar voice in front of him. *Was that Brenda Kato? It was!*

"Excuse me, young lady. May I buy you a drink and a pastry?" Joe asked, tapping her on the shoulder.

"Oh—hello there, Joe. Fancy meeting you here. I'm actually here on a work errand, more or less, but thanks for the offer."

"Oh, okay, I just thought it would be nice to catch up. I haven't seen you in a while. Say, did your injuries heal okay?"

"Um, yes, thanks. It's all in the rearview now, Joe. Oh—

excuse me. I need to speak with Mallory here." Brenda's tone was a little curt.

"Gotcha. Nice seeing you, Brenda," Joe replied, forcing a smile to hide his disappointment.

Steaming latte in hand, Joe headed back to the car. The wind had picked up in the short time he'd been inside Mallory's, and he pulled his wool coat more closely around him. He took one last look at the part of the sidewalk where he had spied Franklin and the rich woman in their cutesy-wootsy, lovey-dovey promenade. Returning his attention to the task at hand, he unlocked the car door and folded his tall body into the driver's seat. The frown he'd been fighting off attached itself to his face. *I should have chosen the mall.*

BRENDA WAS both satisfied and irritated by the way her day was turning out. Mallory had agreed to give the library a terrific deal on upcoming catering jobs, even offering to donate two dozen blueberry muffins. However, Brenda wished she hadn't encountered Joe West, a man with no filters.

If I'd wanted all of Chapel Bay to know that I got hurt while running, I would have taken out an ad in the local paper. No need for that now, as Joe's loud voice announced her trail injury in the town's most popular coffee shop during one of the busiest times of day. *Harrumph. I hope I don't turn into one of "those" old people someday...*

Shifting focus, she placed a call to Deirdre and Jane, two old friends who had invited her up to San Francisco for Christmas. She was to drive up just before Christmas, staying with them through the twenty-seventh, and possibly spending one or two more days in the Bay Area if she could find a clean, out-of-the-way bed-and-breakfast that still had a spot available.

It was going to be really nice being with other lesbians for a change, and she was looking forward to hanging out with

Jonathon as well. Staying at Jonathon's place was out of the question, because of her cat allergies. The three of them—Jonathon, Deidre, and Jane—were the closest thing she had to family. She winced, realizing she'd mentally conjured up the "f" word. Oh well, now was not the time to dwell upon that which was lacking.

With a start, Brenda saw it was nearly time for the monthly staff meeting to begin. Face mask in hand, she walked down the hall, away from the circulation area, and into the library conference room. *Great, another long meeting. This time, the added fun of a budget shortfall will be the icing on the cake.*

She selected a seat near the middle of the long conference table. A few watercolor seascapes graced the long wall she was facing. Local artists had contributed works that celebrated the area's natural beauty. In this mural, blues and greens of the ocean contrasted with pink ice plants and orange California poppies.

The door opened, and a shuffling of feet and snippets of conversation brought Brenda out of introspective musings. She allowed her eyes and forehead to relax. The library staffers were fortunate to call this little town home. The hateful email she'd received a few weeks ago still weighed on her mind, making her aware of her "otherness." However, that was no reason to project a sour attitude. Brenda turned to her left and saw April, the volunteer coordinator. She made a point of speaking in a sweet, gentle voice.

"Well, hello there! How are things going in the world of volunteers?"

"Hi, Brenda ... going well, though I need to find more people to help with the Saturday morning kids' reading group. Let me know if you hear of anyone who's interested. Oh, it looks like the boss is about ready to start."

They turned their attention to the end of the table, where Justin stood.

"I know I have individually briefed you all on our budget issues, so I won't go into that too much. We've had times of belt tightening before and have eventually come out of them okay. I have full confidence that this time, it will be no different. But I want to spend a little time this afternoon on a different subject, one that I think will be more inspiring," he offered.

On the screen directly opposite, a black-and-white image of an old fishing village appeared. The sounds of meeting attendees shifting in the padded chairs took the place of muffled conversations. All eyes focused on the photograph.

"The library has a collection of photos such as this one, documenting the history of the Chinese fishermen who once populated these shores."

A photo of two men in a small boat popped onto the screen.

"Ample stocks of abalone made this area a favored spot for fishing, starting about one hundred years ago. History tells us that several things altered this situation," he added, flipping to a photo that showed empty warehouses on the wharf.

"First, overfishing reduced the number of abalone in the bay. Second, a fire along the wharf destroyed many of the homes and boats upon which these folks depended," Justin continued, showing a photo with a pile of abalone shells in the foreground and burned out homes in the background.

"Several years later, in well-meaning but deeply flawed efforts to honor this heritage, the good people of Chapel Bay began a yearly Festival of Lanterns," he said, showing another black-and-white picture with what were obviously white people dressed in kimonos, wearing pancake makeup.

"It took until last year to end this tradition, which had involved little skits, musical performances, and food. None of it, might I add, prepared or performed by Chinese Americans," he continued.

"Which brings us to the present day. As some of you may recall, April is National Poetry Month. Then, during May, local members of the Asian Pacific Justice Coalition will honor the true cultural heritage of their ancestors with a Walk of Remembrance," he announced, flashing to a color photo of people marching along the wharf, carrying signs that read "In Honor of My Grandparents" and "Real History Must be Told."

"We have an opportunity to contribute to this wonderful celebration by highlighting the poetry of the Asian American members of our community, both past and present. I think this deserves consideration during both April and May, perhaps focusing on novels and nonfiction works during May. I'm planting this little seed with you talented, literary folks so that you can think of ways you—and the library—might like to contribute to the celebration."

"As you know, Chapel Bay's library is now the Best Small Library in California. It's time to take that momentum and use it to become an even better member of this wonderful community," he said, ending the slide show.

Applause followed, along with a spate of questions.

I didn't know most of this history before now, Brenda realized ruefully. *It's great that my coworkers have an interest in honoring Asian Americans who've made homes in Chapel Bay.*

Her thoughts turned to readings that she could spearhead, local authors whom she might invite to take part. *This is a true holiday gift.* When the meeting ended and most people had left the conference room, Brenda approached the librarian.

"I've never mentioned anything about this before, but did you know my mom spent time in the Japanese internment camps as a child?" she asked.

"Wow. That makes sense, because I know thousands of Japanese Americans were locked up during World War II," Justin said. "It makes me wonder about the history of those from Chapel Bay and surroundings—did they return after the camps? Were they welcomed?"

"I don't really know much about that, but maybe we can work with the history museum and find out a little more," Brenda said.

"Yes, it would be good to do that. Kind of like genealogy research on a slightly larger scale," Justin said. Brenda thanked

him for the conversation and returned to her office. Closing the
door, she dismissed the recurring questions she had about her
own family. She gathered her leather purse and fleece jacket, shut
off her computer, and headed out for the day.

"Thank you again for a wonderful meeting, Justin," she added
before exiting the building.

"Oh, it's my pleasure, and I hope you'll follow through on
that research!" Justin replied, donning his windbreaker. "We need
more local writers from all backgrounds to be featured."

Justin's words about increasing the diversity of people being
showcased by the library gave Brenda a bit of hope. Walking out
the door of the conference room, she held her yellow legal pad and
pen a little closer to her chest. *They say that the best defense is a
good offense,* she thought. *A show of inclusivity could be like spitting
in the eye of those who would silence our voices.*

11

It was Monday, December 19th, and Joe West needed a distraction. Other than the little neighborhood gathering on Christmas Day, he really had nothing to look forward to over the next few weeks. He wasn't one to begrudge others their family gatherings, those long expected annual get-togethers which, in his experience, rarely matched expectations and were sometimes downright terrible. How many clients had he seen coming away from family holidays anxious, depressed, or angry?

With families, it seemed as if people wanted what they didn't have. Those with big families craved more one-on-one time with favorite family members. Those with small families felt they must be missing out on bunches of fun with a house full of near-and-dear ones. Ah, the human condition. *Dissatisfaction runs through our very bones.*

Back to the issue at hand: How to entertain himself over the next several days? He loved bird watching but couldn't very well take the dogs along on that kind of adventure. No downy woodpeckers or red-shouldered hawks or even scrub jays would hang around his dogs long enough for him to get a good photo.

If he'd done more planning, he could have rented a cabin at Big Bear or Lake Arrowhead, but those were not first come, first

served kinds of spots. Besides, he wasn't much of a skier, and
didn't really care for the hoity toity types who frequented the bars
and restaurants in the resorts during ski season, snow or no snow.
He snorted, making Kibble bark. *Franklin would be right at home
in that crowd.*

"Well, this is just a bunch of bullshit," Joe muttered. As a last
resort, he looked up the number for the local state park, just four
miles from his bungalow. The park featured accommodations in
cabins directly across the road from the beach. It felt like a bit of a
longshot, but if there were any cabins available, he would get a
change of scenery, at the very least. Also, they permitted dogs on
the grounds.

He punched in the number to the park office and was immediately put on hold. What felt like thirty minutes later—but was
really ten—an actual person came on the line. It took a few addi-
tional minutes, but at last the operator found him a spot for
several nights around Christmas.

Gathering up the dogs' leashes, he called them to the door.
The three of them headed out for their daily walk. *May as well
enjoy this beautiful, sunny weather. It feels good to have a holiday
plan. But will the cabin have a fireplace? Can I get meals in the
dining hall?* He was so caught up in these thoughts that he failed
to notice that a woman had approached him from behind.

"Joe, is that you?" said the voice.

Joe jumped when he heard the lady's voice. He turned,
smiling reflexively.

"Oh—Oh, hi! Yes, it is. You're the lady with the lovely roses!"
he said, remembering that he'd seen her in her yard recently. The
gray streaks in her dark brown hair shone in the sunlight.

"Yes, those were my mother's pride and joy. She's deceased
now, and I've moved into her place full time. Oh, and my name is
Sally. Sorry for not introducing myself right away!"

"I can place you now. You and your mother came to the
neighborhood Christmas lunch, right? Will you be coming this
year?" asked Joe.

"I will. Mom is no longer with us, but I hope to see you there, Joe!" Sally said, smiling.

The little lines around her eyes were so charming.

"Yes, I'm definitely coming this year, Sally. Say, it's been nice chatting, but this is where the little monsters and I turn," Joe said as they came to the end of the block. He couldn't help but notice the pleasant, woodsy smell that wafted from Sally as she waved goodbye. *Reminds me of a pine forest. I'd enjoy getting lost in those woods ...*

Crossing over Barnacle Avenue, Joe decided that this had, in fact, turned out to be a wonderful day. *Is Sally always this friendly, or do I detect a tiny spark between the two of us?* He never was too sure what he was feeling these days and couldn't pick up on the vibes women put out. *But maybe ...*

It felt good to get encouragement from the opposite sex. He pictured a note in a tiny bottle that had washed ashore. Mentally opening the little note, he read, *"Joe is not insignificant."* He could almost imagine being free of Franklin's threats to disclose his affair with Pat Star. Almost, but not quite.

FROM BEHIND THE wheel of her Volvo this Christmas Eve, Harriet began considering her heritage. She was, after all, en route to Ventura to see a cousin on Mom's side of the family. They were Italian—the Sabatinis. Dad's side was English—the Stars. *Why haven't I spent more time digging into family history?* Her entire reason for writing was to connect the past with the present, to leave a legacy of sorts. That made little sense if she didn't clearly understand her own heritage and family background.

Harriet's knowledge came primarily from stories she'd heard growing up. The Stars arrived on the Peninsula in the early 1800s. All the men in the Star family had been prominent members of the community, practicing law, medicine, or running commercial establishments. *To the manor born.*

Her mother's people came from a much more difficult set of circumstances. Emigrating from Genoa during World War II, Grandfather Sabatini was a fisherman like his father and grandfather before him. Settling first in the Bay Area and then, once the whole family had emigrated, moving down the coast fifty miles, they were a tight-knit clan.

Several generations later, her own mother emerged as the third of six children. Her parents had met at a dance in the valley, about twenty miles from Chapel Bay. According to the story, it was love at first sashay. But Harriet had many questions about the previous generations on both sides of her family. What were they like? What did they do for a living? *Maybe the cousins will know a little more about Mom's side.*

Darkness was encroaching. Harriet checked her GPS. Only twenty more miles until the turnoff. Soon, she pulled into Angela's sloping driveway. *Well, here goes.* She pulled her suitcase and bag of gifts from the trunk. A minute later, her favorite cousin opened the front door wearing a big smile. All throughout dinner, Harriet got the distinct impression that something troubled a young niece who was also visiting for the holiday. Later, when they drove to the harbor to watch the annual parade of boats, Harriet talked with the young woman while her cousin fetched hot cocoa for them.

Shivering and rubbing her hands together, Harriet asked, "Honey, is everything okay? You've been really quiet. What's on your mind?"

I hope Angela hurries up with the cocoa! It's freaking cold!

"Yeah, I'm feeling unsettled, Harriet. You know that my degree is in cross-cultural communications, right? Well, I'm working as a diversity and inclusion manager in a company in San Diego. I'm in charge of staff training and I'm supposed to help everyone understand where team members with different backgrounds are coming from." Her niece sighed. Harriet sensed the girl felt overburdened by this task.

"The trouble is, I grew up and attended school with people

almost exactly like myself. I don't feel qualified to give the training." The young woman finished, shaking her head. "Classroom lessons aren't the same as really knowing something in my bones."

They stood together silently, watching as the houseboats and fishing trawlers paraded by. The flashing red and green lights and Santas on board formed a stark contrast with their serious conversation.

"In my experience, it can often be more helpful to find ways in which people are similar, rather than different," Harriet said, adding, "but I can see how knowing about different cultures and backgrounds could also be helpful."

That was probably not great advice, she considered after blurting that truism. Before she could amend her words, a loud blast came from the approaching speedboat. *Saved by the horn.*

Back at the bungalow, Harriet went to the guest room and changed into her nightclothes. As she looked around the room at the framed photos of family members, it occurred to her that each one of those people may share DNA, but not a common outlook on life. People could be so different from one another and never even question how or why that was. *And I suppose the opposite is true. Complete strangers can have more in common with us than we ever would have imagined possible.*

Realizing how tired she was, Harriet turned back the quilt on her double bed. It was a quilt her grandmother had made. As a bonus, the pale-yellow sheets were extra soft. As she switched off the bedside lamp, gratitude bubbled up. *A high thread count is a first-world luxury.*

Two days later, Harriet prepared to go back to Chapel Bay. The visit and exchange of gifts had gone well. She rested in the contentment and peace that settled over her. Families ... such curious entities. What did the Russian author, Tolstoy, say? Something about how all happy families were alike, but each unhappy family was unhappy in its own way. Huh. *Grist for the old literary mill,* Harriet thought.

Driving up Highway 101, Harriet tried to decide whether her

own family had been a happy one or an unhappy one. She concluded that even if hers was a happy family, it couldn't be just like other happy families. And if it was an unhappy family, surely it bore some resemblance to other unhappy families. Thinking about the whole concept gave her a headache, so she focused on something more concrete.

The New Year's Eve party was coming up in just a few days. *Was she ready?* Also, she had to check emails for RSVPs. She'd invited nearly fifty people. Hopefully, most had responded by now. Her phone rang. Sally's voice filled her car's speakers. Coincidentally, she was asking about the party, wondering whether Harriet had enough chairs for everyone. Then Sally came to the real reason for her call. She told Harriet that she "really hoped" that only locals would be coming.

"Sally, what on earth are you talking about?" Harriet asked, swerving the car to avoid a collision with a driver who changed lanes without signaling.

"Oh, Harriet, you know what I mean. You have so many friends from so many backgrounds. I just hope that you aren't mixing things up too much. For the sake of keeping everyone comfortable, you understand ..."

Why was Sally trying to micromanage the guest list? Harriet shuddered at the thought that her best friend might be a bigot or a classist underneath her beautiful veneer.

12

D riving up to the Bay Area on December 23rd required more patience than Brenda normally possessed. Traffic snarled for miles, and the drawn and tired faces of the other drivers told its own tale. Once she arrived at Jane and Deidre's apartment in the Bernal Heights neighborhood of San Francisco, she was ready to settle in for the rest of the day. Pulling her black Camry to the curb in front of their Ripley Street address, she shut off the engine and didn't move for three minutes.

While the slight vertigo from hours of driving subsided, she recalled the many parties, festivals, and dances at lesbian bars she'd attended with Jane and Deidre. Jane, tall, slender, dark-haired— always ready for whatever any of the others wanted to do. Deirdre, short, stocky, red-haired — stirring up mischief and wanting to be the center of attention. They'd been together for nearly a decade and were a cute couple. It wouldn't be a boring visit, that was for sure.

After a cup of hot tea and a chat—during which, of course, romance came up—the gals asked whether Brenda was up for going out to one of their old haunts for dinner. After reassessing her level of fatigue, Brenda gave them a thumbs up on the idea. *What the hell—I haven't been here in nearly two years.*

"Brenda, you always loved that pizza place on Castro Street— The Sausage Factory—and I don't know about you, but I could make a few slices disappear in the relatively near future," said Deidre.

"That sounds great. Do you want to phone in our order, so the wait won't be so long?" Brenda asked.

"Good idea. Do you still like your pie with Canadian bacon and mushrooms on top? Extra cheese?" asked Deidre.

"Oh my God, yes. Just the thought of it has me swooning," Brenda said, laughing. "Although I'm not sure I'd know how to conjure up a good swoon at this point ..."

Deidre placed the order, then jumped right back into Brenda's romantic situation.

"Are we to understand that you really haven't dated at all since we last saw you ... two years ago?" Deidre asked.

"Correct. That brief fling I had in the fall of 2019 was just that—a brief, painless fling. It's not exactly easy to meet single lesbians in Chapel Bay. I've never been one for online connections, and since the gay bar closed, well, let's just say I've been having a dry spell, no pun intended," Brenda said.

"Well, don't give up hope. You're still a beautiful woman, Brenda. Don't close your heart to the possibility that one or more Ms. Rights are out there, just waiting for a chance to get together with the librarian of their dreams," Deidre said, raising her eyebrows suggestively.

"Yeah, yeah. Ms. Right, whomever she or they may be, needs to put the brakes on. I'm really busy with work and running and my piano teaching. Life is good, Deidre."

The three friends donned coats and headed out to the restaurant, miraculously finding a parking space only a block from Castro Street. Walking to the pizza place, they passed several wonderfully decorated Victorians, done up in a truly "extra" manner that only gay men seemed to concoct. Approaching one three-story home on Castro, Jane reached out and placed her hand on Brenda's sleeve.

"Do you see what I see?" Jane gasped.

"Said the little lamb to the drummer boy ...." Deidre sang.

"No, for real. Three balconies, each one hung with more lights than an entire small town. And that Santa, swinging in his sleigh from the second story! I swear, if he drops on top of me, it will be the last anyone ever hears from me." Jane's eyebrows shot up.

The red neon sign of the Sausage Factory beckoned them in after another half block; they paused to allow five chatty diners to leave. The waitperson soon motioned them back toward an empty booth. The warmth of the restaurant, the red satin wall covering, the smell of Italian food—it was like being in a gastronomic bordello.

The pizza and drinks came to their table only minutes later, and the collective desire to fill empty stomachs overtook all other needs. After each of them had enjoyed that first, indescribably delicious slice, they made eye contact once more. Deidre nodded at something behind Brenda, causing Brenda to wrinkle her brow. Once she had finished chewing, she spoke up.

"What, Deidre? You look as if you just saw a ghost." Brenda looked directly into the eyes of the redhead.

"Only the ghost of your longest relationship, dear. Don't turn around now, but Cynthia just walked in on the arm of another woman," Deidre said, keeping her voice down.

"Shit! I did not want to run into her on this trip. I hope she doesn't see us!" Brenda's voice quivered the slightest bit, enough to generate a sympathetic look from Jane.

Not thirty seconds later, up sauntered Cynthia with her very attractive date in tow. Cynthia stopped, ogling her former lover from head to toe. Her blue eyes sparkled. Brenda shivered, feeling like a discarded toy on a shelf. She quickly took in Cynthia's lady friend—medium height, long blonde hair, expensive clothes. *Great, just great.*

"Brenda! Is that you? Shoot, I've been thinking about you. How've you been?" said Cynthia, still fixing her gaze upon Brenda.

Brenda felt her cheeks flame. A flood of unbidden memories tumbled forth. Pictures of the two of them dining in this very restaurant. *Damn it, why does she have to be here? Don't cry, don't cry...*

Cynthia introduced Brenda to her new girlfriend. In the course of their exchange, Brenda learned Cynthia was now working for the District Attorney's office and that her date was an assistant district attorney. *Way to be replaced by an upgraded model.*

After the couple moved on to their own booth in the adjoining room, Jane leaned across the table toward Brenda, a caring look in her eyes.

"None of us expected to see her here, I'm sure. In fact, I'd heard that Cynthia had moved to Portland. I guess not, though."

Brenda averted her eyes. Jane was well-intentioned, but her sympathy only made Brenda feel worse. She was so tired of being in a one-down position. Being vulnerable once again was triggering so many emotions. Seeing Cynthia and her new love was devastating. But that wasn't the only thing weighing on her heart. Threats from the anonymous Lovers of Literature book banning advocate, wounds from being plowed into on the Chapel Bay running trail, shame and humiliation made worse by Harriet's kindness in the aftermath—it was all just too much. She took a breath, tried to refocus, and turned back toward her friends at the table.

"Doesn't matter. Let's keep our focus on the three of us. This pizza is beyond good, and I, for one, will not let it get any colder," Brenda said.

They finished their meal, paid, and left. Along the crowded sidewalk, Brenda was suddenly hyper-aware of all the couples holding hands, laughing, and scooting out of the way of equally mirthful people coming out of shops and restaurants.

Memories of her own San Francisco days assaulted her brain. Not only memories of Cynthia—they had met years after she had moved to the city—but also other women whom she'd dated and with whom she'd enjoyed the freedom of this gayest of all cities. Shaking her head, she refocused upon the present, as her meditation training had taught her. *That was then. This is now.*

"Hey, I remember reading that there's going to be a Holiday Spectacular, some kind of live event with singing and dancing at the Castro Theater tomorrow night. Do we think there may be any tickets still available?" Brenda asked.

"Girl, I was going to wait and surprise you, but yes, we have tickets for that already. In fact, my buddy Joel is a member of the Holigays and he assures me that this one is not to be missed," Deidre said cheerily, dropping her wrist in an imitation of the effeminate Joel.

They arrived back at the car. Deidre started the engine. KBOOM! The engine roared like it was ready for the Indy 500.

"SHIT! They took my catalytic converter!" Deidre shouted, pounding her fists against the steering wheel.

"Oh, no! What do we do now?" Jane asked, grasping her wife's hand.

"Do? There's nothing to do but drive home and call the repair shop in the morning. This freaking city—crime has gotten out of hand. Brenda, you're lucky to live in the boonies," Deidre said, practically spitting out her words.

"I guess, although we have our share of crime," Brenda said, trying hard to sound sympathetic.

"Oh really? I remember reading your local newspaper when we visited three years ago. The police reports were hilarious. 'Man locked out of his own house,' 'Mail incorrectly delivered,' "Raccoon seen crossing the road after dark; residents asked to drive carefully.' Yes, you Chapel Bay residents really have your hands full with those problems. I'm surprised we haven't had episodes of Crime Stoppers devoted to your town's issues," Deidre said, her voice dripping with sarcasm.

"Well, you're right. But sometimes the isolation can be a bit much." *They have no idea just how isolated.* Looking out the car window toward the lights on Market Street, she fervently wished for a change in subject.

"Uh-huh. To each her own, I guess. We choose to live here, and the benefits of big city life usually outweigh the drawbacks. Just not tonight," Deidre said with a sigh.

The three gave up on trying to talk over the loud muffler. They rode back to the apartment, each lost in her own individual thoughts. Brenda couldn't help but wonder whether Cynthia was truly happy with her life. Deciding to let that thought go, she suddenly realized just how exhausted she was feeling.

AFTER SLEEPING LATE, Brenda rose, had some toast, and strolled around the neighborhood by herself. It was a mild, sunny day—perfect sweater weather. She walked past the apartment she had inhabited for fifteen years while living in the city. It was just around the corner, at the very top of Folsom Street.

Such a great view from the second-floor balcony. On clear days like this one, Cynthia and I could see both the Bay Bridge and the Golden Gate. A bus groaned going up the hill, snapping Brenda out of her flashback. *City life.*

She and her friends went for a late lunch near Ghirardelli Square and then took the festively decorated cable car up and over the hill to Union Square. Dusk was falling, and the lights on the giant Christmas tree were stunning.

Ice skaters glided around the rink near the tree, and the Macy's windows were fabulous, as usual. Brenda could see giant wreaths in twelve windows that towered over the square. The center of the display was done up to look like a giant roll of Christmas wrapping paper. Vertical stripes in green, yellow, and red greeted onlookers.

Street vendors were selling coffee and hot cocoa. Carols rang out over the loudspeaker, and tourists and locals alike seemed to buzz with the excitement of the season. Brenda beamed. *This is why I love coming to the city during the holidays.*

As the three turned the corner from the main square, they came upon a large homeless encampment. Blankets were strewn over shopping carts. Men and women without shoes. A pit bull chained to a lamp post. This was such a stark contrast with the upbeat and festive happenings. Jane looked over at Brenda, and Brenda could see tears in her eyes.

"It's awful that people have to live in these kinds of conditions. Do you have any homeless in Chapel Bay?" Jane asked.

"We have a small group, mostly clustered around Fisherman's Wharf. I'm not sure where they sleep, but I know volunteers bring them meals regularly. It's really different from this; I'd forgotten how many unhoused people are here in San Francisco," Brenda said.

"I know it's outrageous, but you realize that over half of these people couldn't stay sober long enough to qualify for most of the housing options available, right?" Deidre said, sounding more than self-satisfied.

"However true that may be, many people don't start out as addicts, D. It's the brutality of life on the streets that drives them to find whatever comfort seems possible, and drugs take pain away temporarily. But of course, drugs make things infinitely worse once the addiction takes hold," Jane said, creasing her brow. "It's not really a moral issue, you know?" she added, tilting her head.

Brenda looked into the eyes of an older woman wrapped in a rough blanket, strands of hair poking out from underneath the filthy sock cap on her head. She saw so much pain and sorrow in those eyes.

"Whatcha lookin' at, lady? Ain't never seen poor people in the fancy part of town before?" said the woman, raising her bushy gray eyebrows.

Brenda broke eye contact and did her best to keep herself from running full speed down the street, away from this hurt.

The stench of unwashed bodies was overpowering. *I must come to terms with my aversion toward this suffering and try to send loving kindness.* She tasted bile in her throat and swallowed hard to rid her mouth of the taste of shame.

At the moment, all she wanted to do was go to the holiday celebration in the Castro, get lost in the merriment and glitter. Running away full speed wasn't an option at the moment, but staying in this place that triggered her wouldn't help either. An unbidden thought scorched her brain: *Mom and my grandparents suffered similar indignities.*

The Holigays performance did not disappoint, with the lavish costumes and cheerful singing. Despite the revelry, Brenda couldn't shake her experience from earlier that evening.

She dreamed of her father that night, but this time he was begging at a street corner in Sacramento. She heard him say to a passerby, "I'm waiting for my daughter. She said she'd be here soon."

THE FRIENDS SPENT Christmas Day in the apartment, opening gifts and enjoying several nice meals. The next day, Jane and Deidre asked if Brenda wanted to go to Japantown.

"You know, I'm no fan of Hello Kitty or Manga. Thanks, but no thanks," Brenda said, wondering if she'd come across too strong.

"I thought you'd maybe want to visit the big Japanese bookstore or grab some sushi. Isn't our Japantown one of the few left in America?" Deidre asked.

"Yes, it is. In fact, all of them are in California. But you realize they redeveloped that area in the 1960s, and what used to be an interesting place hosting families and small businesses is now mostly just a mall, right? I guess I'm just not that interested in supporting a sanitized version of what used to be real. White men bulldozed people's houses, and for what?" Brenda said, sparks flying from her brown eyes.

"Whoa. Okay, okay. I don't condone the erasure of culture. I'm not sure I've ever seen this side of you, Brenda. When you lived here, you never seemed all that political. But good for you, taking an interest in history," Deidre said.

Brenda took a breath. *Are these two aware of the pain I've felt —am still feeling—over being a double minority? Is intersectionality really that strange a concept for white people?* She dropped it for the time being. However, she made a mental note to get back in touch with a few of the Asian American lesbians she'd met at a conference a few years ago.

"You know what? Let's drive over to Muir Woods. It's still early enough that we ought to find a place to park. And, of course, I'll drive. Your poor car sounds like it's carrying a bomb in its tailpipe!" Brenda added.

They made the drive across the Golden Gate Bridge to Marin County. The many redwoods in the park reminded Brenda that life could be both precious and sturdy, delicate and strong. The trees last hundreds of years, providing homes to countless generations of animals and insects and taking in carbon while releasing oxygen—over and over again. *That is real commitment.*

Brenda noticed that some of the tree stumps had little seedlings growing in circles around their huge trunks, called "fairy rings." She remembered explaining these circles when she worked for the parks department. Once a mature coastal redwood falls, its roots begin to re-sprout from the decay and will often leave an almost perfect circle of new trees in its place. Amazing. *It's sure a lot easier for trees to find their roots.*

Late that afternoon, sitting on Deidre and Jane's deck, Brenda's thoughts returned to experiences and feelings from the past several days. As the sun disappeared over the buildings, she allowed herself to close her eyes and become quiet.

Thoughts came into her field of awareness, some gently

passing through like white clouds moving across a clear blue sky. Other thoughts were heavier, darker, more like thunderheads laden with moisture. The heaviest of them all carried the word "belonging" across their centers like a banner on a giant skyscraper.

Belonging. Belonging. Belonging. It was so easy to spot those who belonged to one another, so easy to see the connections. Cynthia and her new lover, walking hand in hand along Castro Street. Deidre and Jane, together for almost twenty years now, sharing a home and a life. The little redwood saplings in the forest, springing up from the mother tree, one generation intimately bound with the next.

Brenda remembered the homeless woman in Union Square, separated from her family of origin. Even she had a little makeshift family of sorts with the other unhoused folks nestled in blankets and under tarps. It wasn't a substitute for a safe and healthy life. But it was a connection with others, something that made sense to the people involved.

Opening her eyes, she saw that darkness had fallen; she much preferred that to her inner darkness. The sweet and pungent smells of roast chicken and mashed potatoes wafting out from under the kitchen door were very welcome, as was the company of her friends once she walked inside.

After the delicious and satisfying meal, Brenda excused herself and called it an early night. Tomorrow would be a full day, and she wanted to be ready for it. With any luck, she would avoid having a nightmare. Just before falling asleep, she overheard Jane and Deidre conversing.

"Boy, Brenda sure got touchy when I mentioned going to Japantown," Deidre said. "I was only trying to find a fun activity for us to enjoy."

"Yeah, well, you can be insensitive, love, and I know you don't mean to be that way. I think you caught her at a bad moment, as well. Let it go, honey," Jane replied, ever the peacemaker.

They really don't get it. Let it go ... let it go ... let it go.

THE NEXT MORNING, Brenda hopped into her Camry, bound for Berkeley. Driving around the corner and down the steeply sloping street, she wondered how her former self had become accustomed to so much traffic. Horns honking, people darting across the street in front of cars, skateboarders riding down the middle of the street. *Ugh.* She couldn't wait to get over the Bay Bridge to the café where she would meet Jonathon for breakfast.

The seven miles across the Bay were not without issues; it was foggy, and there were at least two accidents blocking lanes on the bridge. A red SUV swerved and cut her off, missing her front bumper by inches. *Shit! Idiot!* As she exited onto University Avenue, an exasperated "Oof" crossed her lips.

The breakfast spot Jonathon had chosen was near the intersection of University Avenue and San Pablo Avenue. There'd been so much redevelopment since she'd last been in this part of Berkeley. *I wonder which minorities have been displaced this time?* Lost in thought, she nearly walked right past the diner.

"There she is! Happy Holidays, best friend!" Jonathon exclaimed as soon as Brenda had opened the heavy oak door.

"Oh, it's so good to see you, J. Last time I saw you, I was in my post-marathon delirium. Better now!" Brenda hugged him tight, not letting go until he squealed.

Shaking his head, which caused his dark curls to bounce, Jonathon stretched out his blue cashmere-clad arms and grabbed each of her arms with one of his hands.

"Yes, you look markedly more alive today than you did after that rainy run, my dear. Are you hungry? I have a table for us right under the window."

They sat and ordered. Blueberry waffles for him, tofu scramble and sausage for her. After the waitress left the table, Jonathon looked at Brenda quizzically.

"Tofu scramble and sausage? Way to confuse the cook! What's

next: gluten-free toast and a side of macaroni and cheese?"
Jonathon said, winking.

"Oh, shut up. I like what I like. I guess that even includes you,
most of the time," Brenda shot back.

They continued their lively banter and ate, Jonathon laughing
so hard at one point that he nearly choked on his waffle. After
paying the bill, Jonathon asked if she would like to go for a hike
before heading their separate ways. Brenda agreed and followed
his car up the hill to Tilden Park.

The fog had given way to sunshine. Light filtered through the
redwoods onto the forest floor, warming them as they walked.
About a mile into the hike, Brenda stopped and took a drink from
her water bottle.

"Hey, did you ever think that we would end up like this,
actual adults with actual lives?" Jonathon asked her, stopping to
take his own drink of water.

"I'm not sure what you mean by 'adults' or 'lives,' but I had
hoped for some kind of a nice future for myself once college
ended. It hasn't turned out to be what I would have expected,
though. What about you?" Brenda asked, taking a seat on a
nearby log.

"From time to time, I think of what my father said to me
when I told him I wanted to major in art and not business, his
choice for me. He told me, 'Son, you're headed for failure. You
need something solid to fall back on, and the arts are anything but
solid.'"

"He woulda been real surprised to see that I've made a good
living all these years. He never woulda dreamed I'd own my
graphic arts studio. Too bad he died before he could see his son
become a successful person."

"Interesting. My mother didn't push me in any one direction
career-wise, but she had plenty to say about how I ought to live
my life. Breaking away from her was terribly painful, yet somehow
I sealed off that part of my heart. And then ... she died."

Brenda let out a sigh.

"Don't get me wrong. I'm proud I've been able to support myself all these years. But there's a big hole in my heart where 'family' is supposed to live," Brenda said, instantly wishing they weren't in a public space.

"Oh, honey, I'm your family. You know that."

"Yes, and I'm so grateful for you, Jonathon," Brenda said, wiping away a tear.

They finished their hike and said goodbye at the parking area. Since Brenda hadn't found a bed-and-breakfast with an available room, she headed back to Chapel Bay.

After deciding on the scenic route—Highway 1—Brenda got onto the 101 and crossed the Bay Bridge. She kept fingers crossed that there wouldn't be accidents blocking lanes. Miraculously, the bridge traffic was bearable, and she connected with I-280 South shortly after reentering San Francisco. Nearing Daly City, she veered onto Highway 1, grateful for the smooth transition.

Pairing her iPhone with her radio via Bluetooth, Brenda found the Beethoven channel on Pandora, always a favorite. Beethoven's Piano Concerto No. 1 was just beginning, replete with rich string sonorities, stirring pulses from the brass and woodwinds, and interwoven melodic and rhythmic structures leading up to the piano's first entrance.

With a gentle, yet decisive touch, the soloist invited the listener into the fluttering heart of the first movement. Freedom within structure; muscle and might knocking on the door of sweet soulfulness. *Could there be anything more sublime?*

The river of music flowed through her heart and mind, and time passed quickly. Before she knew it, Brenda was at the turnoff for Moss Beach and the Fitzgerald Marine Reserve. After parking in the reserve lot, she grabbed her water bottle and donned her gray Patagonia sweater and headed out onto the bluff trail.

The path led her uphill through cypress trees, and she inhaled their smoky, spicy scent as she walked. The Greeks thought cypress could clear the mind and comfort those who were in mourning. As she stood on the 100,000-year-old cliffs that overhung the beach, Brenda found her heart expanding. She observed what must have been at least fifty harbor seals sunning themselves upon the sand and sediment.

Remembering the Buddhist belief in non-self, known as *anatta*, it became clear in this moment that the lovingkindness which she felt for these creatures was part of a connection that went beyond the confines of her small body and mind. A giant self, composed of all the little selves. Closing her eyes, she took in the sharp scents of conifers and the moans of harbor seals. A brisk, chilly wind blew across the water from points unknown and whipped through her hair. She grew cold. Eyes open, she continued down the path, winding back toward the car on the Coastal Trail.

Beach, Beethoven, Buddha. Her very own Three B's. How much social interaction did she need? Not much. Feeling more peace than she had since the end of the marathon several weeks ago, Brenda continued along Highway 1, enjoying her view of the ocean as the road wound along the very edge of the continent.

Finally, she was back in Monterey County and heading toward the iconic Bixby Creek Bridge, the one that local marathoners loved to run across while listening to a pianist performing upon a grand piano hauled there from God knows where.

Piano had always been Brenda's escape before she discovered running. As she continued listening to classical music while driving up, down, and around the curves on the road, she realized she needed to spend more time at the keyboard. Pulling onto her own block in Chapel Bay, her thoughts turned momentarily to her piano student, Michaela. That little girl was as driven to succeed as Brenda herself had once been.

The conversation she'd overheard in the Muramoto's house after Michaela's lesson troubled her still. Her student was suffering as she had once suffered. Being doubly different—Asian American and lesbian—was its own very special challenge. As she walked into her chilly cottage, Brenda resolved to do whatever she could to ease this young woman's burden. *I won't allow her to be misunderstood the way I've been.*

13

P arty day, at last! After ensuring that both refrigerators had space for the caterers' platters of hors d'oeuvres, beverages, and desserts, Harriet mentally reviewed other items from her last-minute list. Gold 2023 centerpieces: check. Champagne glasses clean and ready: check. Tip envelopes for catering staff: check. House clean: check. It seemed like she really *was* ready for this shindig.

By noon, Harriet's arthritic hips sent a clear message that they needed a break. Reclining in her favorite chair, she closed her eyes. It felt so good to put her feet up and relax into the supple red leather of the La-Z-Boy.

Bathed in a pool of sunlight streaming through the bay windows, Harriet felt her heart rate slow. The curtains over her eyes closed; she began snoring. Suddenly, she was thirty years younger, sitting in the kitchen. She and Arthur were visiting her parents over the holidays, and they were getting ready for the New Year's Eve bash.

Dear Aunt Elsie sat across the round oak kitchen table from her. Looking at Harriet over the top of her half-moon readers, Elsie arched her left eyebrow. Her finger stabbed at the air as she leaned across the table toward Harriet. Just then, a caterer knocked at the back door. The door flew open. In came the caterer laden with trays, and right behind him, an elephant. As if inviting an elephant into one's kitchen was the most natural thing in the world, Elsie reached into her pocket and pulled out a handful of peanuts. The elephant raised her trunk and took the nuts.

Harriet awoke with a start; the knocking continued. She rose and let the flesh-and-blood caterer in, still shaking off the weird dream. *Elephants don't eat peanuts in real life!* She remembered reading in *Smithsonian Magazine* that peanuts contained too much protein for elephants' diets. *Sheesh! So much for truth in dreams!* But Elsie—Dear Aunt Elsie. *Why was she so angry in the dream? Or was it something else besides anger? What could it possibly mean?*

By FIVE THIRTY, it was all systems go. Harriet walked upstairs to change into her long green gown and flashy gold earrings. Achy hips notwithstanding, she couldn't keep a smile from forming. This was the first party that she had hosted in four years, and it felt like she was getting back on a bicycle.

Downstairs again, Harriet watched as Sally directed the caterers. Chafing dishes were being set up for the turkey and ham, and all seemed to go to plan. Sally sat down on a kitchen bar stool while the caterers continued working on the food.

"Mind if I ask whether Joe West is attending?" Sally looked every bit like a smitten schoolgirl.

"Joe is a 'yes,' dear. I still don't know why you get all worked up over that guy. I mean, he's good looking and all. But what do you two have in common, anyway?"

The doorbell rang, cutting the conversation short. It was Scott, Jenny, and Michaela Muramoto. Brenda Kato trailed behind.

"Oh, welcome all! Did you drive in one car?" Harriet asked.

"No, we just arrived at the same time. I have to make an early evening of it, but I wanted to make an appearance. Thanks again for helping me when I got hurt on the trail six weeks ago."

"Brenda, I didn't know you got hurt! What happened? Are you okay?" asked Jenny.

Brenda gave the Muramotos the short version of her encounter with the bike, and how Harriet had played a key role in getting the EMTs to take her to the hospital for treatment.

More folks arrived, and by seven thirty, the house was brimming with party guests. Joe West got there around eight, and he wasted no time finding Sally and engaging her in conversation. Franklin Fargo, all gussied up in a tuxedo and red scarf, scooted through the front door and down the hallway. Harriet saw him shoot a look at Sally and Joe. Too busy to give any thought to that dynamic, she circulated between kitchen and living room, joining one conversation after another.

By twenty till nine, Brenda was saying her goodbyes. As she walked toward the door, raised voices came from the study. Brenda kept walking. The Muramotos followed her, and they all exchanged New Year's greetings. Michaela looked as though she couldn't keep her eyes open much longer. As the front door slammed shut, Harriet heard something crashing down from a shelf.

~

HARRIET RUSHED into the study just as Joe was backing Franklin into a corner.

"You damned deceitful idiot! Not only do you pretend to be ss-somebody you're not to your so-called *public*, you have the ... the audacity to bring my lady friend into your web and get her to b'lieve that you're worth her time!" Joe shouted, slurring his words and sweating.

"Joe, Joe, stop this! Whatever you think Franklin has done,

please take it up with him in private. You're making a spectacle of yourself!" Sally placed a hand on Joe's forearm.

"Sally, y-you don't know who this guy really is! I've had 'nuff of his arrogant prancin' and romancin'. I saw how he was looking at you, puttin' his arm on your shoulder. He's no good for you! Wait until I tell you his real back story. The REAL truth! That will make you think twice 'bout goin' out with him!" Joe's voice was louder than ever.

"Guys! This is a celebration, not a high school fight club! Knock it the HELL off!" Harriet fumed.

"Joe, leave me alone! Sally and I were only having a friendly talk!" Franklin sputtered, eyes wide. "Friendly" came out as "fenly."

"Yeah, well, it looked like a hell of a lot more than that, pal!" Joe shouted.

The room filled with onlookers, many covering their mouths in surprise. Conversations halted mid-sentence. In the void, the only sounds were a saxophone and guitar duo playing the jazz standard "Misty" through Harriet's Bose speakers. Although few knew Joe, they all at least knew OF Franklin Fargo. This brawl was unexpected, unheard of at a Chapel Bay soirée. Though the night was still early, both men seemed to have had too much to drink; neither was handling their liquor well.

Sally walked from behind Harriet and took Joe by the hand, leading him back into the living room. Eyes cast downward, everyone could tell that Joe realized how badly he had messed up.

"Joe, I think you had better leave. But you seem too upset to drive."

"Oh, no, Sally. I'm gonna walk. S'only seven er eight blocks. I can get the car in the morning. Sal—I'm ... uh ... terribly sorry you had to witness that. I can't ... I can't believe I did that. It's a long story," Joe wiped his face on the back of his plaid shirt sleeve.

"No need to explain right now. We'll talk tomorrow, okay?" Sally said while walking him to the door.

"If you wait a minute, I'll grab your coat from upstairs," she added.

No sooner had Sally turned her back than a clang, then a thunk, reverberated through the house. Joe lay on the floor, head bleeding. Franklin was holding a brass urn over Joe's prone body, eyes wide, spittle flying from his mouth.

"Oh my God! Somebody call 911!" Sally blurted.

Someone found a towel for Joe's head, another person grabbed their phone and dialed.

"For fuck's sake, Franklin, are you insane?" Harriet screamed in his face. "The man shouted at you, yes, but why on God's green earth did you attack him from behind? And with one of my prize urns? You're a monster!"

By then, two burly men had grabbed hold of Franklin, one on either side of him. Sally, the apparent object of both lust and fury, slowly inched her way out of the study and into the kitchen, where she poured herself another glass of wine.

Shaking her head from side to side, Harriet saw her friend sneak out the back door with an unlit cigarette dangling from her lips. Within a minute or two, Harriet heard sirens screaming toward the house. She sighed. *Love is perhaps just not worth the bother anymore.* She returned to the living room just in time to see Franklin being hauled out in handcuffs.

By the time Sally was back inside, tobacco smells following her in from the cold, Joe was sitting on the gray velvet sofa. He cradled his head in his left hand. The bleeding had stopped, and his right hand held an ice pack.

"Joe, are you absolutely sure you don't want to get checked out at the hospital?" an older man said.

"No, really. I'm gonna be okay. I need a ride home, though, if someone can take me," Joe replied, sounding more sober now.

"Joe, I just called you an Uber," Sally said charitably.

"I won't refuse, Sally. I acted like a complete fool."

"You did, but let's not discuss that right now." Sally's voice had resumed its usual even tone and timbre.

The Uber arrived in front of the house, and Sally helped Joe up and out the front door. With an involuntary shudder, Harriet looked around at the twenty-some people who were still trying to have a nice New Year's Eve. Thinking that she had better elevate the mood, Harriet selected some old Big Band music for the CD player. As soon as Glen Miller's "In The Mood" came on, everyone seemed a little more cheerful. They parked drinks on coasters. A few couples began dancing in the hallway. There was nothing like invoking the music of the past to help soothe life in the present, it seemed.

"Whew. I can't believe any of that just happened. In MY HOUSE, for God's sake!" Harriet said to Sally once they had walked back to the kitchen, out of earshot of the others.

"My friend, I feel like we were on the stage of a movie. I'm not sure who the villain was—both of them, I guess. But it's over, and you still have guests, so let's party!"

Sally poured herself another glass of wine—cabernet this time —and lifted it for a toast.

"Whatever. You're right, as usual," Harriet poured herself a drink from the same bottle. She met Sally's raised glass with her own.

The party continued, and by the time the grandfather clock struck twelve, the final three guests were saying goodnight. Exhausted, Harriet told Sally not to worry about helping with the cleanup. For once, Sally agreed.

"Hey Sally, before we go upstairs, I have a question. When you asked earlier about whether I was only inviting locals to my party, did you mean I shouldn't invite Franklin?"

"Oh, no, Harriet. That never crossed my mind. Although, in retrospect, it may have been the best plan. But I was concerned that people from different cultural backgrounds may have their own expectations of how to celebrate the New Year. I was only trying to help you keep things traditional, you see?"

Harriet didn't "see." However, she knew Sally was slightly drunk, a bit traumatized, and exhausted. Best to let it go.

Sally turned around, stumbling slightly. Focusing her bleary eyes as best as she could, she looked back down the hallway toward the kitchen, where Harriet still stood.

"Oh, one other thing ... just before Joe started yelling at Franklin, Franklin was telling me something about your mother having an affair. He didn't finish his comment, but it shocked me to think ... " Sally didn't finish her remark.

"What?? That's insane. Mom was completely devoted to dad and would NEVER have had a love affair!" Harriet felt herself sobering up, none too happy that this far-fetched accusation, this ugly rumor, was capping off an already disastrous evening.

"Well, I don't know what to tell ya, sis. Maybe you ought to give Franklin a call and try to find out what his problem is. I can't think of a single reason he would have to fabricate stories about your mother, can you? I mean, did he even know her?" Sally turned around once more and grabbed the banister, slowly weaving her way up the stairs to Harriet's guest room.

Harriet sat down at her kitchen table and put her head in her hands. *Is this the cause of Aunt Elsie's wild gesturing in that crazy dream I had before the party? Was she warning me of some bad news I was about to receive?* Exhausted, she allowed her head to drop onto the table, where she slept for several hours before going upstairs and tucking herself into bed.

14

Brenda sipped her chamomile tea while staring through the front window on this New Year's Day. Although there was plenty to see outside, her inner landscape was the object of her attention. The threads of thoughts and events that had been spinning over the past couple of weeks were creating a tapestry unlike any she'd ever seen.

With a shudder, she closed her eyes and let her imagination take over. In the top left section of the fabric, she saw bright oranges and yellows heralding exciting new research projects, chances to dive deeper into the history of her community and connections with Japanese Americans who had come to Chapel Bay years ago. Her heart swelled with excitement, pride, and hope.

Deep shades of blue mixed with iridescent lime green appeared to the right of the oranges and yellows. This more muted corner of the tapestry brought about feelings of emptiness and sorrow. For Brenda, these colors symbolized a fixation on her past, with the family she'd never known, a mysterious and mesmerizing mélange.

The ten-year anniversary of her mother's passing, along with Anti-Asian sentiment—put into motion during the beginning of the Covid pandemic—made her acutely aware of a need to connect with her origins. The hateful, anonymous email she'd received added a chilling sheen to the blues and greens.

Brenda's boring social life appeared in tones of beige and gray. These shades popped up around the edges, their threads keeping the fabric from fraying. Music, running, and religion were showing up in browns and deep purples—solid, grounding earth tones—appeared in the bottom half of the fantasized cloth. Finally, dark red filaments fanned out from the center and crisscrossed the panels. They represented nurturing feelings Brenda had toward young Michaela Muramoto.

Opening her eyes, Brenda inhaled, feeling the cool morning air coming in through her nasal passages and settling in her lungs. Slowly exhaling, she smiled as she came fully into her body. The bright sunlight now streaming through the glass warmed her arm, inviting her to get up and move out of her comfortable chair, to join nature's own celebration. The first run of the year always set the tone for more good runs to follow.

Dressed in black leggings and a long-sleeved top, Brenda grabbed her water belt and jetted out the door toward the waterfront. January at the beach was a quiet time, tourist-wise. Locals enjoyed this brief hiatus between the winter holidays and the spring break rush, a time when the beachfront, the downtown cafés, and the chilled-out vibe of Chapel Bay belonged to them.

Nature, however, was far from quiet during the winter months. Giant waves crested and broke, marine mammals scooped up the fish brought to the surface. Shorebirds were vociferous. In this cascading cacophony, the protean energy of the planet pulled Brenda onward toward the water's edge.

A languid pace felt perfect, and Brenda was content to just keep moving, allowing herself the luxury of observing whatever crossed her path as she ran. Her footsteps slapped the pavement, each one a purposeful testimony, a statement of belonging to the wider world.

Coursing downhill, passing colorful cottages fronted by driveways hosting hybrid Hondas and larger luxury SUVs, the benefits of being part of the monied class were on full display. But this wasn't the time to dwell upon the history of privilege or the historical racism that propped it up. Brenda turned her attention instead on the beauty of the surroundings.

Near the boardwalk that connected parts of the beach further north with the State Park property, she paused, taking in the sun's warmth and the salty smell of sea air. *What a luxury to be connecting with life on the very edge of the continent.* Her mind felt like it was merging with the open sky, opening to what felt like a giant smile. Life coursed through her heart, lungs, and limbs. Pausing, eyes closed, Brenda felt a connection with all seekers.

Slowly opening her eyes and taking a swig from her water bottle, Brenda was ready to continue her journey. A left turn took her onto the wooden planks of the boardwalk. With each twist of the path, blue-green mounds of ice plant, not yet in bloom, jutted toward her moving legs.

Gulls shrieked overhead, then plunged into the receding waters, a New Year's fish feast on their minds. Willets, sandpipers, and sanderlings played tag with the sea foam as they sought tiny crabs and other invertebrates. The intertidal ecosystem was a blessing, pure and true, a setting of such incredible interspecies commerce and cooperation. *If only human commerce could be so seamless, so dedicated to taking what each one needs but allowing others to freely take as well ...*

One mile became two. The boardwalk wound away from the beach and toward the road fronting the state park. Beads of perspiration dripped from her face to her arm, and Brenda grabbed her water bottle for a drink. Looking up, she saw a familiar figure seated yards away on a bench overlooking the path. Actually, it was three familiar figures: one human, two canines.

Oh, brother. What were the odds of running into Joe and his mongrels today? With no way of avoiding the little cluster, she turned toward them and made eye contact with the human member of the tribe.

"Happy New Year, Brenda," Joe said, nodding in her direction.

He looks like hell.

"Happy New Year, Joe. I'm surprised to see you out here, but honestly, grateful that the dogs aren't trying to trip me, for once."

"Hey, that's not fair. We all have a right to use the paths around here. That's what the regulations say. I think it's great that you runners are getting your endorphins going, but we regular folks like to go at a more leisurely pace, don't you know?"

Joe's face was wan and pinched, and Brenda could tell something was wrong. Regardless, this conversation was getting on her nerves. How was she supposed to keep her compassion intact when she was always being attacked by the ignorant of this town? She wondered if Joe was the one who'd written the ugly homophobic, anti-Asian, anti- "everything that's not straight and white" email.

"Ok, then. I think I'll be on my way. Please keep your dogs leashed and away from the rest of us." Every time she saw Joe, she got triggered. *Damn that Joe and his two dogs! Damn my fear of dogs!*

She spent the three-mile run back to her cottage saying the Green Tara mantra: *Om Tare Tuttare Ture Soha.* I prostrate to the Liberator, Mother of all Victorious Ones. By the time she arrived back at her doorstep, she could at least breathe freely again.

PICKING himself up from the sandy bench, Joe wondered whether it was even possible to feel more dejected than he did at present. Dogs' leashes in hand, he meandered up the twisty path back to the main road, too lost in his own quagmire to even care that brambles were bumping up against his khakis and depositing burrs in his socks and on his companions' tails and belly hair.

They crossed the road and made their way to the parking lot, gravel crunching beneath Joe's boots. After wiping down Kibble and Bones and loading them into the rear of his Subaru, Joe leaned against the back of the vehicle. What, he wondered, brought about so much bad karma, so much relationship rancor that was popping up everywhere?

Joe shook his head and tumbled into the car. Brenda felt discounted. That was the problem. What was it was like to be a female, let alone a female of color? Kibble and Bones shook, rattling their collars. *How in the world can two such loving creatures annoy Brenda so much? Are they tainted just because they're my dogs?* They had done nothing that any other ordinary dogs hadn't done. *So they got in her way once or twice. So what?*

Back at his humble abode, Joe fed the dogs and then warmed up a can of chicken noodle soup. Brenda's impression of him was the least of his worries at the moment. How much damage had he done to the relationship with Sally? She had witnessed him in full verbal attack mode with another man. Not a good look. *Screwed royally, no matter how I slice it.* Ha. He had been so tickled with the mantra, "Joe is not insignificant." Now, he'd better change it to, "Joe is a significant ass."

Was there a chance for damage control? What approach should he take if he tried to mend things with Sally? Maybe Harriet could help him. She and Sally seemed to be really close, after all. Joe's mind was racing out of control. *Maybe I can call her, apologize for ruining her party, then casually ask if she thought Sally would consider speaking to me again. Maybe that would work.*

Joe bit his lip. The torrent of unsettling thoughts continued. *Am I playing with fire? What if she knows about me and her mother? Has Franklin told Harriet about my affair with Pat? Surely, I wouldn't have been invited to her party if she already knew about it. Maybe I can come up with a way of finding out what Harriet knows ...*

Unsure what he should do, Joe's gaze came to rest on his spoon. His soup had grown cold, but no matter, as he'd lost his appetite.

It had been too long since he'd seen his own therapist (physician, heal thyself!). He went to the list of contacts on his phone and pulled up Dr. Graves' number. Joe fully knew how dangerous unchecked depression could become.

~

THE AFTERNOON after her big party, Harriet could only wonder at the social mess it had created. Joe's angry outburst had caught everyone by surprise. Franklin's pugilistic response was even more startling, given the fact that he had always seemed like a person of refinement, a cool customer of sorts. Interesting as this all was, more important issues than the relationship between Joe and Franklin troubled her.

Did Mom have an affair? Why would she have done that? Did Dad know? How would Franklin have known anything about it?

Red-faced, she picked up her cell phone and punched in Franklin's number.

"Hello, Franklin—Harriet Conley here. Do you have a few minutes to talk?"

"Harriet! Oh my gosh, yes. I've been meaning to call. I am SO sorry for my behavior at your party! I wasn't myself at all last night!" Franklin said, sounding for all the world like a little boy caught with his hand in the cookie jar. Harriet could just picture his puppy dog eyes and trembling lip.

"Your behavior was truly abominable, that's true. I hope you were humbled by being hauled off by the police. But that's not why I'm calling," Harriet sighed.

"Yeah, well, Joe started it!" Franklin's voice rose a full octave.

"There's something else I need to say, Franklin. Sally said you were about to tell her something to do with Mother and an affair. Let me tell you something ..."

Franklin interrupted her, "Yeah, but Joe and your mom, they were lovers, and I just thought that Sally, being your good friend and all ... well ...."

Harriet sucked her teeth. The room spun. *Joe? Joe WEST? How is this possible? Isn't he a retired psychologist?* She stopped listening to Franklin, and when she tuned back in, he was mumbling something about Joe. Harriet lost patience for this ridiculous diatribe. She needed to shift the focus back to the original reason for her call to Franklin.

Cutting him off mid-sentence, she said, "Let me finish! As I was saying, you are absolutely NOT to spread malicious gossip involving my mother or ANY member of my family. If I ever hear that you've done so again, I will have no choice but to reveal that you have been in several altercations over the years that have landed you in jail. Am I clear?"

Harriet was exhausted. She hadn't planned to use this trump card, but Franklin's belligerence and the revelation about Joe and her mom left her no choice.

Again, Harriet asked, "Franklin, DO I make myself clear?"

Franklin cleared his throat, and Harriet could hear a woman's voice in the background, asking if everything was okay.

An uncomfortably long silence ensued. Eventually, he spoke. "Yes. But let me ask you this: How do you know about my time in jail?"

"I was cleaning out the attic just a few minutes ago, looking for some books. I came across a box of my father's legal files, stuff I thought he'd shredded years ago. I opened one box, and there it was, plain as day: proceedings of a court case in San Francisco in which YOU were charged with assault and sentenced to six months in jail. There were files on two other situations, disorderly conduct charges. Dad got the charges dropped." Harriet finally took a breath. She was certain her anger had come through loud and clear.

"Oh, I see. Well, considering that, I have no choice but to agree to your terms, Harriet. But do your friend Sally a favor and let her know Joe is not the honest man he portrays himself to be ...."

Harriet cut him off once more.

"Listen to me, pal. It is not your job to interfere with Sally's, or anyone's, relationships. I will certainly not convey salacious gossip and half-baked stories to her. You've done enough of that already. And mark my words, if I think you've been running your damned mouth off again, I will NOT hesitate to spread the stories of your sordid criminal past. I'll do it quicker than you can turn around."

Harriet hung up.

Was there any truth to Franklin's claim that Joe and Mom had an affair? If so, maybe that's why he looked familiar to me the first time I spotted him on the walking path. Maybe he's the guy I saw leaving the house once or twice when coming to visit Mom, while I was still living in San Francisco.

Frustrated, she wondered how she might sort this out. Remembering that there was one more unopened box in the attic, she limped upstairs to the second floor. The folding ladder to the attic was still leaning against the wall in the hallway, trapdoor down. She switched on the attic light and grasped the sides of the ladder, taking one rung at a time up into the musty attic.

Harriet spotted it right away, just next to the box holding her father's old legal briefs. Labeled "Patricia," the box had less dust on it than the one that contained her father's papers. Dad had passed away a few years ahead of Mom, so it made sense that her mother's memorabilia box would not be as dusty.

The brittle masking tape cracked as Harriet pulled it off, and she placed a shaking hand atop the lid. She paused, heart beating rapidly in her chest. *Do I really want to know what's inside the box?* It could be anything, really. Old family photos, her mother's high school yearbooks, even clues about generations past. Exhausted, Harriet picked up the box and schlepped it back downstairs. She couldn't open it just yet. She placed it underneath the secretary in her office. *There will be time enough to sift through the contents tomorrow.* All she had energy for tonight was eating a sandwich and watching reruns of *The Golden Girls*.

15

Sitting on her meditation cushion the day after her run-in with Joe at the beach, Brenda's eyes rested on the six-inch Buddha figurine on her altar. Recognizing her suffering, allowing the pain to be just what it was—Brenda didn't have to dig too deep to know why she was hurting. A distant mother who constantly judged. A father who, for whatever reason, had abandoned her. The recent incidents of bigotry in America, including the banning of books written by minorities. The anonymous email from book banners. A physical assault on the running trail.

Twenty minutes of introspection passed. The last rays of sunlight receded from the window, turning the top of her spinet piano from walnut to black. "Hello, old friends," she said to the white and black keys that had kept silent vigilance—had it really been over a month since she'd touched the keyboard?

Taking a deep breath, she lowered herself onto the old wooden piano bench. It creaked, and her body responded by releasing the tension in her neck and shoulders. Eyes closed, she allowed herself to fall into a state of repose, a musical meditation. Here, away from other worries, was a river of tranquility. As the waters settled, she sensed the world of melody, harmony, and rhythm.

With another breath, she lifted her hands from the keys. Quick, punctuating notes flowed from her fingers as she launched into the Prelude of Bach's English Suite Number 3. The lines of melody went from left hand to right hand and back again, pulsing and turning and finally ending as the graceful allemande began.

Pulling long, delicate lines from the piano, Brenda saw a scene appearing before her mind's eye. So lovely, so regular, the strands in the imagined tapestry which she'd previously woven came more vividly to life. The oranges, yellows, blues, greens, reds, and purples all appeared along with the feelings each denoted.

Next, the rapid courante poured out of her like a torrent, almost fugue-like in its design. This was release, salvation, celebration. Each repetition of the theme required a slightly different touch, ending in an upward flourish. The sarabande began with a somber and serious declaration. Quietly, the clustered notes invited the listener in. Embellishments over the plain theme gave texture and purpose to the mournful feelings aroused.

The sarabande came to a subdued end and transitioned to the more playful gavotte I and gavotte II. The effect was like sunlight peeking through the dark clouds. *Oh, the joy of losing myself in the simple, almost childlike melodies and harmonies, regular rhythmic motifs pulling along like a horse leading a wagon.* Brenda smiled.

Nearly breathless, Brenda allowed her hands to drop to her sides once the final bars of the gavottes receded. Her body shook, and tears streamed down her face. This was the catharsis she had been seeking. *So much better than interacting with people ....*

Just then, a loud pounding on her front door made her heart skip a beat. *So much for having a quiet dinner. Brenda* peeked through the sheer curtains framing the door. Franklin Fargo stood on her stoop.

"What on earth, Franklin? How did you know where I live, and why are you here now, for God's sake?" Brenda asked, opening the door just wide enough to accommodate her face.

"I tried calling earlier, but you didn't pick up. I Googled you and found your home address," Franklin blurted, rapid-fire.

"What? Why would you do that? What's the big emergency?" Brenda asked, eyebrow arched. She stepped onto the porch, hands on hips.

"I ... I ... well, have you talked with Harriet? Has she mentioned me? I was hoping ..." Franklin swayed and grabbed onto the iron handrail. Regaining his balance, he took a step closer to her. Alcohol wafted from his pores, and his eyes were bloodshot.

"It's just ... since you're some sort of Asian you must understand how the law can go against a person. And me, I'm not even a minority, just being treated like one ... and, you know, I wanted you to have my side of the story ...." Franklin careened again, nearly falling over backwards this time.

Brenda crossed the threshold of anger and stepped into the land of rage. Thoughts raced. She shut her eyes. *Oh My God! Is this fool trying to get me on his side by insinuating that his issues are equal to the generational discrimination and trauma I have experienced? And is he really putting all Asians into one category? What the hell!!*

Realizing that this wasn't the time for a lesson in cross-cultural sensitivity and communication, she opened her eyes and spoke.

"You're drunk, Franklin! I'm going to ask you to leave, or I'll call the police! I'm sure they would be most interested in your side of the story!"

"Oh, no need for that at all! I can go, yes, I can go. I just wanted to let you know ..." he sputtered.

"GO!" Brenda shouted.

Franklin raised a hand, turned precariously on his heel, and somehow made it down the two front steps to the sidewalk without falling over.

Watching to make sure that her unwanted guest actually made it down the sidewalk and around the corner, Brenda sighed in exasperation.

What a piece of work that guy is! "Keep moving, asshole!" she shouted, not caring who heard her. "And don't come back!"

More confirmation that human interactions are often over-rated. If I had any trouble recognizing the causes of my suffering earlier, that whole puzzle just became much easier to solve ....

She had forgotten, for the time being, about not blaming her discomfort on others' flaws. Shivering, she came inside and slammed the door.

∼

FOR WEEKS, Brenda had awaited the Writing Wrongs Conference. It began the day after Franklin's unexpected visit, and featured writers from many cultures. Besides current work, the program also included poetry and prose written in the past. The drive from Chapel Bay to Sacramento would take four hours, and Brenda started her drive before the sun rose. Her mind blossomed with ideas. *I hope I can make some contacts that will bear fruit. National Poetry Month is coming up in April, with Asian American and Pacific Islander Heritage Month in May.*

While driving, Brenda also continued to think about Franklin's drunken demeanor and the micro-aggression he'd tossed in her direction. And saying she was "some sort of Asian" ... *What a jerk!* Circling back to the anonymous racist and homophobic email she'd received before Thanksgiving, she saw he fit the profile of one who might send such a missive. He was insecure, lacked proper boundaries, and seemed desperate. *I hate to think that a published author would stoop to something as heinous as espousing book banning, but stranger things have happened ....*

Pulling into the conference center parking lot, Brenda grabbed her bag and practically skipped to the center's front door. Within moments of entering the cavernous front hall, she felt a sense of peace and belonging. She was about to spend a day and a half with others who understood what it felt like to be revered as a member of a "model minority" yet invisible as an occupant of the "white adjacent" category. Picking up her name badge and program, Brenda hustled to make the first workshop she'd chosen.

"Oh, hi, is this the right room for the poetry forum?" Brenda asked a friendly-looking woman wearing a kaftan.

"Yes, I think so. I guess they forgot to put the sign on the door," the woman replied.

Once inside, Brenda took a seat in the front row. Pulling out her pad and paper, she looked once more at the program notes. Surprisingly, there was a reference to a publication called Sinister Wisdom, an American lesbian literary and art journal. One presenter had written an article appearing in the recent "Asian Lesbians" issue. Brenda couldn't keep a smile from decorating her face. *This is awesome!*

She turned the page and noticed that another presenter was sharing poems from an internment camp. If she'd needed any more proof that she was in the right place, Brenda couldn't imagine what it would be. The room filled, and the presentations began. Each author spoke straight from the heart, telling truths both painful and joyous. Filipinos, Vietnamese folks, Chinese women and men, the list went on. Brenda made notes on speakers she wanted to contact for help with her upcoming events.

The next-to-last speaker was an older Japanese woman by the name of Ruby Yamamoto. She was a native of Sacramento and was sharing poetry written in an internment camp. From 1942 to 1945, the American government had confined her and her family to Camp Tulelake, just as Brenda's mom and her family had been. Ruby spoke briefly of her own life and then shared poems written by her father, John. His haikus sounded lovely in both Japanese and English. He portrayed horrors of life alongside the ever-present beauty of nature.

Ruby finished, and everyone in the room rose to their feet. Tears flowed freely. Although one speaker had yet to present, Brenda felt compelled to follow Ruby out of the room and into the hallway. Introducing herself, she asked whether Ruby had time to chat later in the day. The older woman said yes, and the two agreed to meet across the street in a café at three o'clock.

The next presentation on Brenda's list was "Literary Responses to Racism." She didn't recognize the presenters' names, but the topic intrigued her. The main presenter, a young Chinese man, shared an essay he'd written in response to Covid. Everyone in the room could relate to the fear that spread when Covid got labeled the "China Virus." A lively discussion followed his reading of the essay. A panel of speakers took to the stage to discuss book banning—its manifestations and effects upon all communities of color. There was time for questions once the six panelists finished interacting, and Brenda's hand shot up.

"I work in a small library on the central coast. A few months ago, I received an email from someone only identified as a member of Lovers of Literature. The tone was threatening and directed me not to feature authors or themes relating to non-mainstream cultures of any type, including Asian Americans and LGBTQ folks. Has anyone else run into this group?"

Immediately, participants began talking amongst themselves and nodding. When the room quieted down, a panelist spoke up.

"Funny you should mention that. I, too, work in an administrative capacity in a library here in California. I received a similar message from that group only last week. Frankly, I'm not sure whether they are all talk or maybe pose a genuine threat. But I'll tell you this: There have been many similar threats and even violence perpetuated by groups just like this all across the country. It's outrageous!"

Other hands shot up, but Brenda had more to say.

"I keep wondering if I'm being targeted because I'm Asian and lesbian. I don't know what to do, considering that I will have authors from a variety of backgrounds, including those communities, speak in the coming months."

A short Korean American woman wearing stylish aviator glasses spoke up.

"I feel you. I've heard of that group. Our best strategy is to collaborate and get some media coverage about the problem. Of course, we don't want to give them free publicity .... I'd be willing to exchange information with anyone who would like to share ideas."

Others nodded in agreement, and before she left for lunch, Brenda had collected contact information from ten people. *Power in numbers.* This was clearly more than a local problem. Although there was no way to determine whether members of the hate group lived in the Chapel Bay environs or who, in fact, had written the email, she felt a stronger sense of resolve now. *These anonymous cowards can't destroy our communities!*

The afternoon session she attended was a good one, featuring young people who were speaking out on social media platforms. Time passed quickly, and before she knew it, it was time to meet Ruby in the café across the street. She'd written her questions out while eating lunch and couldn't wait to talk with this wonderful woman. She walked into the small café and she was pleased to see their rendezvous was taking place during a lull in business. Ruby had already arrived and sat at a table toward the back of the dining area.

Brenda ordered a coffee and took it to the table, and the women greeted one another. She looked at Ruby and marveled at the strength of character she'd shown all throughout her long life. After taking two sips of coffee for courage, Brenda launched into her questions.

"I really enjoyed your presentation, Ruby. Your dad's poems were remarkable! Is there any chance you'd allow me to share them during National Poetry Month? I coordinate events down in Chapel Bay and we're featuring Asian American poetry in April."

Ruby smiled. Her words were slow and measured. "I'd be delighted to share his work with you. Why don't we exchange information, and I will send you a digital copy of the poems I shared this morning? I have also written a book about my family's life, and many of the poems are within the book. Maybe you would like to acquire a copy for your library," she added.

"Yes, that would be lovely. If you don't mind, I have a few more personal questions for you," Brenda said. She hoped she wasn't overstepping.

Ruby raised her eyebrows and leaned forward. Brenda took that as a sign to continue.

"My mom grew up in Sacramento and went to Camp Tule-lake. I just wonder whether you knew her. Her name was Toshi Kato."

Asking this question had left Brenda breathless. She was afraid of what she might find out and just as afraid she'd learn nothing at all.

"Toshi Kato! I haven't heard that name in years! Yes, we knew each other from the camp, and then later on we went to the same dances in town. My brother tried to date her! She wasn't inter-ested in him, though. Haha—you're really taking me down memory lane!" Ruby's eyes shone with delight.

Brenda felt the air change around them, becoming heavier, thicker, and darker. Ruby's aura magnetically pulled her in, tugged at her whole being. *This is something I've waited for my whole life ... a chance to talk about Mom in the camps with someone who knew her, who lived that experience with her!*

"I know it's painful to speak about times in the camp, but can I ask you a few things?" Brenda asked, chewing her lip.

"Oh, my. Yes, it's difficult, but I can see that you're dying to ask about your mother. What would you like to know?" Ruby placed her warm hand over Brenda's cold one.

"Tell me what your days were like in camp. Was it one terrible thing after the next? Were you afraid all the time?"

Ruby described the cold nights in winter, the heat in summer, and many of the deprivations families had to endure. There was enough food, but not the food their bodies had been used to. Many, including Toshi, had bouts of flu and pneumonia.

"I recall the summer and fall of 1942. Japanese farm workers went on strike for several days because their breakfasts were inadequate for the hard labor they had to perform. Then, over Labor Day, the camp supervisors held a big celebration. Your mom and I watched the older kids and parents having fun at the dances, and there was even a Labor Day Queen and her court," Ruby said.

Brenda could easily picture these scenes; it seemed like the camp supervisors were doing everything possible to keep internees off balance.

"Kids thought it was one big party. But later on, we found out that our parents who worked in the camp had to make up all the time they'd taken off to celebrate. And there were more strikes that fall, too. It was really a tense time. Not too long after the strikes, Toshi's dad and my dad were put in a compound, kept separate from their families and treated very poorly. Toshi and I cried and cried, calling out for our fathers. . . ." Ruby paused and folded her napkin into thirds.

"But I'll tell you this, Brenda," Ruby added. "We found time for fun—we were kids, you know! Toshi was a kind of instigator in our friend group. I remember the time she snuck into the mess hall after dark and came out with candy bars for five of us. They must have been from a secret stash the guards had!" Ruby's face broke into a broad smile; her eyes sparkled.

So Mom grieved for her father, who'd been locked up, but also had a playful side! Who knew? Encouraged, Brenda kept going with her questions.

"Wow! Okay, here's something else I want to ask. Do you know anything about a man she became very serious about after high school? Mom got pregnant with me during that time, and I've never been able to find out who my father is ...."

Brenda averted her eyes. A deep and familiar shame, not hers to bear, crept in.

"Oh ... well, she and I attended the same Buddhist Church. Now that you mention it, she showed an interest in one particular young man. I'm sorry, I don't remember his name, though. I do recall that he was good looking. And he seemed really friendly to those of us in Toshi's circle. But I stopped attending the church shortly after that, and she and I lost touch. It's not like today, with everyone texting all the time!"

Ruby took a sip of her coffee and sat back in her chair. Her face sagged with fatigue. Brenda was still processing this information, not sure how to respond. She closed her eyes. *This is a lot to take in ... but who was this man?*

After a moment, Brenda spoke.

"Thank you for meeting me, Ruby. You are a true inspiration, and I look forward to receiving the poems and a copy of your book. I'm glad you knew Mom. I'm so grateful for the stories you've shared with me," Brenda finished.

As she rose to leave, Brenda was sure that the contacts she'd made this day would be important in the upcoming months. Driving to her hotel, she pondered the new information she'd received about her father. *They went to church together; Dad was a looker, and nice to folks ... that's more than I knew before, but it feels like a sort of dead end.*

~

"Hey there, Brenda—got time for a quick chat?" Justin asked, appearing at Brenda's office door the following Tuesday morning.

"Oh, hi Justin. Yes, I can talk with you in five. Just finishing up this email," Brenda replied.

Last week's meeting with the Chapel Bay Asians—as she learned the group was affectionately called—had gone really well. She was responding to a request for her participation with the Day of Remembrance of Japanese Internment, celebrated every February 19. She recalled that had been the day in 1942 when President Franklin D. Roosevelt had signed Executive Order 9066, ultimately putting over 120,000 Japanese Americans in one of ten camps in America.

Yes, of course I'd like to attend the memorial gathering. In fact, she offered to speak about her own mother's incarceration at Tule Lake. It would be difficult, but perhaps rather healing. Interesting to note that the club's president was none other than Scott Muramoto, the father of her piano student, Michaela.

Finished with the email, Brenda closed her laptop and went to speak with Justin. He had a calendar pulled up on his computer screen. Taking a deep breath, she put a smile on her face and rapped lightly on the wooden doorframe to his office.

"C'mon in and have a seat," Justin said cheerily. "I'm just working on the library calendar for the next two months and need to see what you'd like to add. I'm aware I usually send out an email request for dates, but it seems like we rely too much on that and don't get to talk often enough. Silly, don't you agree, since we're just down the hallway from one another?"

Brenda nodded and told Justin that she still needed to find speakers for the February and March time slots. She noted that her membership in the Chapel Bay Asians group and experiences at the conference she'd just attended brought promise for the April gathering.

"Well, that's great, Brenda—the part about finding poets for our big April display and talks. But it's the February to March timeframe that worries me. When do you think you'll have something for me?" Justin asked, head tilted, eyebrows raised.

His expectant expression made him look a little like a dog begging for its treat.

"I'll get on that today, Justin. I may know someone local— one of our library volunteers—who can help find speakers. I hope to have the gaps filled by the end of the week," Brenda said.

"Terrific. I was sure I could count on you! And if it helps, I can kick in a small honorarium out of my own pocket to entice the speakers," Justin put in. "Anything I can do, I'm more than happy to."

Back in her own office, Brenda bit the bullet and gave Harriet a call. This was sure to tickle Harriet's busybody bones, but it was the only way forward at the moment.

"Hi Harriet—Brenda Kato here. Do you have a moment to talk?"

Harriet replied in the affirmative.

"Great. It's about the Meet the Author talks that I organize. You mentioned that you have an in with a group of local writers, and I wanted to pick your brain a little. I placed calls to three local authors but haven't heard a peep from any of them," Brenda said, giving Harriet the three names.

"Oh, let me see. As I recall, one writes about the plant and animal life in the area, but the last time I heard anything about her was over five years ago. Someone told me she's moved out of the area, come to think of it. Or did she die? Something like that. The second one you mentioned I've seen from time to time. Boy, he's really making his mark these days! I've seen his name on posters announcing book signings at various locations. Oh, and Frances Wong, the third one? No, I'm afraid I'm not familiar with her. What does she write?" Harriet asked, finally running out of steam.

"Frances Wong is a cookbook author. Well, from the sounds of things, the first two are unlikely to be available. I'll keep trying to reach Frances, though."

"Oh—you know what? It's been some time since I was a regular attendee at the Wednesday book group's monthly gatherings, but I remember they used to feature members reading from their latest work. Would you like me to see whether one or more of the active participants wants to do a reading at the library?" Harriet was clearly trying to be helpful.

"Sure, why not? I'd need to meet with them in advance, of course, especially if the work is unpublished. We're trying to keep the focus on published work,"

"Okey Dokey! I'll make some calls and get back to you shortly. Thanks for letting me be a part of your process. Maybe one day I can show you some of my writing."

"I'll look forward to hearing from you, Harriet, and thanks again," Brenda said in closing, ignoring Harriet's self-promotion.

BEFORE SHE KNEW IT, Brenda had come to the turnaround point of her Tuesday afternoon run. As she paused, catching her breath for a moment, she noticed a somewhat familiar-looking blonde woman. *It can't be! It is!* Tara, the woman she had seen at the end of the local half marathon and then once more, at the finish line of the California International Marathon, was rapidly approaching. Her hair glowed golden in the waning light of the day, making her appear quite angelic.

"Well, hello there! We meet again! How far are you running today?" Tara Winslow, suddenly right in front of her, stopped for a sip of water.

"Hi! I'm about to turn and run back to the house—the second half of my usual six- miler." Brenda's bottle was nearly empty, but she tried to pretend otherwise by only tipping it half-way. Tara seemed in better shape than she was and probably didn't need to gulp down three quarters of a bottle of water on a three-mile stretch.

"I've got one more mile in this direction before turning around myself. Mind if I join you for a bit?" Tara asked, flashing a smile while adjusting the water belt on her shapely hips.

Brenda felt an internal flutter, but she couldn't tell whether it was butterflies in her stomach or something more primal originating from a slightly lower body part.

"I'd love the company, but we'd probably better go single file since the path narrows just around the bend." Brenda pointed out the part of the trail that turned toward the cliffs overlooking the water.

Just keep breathing.

"Agreed. I'm ready when you are! Oh—and you're Brenda, right? I'm not the greatest with names, I'm afraid," Tara said, grinning shyly.

This woman might be my undoing.

"Yep. And how could I forget your name, Tara, after you overheard me talking to the mythical Green Tara the first time we met?" Brenda chirped.

"That's right! Well, lead the way, Brenda." Tara's thousand-watt smile made Brenda forget which direction to head until Tara pointed the way.

They ran without conversing. Brenda couldn't help but feel Tara's eyes on her backside, a sensation that made her whole body sweat. It wasn't easy to stay focused on a pace when all she wanted to do was turn around and look into the green eyes of the fetching woman on her tail. Much too quickly, they came to the end of the mile.

"This is where we part ways, Brenda. I hope we can run together again sometime. Can I give you my number?" Tara reached for her phone.

Heart pounding, Brenda gladly rattled off the phone number. Seconds later, her own phone buzzed with a text from Tara.

"There, now we each have a way of contacting the other. Take care, Brenda, and let's get in touch soon!"

Whoa ... did that gorgeous woman really just give me her number? Is this for real? Brenda mentally pinched herself, unsure of what exactly had just taken place. As she watched Tara turn and run back along the path, she briefly daydreamed about the possibility of being friends. More than friends, if she was being honest with herself.

Two miles to go. Looking out over the ocean, Brenda noticed how each wave seemed to come out of nowhere, crested, and then returned to its watery home once the energy had subsided. The greens and blues of the water also shifted with the changing light, an ever-changing palette of cool color. Everything seemed fresher, brighter, more vibrant than it had earlier.

As she turned her attention back to the path, a sudden pain struck her quadriceps. *Shit! Not again!* Yowling, she stopped in her tracks. This betrayal of the body was really beginning to piss her off.

Limping home, Brenda's thoughts went from the fun of

meeting up with Tara to the dismay of not being able to run. Whenever she got sick or hurt, she thought that this illness, this pain, would last forever. Darker and darker her thoughts became as she trudged up the three steps to her front door. *Shit, shit, shit.* Dragging her sorry self to the lounge by the door, she plopped down, utterly defeated. *So much for freedom, joy, and immersion in the planet's energy.*

"Great, just great. I meet up with a pretty woman who wants to run with me, then turn around and screw up my leg. Damn it all!" Brenda sputtered, tears flowing down her cheeks and falling onto her stretchy black running pants.

Putting her face in her hands, Brenda reflected upon her life. *Can't run, can't find speakers for the author events, don't even have a family to call my own. This really sucks!*

As the sun set, Brenda slowly rose from the La-Z-Boy and limped to her bedroom. *What on earth am I supposed to make of this situation? Is this a punishment, a karmic result of past misdeeds? If so, what were they?*

After showering, she pulled out a book she had been reading and retired to the warmth of her queen-sized bed, pulling the blue and white quilt that her mother made so long ago up around her neck. It wasn't a substitute for actual love, she mused, but maybe some of the initial feeling Toshi put into the quilt during its creation would still be there, moving outward into the cosmos like pieces of atoms during the radioactive decay of elements.

Her last thought before falling asleep was that it was a good thing she'd hurt herself. *I can't open my heart to a new love now. Not with the shadow of the Lovers of Literature hanging over my head. Not without knowing who my father was.*

16

A week after her big party, Harriet got to work on her fledgling writing project. It felt good to be back at her writing desk. She retrieved a yellow legal pad from the center drawer and began brainstorming. She recalled a writer's workshop she'd taken in San Francisco twenty years earlier. The instructor had asked the students to come up with a main idea and place it in the center of a circle. Then, as sub themes came to mind, they put those in smaller circles and connected them to the center and to other circles in whatever way made sense. *Why not try it now?*

In the center of the fresh page of paper, Harriet wrote the word "Italy." Although she had yet to open the box of her mother's keepsakes, just the idea of the dusty box under her desk nudged her toward her family heritage. In just a few minutes, ideas were popping into her head and making their way onto the page.

Religion
Family Drama
World war II
Crime
Romance
Immigration to the U.S.

Interesting. Relying upon her memories of stories told to her as a young girl, she opened her laptop and set the timer on her phone for ten minutes.

It is Genoa, Italy; the year is 1915. After a long day on the water, Giuseppe Sabatini is bringing in his fishing nets and looking at the daily catch. Not bad for a winter's day, he thinks. As he lifts the heavy buckets of fish from the boat onto the deck, he takes in the smells and sounds of the dock, so familiar to him by now. Smiling, he remembers how the pungent odors of perch and pike, the insults of fellow fishermen comparing their catch with that of their rivals, how all of this was a shock to his system when he began working the boats.

That was thirty long years ago, and what he lacked in experience, he made up in enthusiasm and the strength of a young man. Now, he was older, more grizzled, carrying a body that spoke to him with its aches and pains at the end of each day. It was a good thing that age and experience had enough redeeming qualities to make up for the suppleness and verve with which youth had once blessed him.

Okay, time was up. That felt like a pretty good start. With childlike glee, she rose from the desk and stretched her neck. Better get some tea and a cookie or two! There was no reason to starve herself, after all. As soon as the kettle was on to boil, the phone rang.

"Hello there, Sally! I was just thinking about you and hoping we could get together."

"Yes, we have some things to discuss, for sure," Sally replied.

"Are you doing anything this afternoon? I'm just taking a break from my writing and having tea. Wanna come over?" Harriet searched through cabinets for sugar while they talked.

"Oh, that sounds lovely," Sally said.

"Terrific! Come on by. I made banana bread yesterday and would love to share it with you."

I MUST keep a lid on what Franklin and I discussed earlier in the week.

SALLY ARRIVED AN HOUR LATER. Harriet poured tea and cut generous slices of banana bread for them. Once they had settled around the kitchen table, Sally began telling her story.

"Well, you'll never believe this, but guess who I saw in the grocery store line yesterday? Nobody but Joe West! I don't think he saw me, 'cause I was several lines over and fairly far behind him. I have to say, he looked really down-and-out. I feel for the poor fella, actually. I'm sure he regrets letting his anger get the best of him in front of so many people, not to mention the physical pain of getting walloped by Franklin!"

Harriet listened and nodded, raising an eyebrow when Franklin's brutish behavior was mentioned.

"Yes, indeed. Matter of fact, Joe called me yesterday, profusely apologizing for his behavior. At the end of our conversation, he asked whether I thought you'd ever agree to see him again. He's super embarrassed, and I can't imagine the courage it took for him to even ask me that question."

"Interesting. What did you say?"

"I told him it wasn't my place to answer that question, since I simply had no idea how you were feeling. But I promised him I would pass along his wish to reconnect and put the ball in your court." Harriet winked.

"Good choice. I'm still wondering how I *do* feel about him, frankly. Maybe I'll call him in a day or so and just check up on him. We can see how things go from there. I'm not totally opposed to us being friends," Sally said, strumming her slender fingers on the oak tabletop.

"Your choice entirely, dear. I know I've sometimes been too harsh with people who made mistakes and ended up regretting the loss of their friendship. We are all just human beings, doing the best we can, after all." *Was Sally taking any of this in?* Harriet paused for effect. "I once heard some therapist on a talk show say that everyone is just doing the best they can with what they know at any one time,"

Harriet continued. "That sounded like a bunch of New Age hooey, but I kind of get it now. It's a lot easier to stand back and criticize someone's life than it is to realize that we are all on our own path. I can't know what another person has gone through, after all."

Sally let out a guffaw. "Well, aren't you just all touchy-feely today? Is this a result of resuming your writing? Are you going deep into the well?"

Their banter continued, and Harriet talked about her interest in exploring her family's roots. Sally nodded while chewing on the freshly made bread.

"Changing the subject: You talked about wanting to volunteer in the community last time we spoke. Any more thoughts on that?" Sally asked.

"Huh. Interesting you should ask. I was returning a library book yesterday and saw a flier asking for volunteers to read to children. I think it's only once or twice a week. I thought maybe I would speak with the volunteer coordinator," Harriet said.

"I can see you doing that, Harriet. I know you've never had kids of your own, but you always said you enjoyed hanging out with your nieces and nephews. Could be a good fit—you, books, and children," Sally said encouragingly.

"Yes, and did I tell you I spent Christmas with my cousin and my niece? You wouldn't believe what a polished young woman she's turned into. She and I had quite a conversation about the fact that people within a family can have very different points of view, even though they all received the same input at one point," Harriet said.

"Yeah, it's the old 'nature or nurture' question, I guess. It must be the same with, for instance, identical twins when one turns out to be gay and the other straight. And speaking of that— do you think Brenda Kato, the woman who came to your party, is a lesbian? I just get a kind of vibe from her. I would never ask, though!" Sally said with a half grin on her face.

I guess being lesbian is one of those "cultural differences" Sally mentally flagged when asking about my party guest list. So much for hoping she'd ease up on her observations.

"I have no clue, but if she is, I guess to each her own. I wouldn't think Chapel Bay would be the easiest place to live as a gay person, but I could be wrong. There are a bunch of well-educated citizens here, after all. Many of them are conservatives, but sometimes education brings tolerance along with it," Harriet replied.

"Ok, well, I was just curious about what you thought about Brenda. She's definitely a little hard to read. Has a bit of a prickly side. But other than that, she seems to be nice enough," Sally said, brushing crumbs from her sweater. Wondering whether Sally had a homophobic streak, Harriet averted her eyes to avoid conflict.

The two said their goodbyes, and Harriet ran her fingers through her short gray hair. She hadn't broached the subject of a likely entanglement between Joe and her mom with Sally, but her anxiety over what Franklin had said was running at a fever pitch.

∾

With Sally gone, Harriet walked through the kitchen, pausing at the doorway between kitchen and office. She had the strangest sensation that she was going from the present back into the past, as if the doorway itself was a portal from what is to what was. A shiver ran down her spine. After a full minute had passed, she stepped through the door and took a deep breath.

Kneeling to retrieve the box of her mom's things stashed beneath her walnut secretary, her knees creaked to let her know that they very much did not appreciate this activity. Shreds of ancient brown packing tape poked up from the top of the box. *Here goes.* Straightening up, she plopped the box onto her desk chair and pushed it across the floor until it was facing the loveseat on the wall opposite the desk. As she took a seat on the well-cushioned sofa, she wondered whether her mom had sat in this very spot as she packed this box over fifteen years ago.

After she removed the lid, the first thing Harriet saw was a high school yearbook, something she had predicted would be in a box of memorabilia. The maroon cover read "South San Francisco High School, 1945." *Jeez, that was when Mom was sixteen years old. Just a year or two after the family arrived in America,* Harriet mused. She opened the cover and located Patricia Sabatini's class photo.

Her mother was even more striking as a teenager than she'd been later in life. Her long, dark, wavy hair and sparkling eyes would have made her stand out in most any crowd, but at sixteen her glow seemed to propel her off the page and right into the viewer's lap.

Setting the yearbook aside, Harriet pulled out her mother's diploma and yellow graduation tassel. Underneath these things she found a few pins from the honor society, a pressed flower, and wedding photos. The next layer contained her diaries. Harriet really wanted to read these. Who knew what she might learn about her family and, well, about her mother's private thoughts and actions?

There was one big problem: They were locked! Harriet

stopped and focused. She recalled seeing small keys, like the type that unlocked old diaries such as these. Where had she seen them? *Aha!* Standing up and walking toward the secretary, she opened one of the tiny drawers behind the fold-down desk front. There they were: four tiny keys inside a small red tin box. Heading back to her seat on the sofa, a weight descended upon her shoulders. *This is the last time I'll be unaware of Mom's secrets, the things she kept hidden from everyone.*

After figuring out which key fit which diary, Harriet began her journey of discovery. Youthful dreams, wishes, and secret crushes filled two of the diaries. The third, written in slightly different handwriting, seemed to come from a time shortly after she and Harriet's father were married. There were entries about the ceremony, the honeymoon trip to Spain, and the excitement Pat felt at moving into her husband's home. Harriet knew Mom had "married up," and these entries conveyed that fact at every point. Finally, picking up the fourth and last diary, she felt more like a voyeur than ever. *I know I'm snooping ... and may not like what I find.*

Harriet skimmed five or ten pages at the beginning of the little green book. There were mundane entries about galas and charity auctions Pat had attended, PTA committees she had chaired, legal dinners during which her husband's San Francisco peers had honored him. Toward the middle of the book, she saw something very different. The color of the ink changed from blue to red, the handwriting cramped and irregular.

Turning to the second page in red, she saw the name "Joe West." *Oh, no ... do I want to read this?* She knew she couldn't stop now. The first two entries in this section talked about him as Pat's therapist. *Wow, that's new to me,* Harriet thought. Lots of people went to therapy these days, she knew. It's no big deal. But in the 1980s, it was something most wanted to keep hidden. It was no wonder she'd written this on pages in a locked diary.

Ok, well, Mom always was kind of high-strung. But it's inter-

esting that Joe West was the person she'd been seeing for help. What a small world.

The next several entries talked about Pat's attraction to Joe. *Uh-oh ... where is this leading?* Harriet suspected she already knew the answer. Hadn't Franklin already told her that Joe and her mom had an affair? She just didn't want it to be true. *I hoped Franklin was lying! Holy Christ!*

As Harriet read through the entries from May through July 1982, the evidence emerged. Page after page of details. Their first time, right here in the family home. The rendezvous in motels, all in other towns. Harriet put a finger to her lip and shook her head. *This is so disgusting! Who WAS my mother?* She fought hard against the desire to throw the diary across the room, to burn it, to deny that she'd ever read those incriminating words. But it was too late for that. Wiping tears from her eyes, she placed the old diary on the sofa.

Five minutes went by, then ten. Holding the damp tissue in her hand, a wave of nausea came and went. She felt her heart begin to soften. *How hard they must have worked to hide the affair from Dad. That may not have been so very difficult, considering he had spent more time in San Francisco than in Chapel Bay during most of the 1980s.* She wondered whether her father had his own clandestine affairs. Banishing the thought, she returned to the pages of the diary.

Harriet found the last entry mentioning Joe. The ink bled. As she read it, Harriet could see why. Joe had broken things off at the end of July 1982. Mom sounded heartbroken. The smears must have been from tears that fell while she was writing. *Shit!* Harriet felt herself getting furious with Joe. *How could he have allowed his feelings for mom to override his professional ethics? How could he have gotten involved with her, a married woman, for God's sake? What made Mom want to have an affair with him to begin with?*

To make matters worse, Harriet despised the fact that Franklin Fargo had been right about this thing. What she still couldn't figure out, though, was his motivation for tipping Sally off to her mother's involvement with Joe. *Wait a minute ... weren't Joe and Sally having a nice chat when Franklin walked into my New Year's Eve party? Franklin either wants Sally for himself or wants to hurt Joe. Or both.* Plus, it seemed like he'd already had a few under his belt when he walked in the door. There was nothing like a mixture of lust, animosity, and alcohol to get people into a dither, especially people with unsavory qualities.

She thought back to what she'd learned about Franklin from her father's legal briefs. The guy had quite a string of charges filed against him in California. Who knew what other skeletons he was holding in his closet? The day they'd shared coffee at Mallory's, he said that he'd grown up in Ohio. *I wonder what criminal acts they charged him with while he lived in the Buckeye State?*

Harriet put the diary down and rose to get a glass of water. The influx of sordid information was making her head pound. She'd been hoping not to find evidence Joe had slept with her mother, but no such luck. Leaning against the kitchen counter, she brought the water glass to her lips. As she drank, she wondered what else she'd find in the diary.

Taking her seat in front of the box once more, Harriet continued thumbing through her mother's private thoughts. Two pages after the tear-strewn entry detailing the breakup, the ink color changed from red back to blue. In an entry from August 4, 1982, she was stunned to read the following words in all caps.

NO MATTER WHAT, I WILL ALWAYS CARE FOR JOE. HE IS TRULY THE KINDEST MAN I'VE KNOWN, AND ONE OF THE BRIGHTEST. IN TIME, I WILL COME TO ACCEPT THAT WE WILL NO LONGER SHARE THE WARM EMBRACES AND SWEET EVENINGS TOGETHER. I ONLY WISH THE BEST FOR HIM.

Wow, Mom really loved Joe. It almost sounds as though they were star-crossed lovers. Her anger with Joe waned. *Even with his breach of personal and professional conduct, he evidently truly cared for Mom, and she for him. I can't condone or excuse their involvement, but I'll bet Joe regretted both getting together with Mom and not being able to love her out in the open.* She realized that it really and truly was not in anyone's best interest for her to share news of this love affair with anyone else. And now she was certain that she really had recognized Joe, albeit in a much younger version, from the time their paths crossed many years ago. *He must have been leaving Mom's side while I was just arriving for a visit.*

17

I t was almost the middle of January, and Brenda was uneasy. *My life is like a roach motel.* Intrusive people, memories, and dreams can get in, but they never leave. Inside the library, Brenda immediately saw a very familiar shape—clad in a dark coat—lurking near the fiction section of the stacks. Hoping to avoid notice, she jogged down the carpeted hallway and into her office. *Whew! That was a close one.* Not a minute later, she knew that her escape plan had failed.

"Brenda! I thought I saw you come in. This is great luck, since I was going to phone you today. Now we can meet face-to-face. Much more civilized!" Harriet said, hovering in the doorway and slightly out of breath.

"Oh, hello there. Aren't you the early bird this morning? Come on in and have a seat while I fire up my computer. I was just about to get a coffee from our lounge. Can I get you anything?" Brenda asked, feigning positivity.

"A black coffee would be lovely, thanks. While I wait, I can pull up the notes I took from yesterday's phone calls. I think you'll be pleased with what I've learned."

Walking down to the break room gave Brenda a little time to consider how to handle this unexpected intrusion into her day.

On the one hand, she had asked Harriet to help her find authors to speak. But she really hated it when people assumed she would drop everything and bow to their agendas. *Oh well, must make the best of things and carry on.* Returning with the coffees, Brenda put on her best "I'm being patient with you" look and handed Harriet her drink.

"Okay, here I am. What did you want to share with me?" Brenda asked.

In her usual rapid-fire talk, Harriet relayed the information that she'd found someone who knew Frances Wong, the cookbook author. It appeared as if Frances was more than willing to speak at the February event. Harriet went on at length, describing Ms. Wong's culinary pedigree, her hobbies, and even the ingredients in her famous fondue. She finally ended her monologue and took a swig of coffee, giving Brenda a self-satisfied smile.

"Wow ... I'm impressed! Well, thanks very much, Harriet. I was hoping for the third Friday in February. Any chance you can give me the correct number for Frances Wong?"

"Yes, I have it right here," Harriet looked at her phone and jotted a number on a sticky note Brenda handed her.

"Now, I do have a favor of my own to ask. I brought some of my work with me today, and I was hoping you would take a little time to look it over," Harriet said, reaching into a voluminous green canvas satchel.

"Oh, gee. Sure, I guess that would be okay. Um ... any particular reason you want to share your work with me?" Brenda asked with slight hesitation.

Harriet held up a finger. Digging into the recesses of her satchel, she produced a file folder, thrusting it toward Brenda.

"Okay, here we are. This manilla folder contains some pages of a book in progress. I just thought that maybe, if you like my writing, well, maybe I could do a reading one of these days," Harriet replied, blushing.

"Oh, okay, thank you. I'll give these a look and get back to you. It may take me a little while, as I have a couple of irons in the fire now and deadlines to meet over the next two weeks," Brenda said, dying a little on the inside.

"Oh, sure. And I really wasn't trying to launch a surprise attack on you, though it probably seems like I am doing that. It's just that I have worked hard at my writing for a really long time, and if I have the chance to share it with neighbors who love books, that will make my whole year!"

Mission accomplished, Harriet rose, smiled, and said goodbye. Brenda sat in a cloud of emotions, ranging from relief at having an author for the upcoming talk to annoyance that she now felt forced to read Harriet's work.

How on earth was Brenda going to let the older woman know that the chances of reading her work at one of their events were slim to none? After all, it wasn't as if people had been clamoring to find out about Ms. Bossy Cow's literary gems. And she wasn't a published author. Deciding to put that problem off until another day, she placed the folder of pages on the small oak table beside her desk.

She'd grabbed a stack of mail from the house on her way out the door, and it sat next to Harriet's work. On top was a piece of bulk mail from an organization. She picked up the red and blue envelope and opened it. The letter inside claimed to help people find relatives through DNA analysis. What the heck? Maybe this was a sign. *Yeah, right! The same sign everyone else who received this junk mail got two days ago ... but really, what could it hurt to try?*

Brenda already knew that her father was Japanese, so a country of origin was not what motivated her to investigate her genetic heritage. She wanted specifics. Had anyone mapped out her family tree? Now that she was officially middle-aged, she had a slew of health questions circulating in her brain. She paused, weighing the pros and cons of sending her saliva to a group of strangers. Maybe it was worth a gamble, after all.

∼

HOLY MOTHER OF GOD. Who *knew* that reading to kids was akin to pulling reluctant rabbits from misshapen hats? Harriet had finally stopped procrastinating and had volunteered to lead the reading group. Her first Saturday reading circle had just ended, and the eight kids in attendance scurried off like savages released from cages. Trying to shed the bits of thread that had attached themselves to her blue angora sweater (a result of too much close contact with children, no doubt), Harriet shook the garment out and groaned.

Was it Harriet's fault if the book they had asked her to read was not as popular as the ones the previous Book Lady had shared with the imps? Not every book could be a carbon copy of Harry Potter. And frankly, that series was way overrated. It had taken just ten minutes for the seat squirming to begin. By the time she'd finished sharing the first five pages of *A Wrinkle in Time*—rather elegantly presented, if she said so herself—the loud whispering had begun.

After finishing the first chapter, Harriet was sure that she, like Mrs. Whatsit in the book, was suffering from a "bruised dignity." However, none of the second graders in the room could sit without moving like the book's fictional Charles Wallace. Surely once they really were hip to the notion of a tesseract, all the kiddos would perk up. Harriet privately vowed to work harder on varying her vocal tone as she switched between characters in the story. And, of course, she was secretly very pleased to be reading from a book that was currently banned in several states!

Pushing open the heavy oak door that separated the reading room from the library's open stacks, Harriet smiled as she glimpsed Jenny Muramoto and her young daughter, Michaela. Backs to her, they were returning books at the counter. When did the girl get so tall? She walked up to the counter and made eye contact with Jenny.

"Howdy, former neighbor! I thought that was you! I didn't get much of a chance to talk with you at my party and surely didn't notice how tall your girl is getting!"

"Oh, I meant to call and thank you for the invite. We had a really great time. We kind of snuck out because Scott and I had promised Michaela she could watch the giant ball drop from Times Square," Jenny replied.

"Trust me, you left at a good time," Harriet said with an eye roll. She did not want to air the details of the hellacious, blood-drawing spat between Joe and Franklin.

"Haha, yes, Sally filled me in when I ran into her the following week," Jenny was skimming over the details due to the proximity of young ears, no doubt.

"Say, how old are you now, Michaela? If you're between nine and eleven, you'd be welcome to help me with the Saturday morning story circle. We've just gotten started, and I'd love to have you join us. The other little girl who'd signed up to assist had to drop out at the last minute," Harriet said with a smile.

Michaela said she was ten. Harriet gave them the title of the book she'd started, noting that the library had at least one more copy in the stacks.

"Super! Let's go look for it, Michaela!" Jenny said.

They bid one another farewell, and the Muramotos went off in search of the book. Harriet left in search of lunch. As she wandered through the library's main doors and out to the street, her own writing came to mind. *Who is my target audience, after all? Other Italians? Older women? Or maybe just folks in search of their own roots?*

WALKING HOME, the beeping sound of a delivery truck backing into a parking stall drew Harriet's attention to the opposite side of the street. Her gaze shifted from the truck to the people on the sidewalk. It was Joe and Sally. Harriet felt stuck. *I won't be able to look at Joe in the same way ever again, now that I know about his affair with Mom.* She did a quick gut check: *How do I really feel about Joe now?* She was swimming in unfamiliar waters, and it would take some time for her to reset her thinking.

How does one reframe a relationship like this one? He's shown himself to be unethical, at least with Mom. Was Mom the weak link in the chain? Was Joe? Were they simply victims of circumstance? What am I supposed to do, all these many years later? The questions echoed inside her mind. There wasn't anyone she could talk with about all of this. It was an empty, lonely feeling and not one that was likely to disappear soon.

Conversely, Patricia's endorsement of Joe's character made Harriet think she should treat him with kindness rather than contempt. It would take effort, no doubt about it. Contempt felt much more satisfying in the moment. An evil thought came to mind, along with a mischievous smile: *Perhaps my kindness will be more of a torture for Joe to bear than my contempt could ever be.*

Home again, Harriet returned to the box of her mother's things and found the place in her diary where she'd previously left off reading. After the breakup with Joe, things appeared to calm down. There were entries about seeing Harriet and Arthur in San Francisco, going out to dinner, attending concerts of the San Francisco Symphony along with her father.

The entries stopped for several months. Then, in October 1982, a new name appeared in the diary: Franklin Fargo. Yes, Harriet remembered the family dinner she'd attended that fall, recalled that her parents introduced her to Franklin. She was alone during that trip, so Arthur must have stayed in San Francisco on business. Her father had come home to do some legal work for Franklin. She recalled overhearing a conversation about an inheritance Franklin had received. There was obviously more to it, though, as the recently unearthed criminal files showed.

Harriet turned the page. *Wait ... this isn't about dad's legal work ... Mom is saying that Franklin lured her into bed ... Oh, no! there's more ... after a few weeks, she broke it off. And right here, in Mom's own writing, is the worst part.* Harriet looked away from the page. Her palms began to sweat. She couldn't believe her mother's words, but there they were. Franklin extorted money from Pat as payment for his silence about their affair. He threatened to tell her father all about it! Pat paid him $5,000 to keep quiet! Harriet felt faint. *How was this possible??* Her mother, obviously no angel, blackmailed by Franklin, the devil himself!

No wonder Mom's health took a turn after that. She recalled the times she'd visited, only to find her mother looking very thin. Her mother said she was taking a new medication for thyroid problems. Looking back, Harriet wished she had paid more attention, asked more questions. It may not have done any good, but she felt a sense of guilt, nonetheless. Putting everything back into the box, Harriet's heart sank. Sad for her mother, angry and aghast at Franklin's outrageous behavior (past and present), confused about her parents' marriage—it was all too much to manage. Her illusions, so thoroughly punctured in only two days' time, dissolved into a sea of tears and confusion. *What in the world am I supposed to do with all of this?* After her sobs subsided, she decided not to do anything at all.

JOE AND SALLY parted ways after their Saturday lunch, and Joe felt taller and lighter as he walked home. It was good to be reunited with Sally, good to feel forgiven for having been such an ass. Their conversation ranged from current events to their individual interests, and he'd been happy to discuss his new counseling gig at the local elementary school. Because of confidentiality requirements, he didn't mention any students' names or their issues. But now that he was alone in his own home, he couldn't help but think about some of them.

Joe put on the brass kettle for his afternoon tea. His thoughts returned to one young person in particular. Michaela Muramoto had come to see him the day before. Such a bright one she was but carrying a burden for sure. Once they'd gotten through introductions and such, Joe inquired how things were going for her. The sun was streaming through the window behind her, and as she dipped her dark head in thought—or maybe shyness— a cloud obscured the sunlight, perhaps mirroring her inner world.

Once she was ready to speak, Michaela poured out her pain. She mentioned being different from the others in her class. Unsure of what she meant, Joe had nodded and waited for her to continue. She said it wasn't just that she was "half Asian," though that apparently was one factor. She seemed to sense that she was too white to be part of the small group of Asian American kids in school, too Asian to blend in with the other white kids. When Joe asked whether she was bullied because of her race, she frowned and shrugged her shoulders.

After a few more minutes, Michaela continued. Haltingly, and with tears pricking the corners of her green eyes, she said there was something more that made her different from the others. She was sure that she was supposed to want to have crushes on boys, just like other girls. Instead, her crushes were on other girls. After handing her a tissue, Joe sat quietly and allowed her to have some time to wipe her tears.

"Why am I having these feelings, Mr. Joe? If I turn out to be gay, I know my dad will get really mad at me," Michaela half-sobbed.

"Why do you think that, Michaela?" Joe asked softly.

"I overheard Mom talking to him the other night. I told him how I'd been feeling, and they were discussing it. Dad sounded angry. He said it was hard enough growing up biracial, and being a lesbian besides was just too much," the girl said, sniffling into her tissue.

Joe told Michaela that people held many feelings for one another, and that it was fine to be attracted to whomever you fancied. Maybe other girls had those same feelings but were covering them up by acting interested in boys. Perhaps her father was just reacting out of love, wanting to protect her from pain. He knew enough not to mention that she might be going through a "phase." No matter what, he didn't want to invalidate the poor child's feelings.

Rising from his seat at the kitchen table, Joe was suddenly dizzy. Whoa! He sat down again and clutched the table with both hands. Taking deep breaths, he noticed that his pulse was racing. "What's going on?" he asked aloud. A minute, then two, passed. His heart slowed a bit. After another minute, the room stopped spinning.

It was time for a checkup. He vowed to call his physician first thing Monday morning. *I've already restarted therapy; now this, too?* Ah, how the body and mind can demand attention. Thinking that he hardly knew who he was anymore, Joe summoned the power to offer gratitude for what seemed to go well for him. Friends, interesting work, his dogs. *About that. Better take a nap before the daily walk.* He rose from the chair without issue and made his way to his bedroom, landing on his bed just as a fresh wave of dizziness hit.

JOE LUCKED into a doctor's appointment two days after he'd called the medical office. Now, sitting in the waiting room early on this Wednesday morning, the third week of January, he wished he could be anywhere else besides here. The magazine he'd picked up from the table next to him was two months out of date.

He sucked in air through his paper mask, and every exhalation made his reading glasses fog up. The hard gray plastic chair faced bright white walls decorated with watercolor paintings of lilies and roses. The faint smell of antiseptic made him anxious. He heard his stomach growling. The culprit was nausea, not hunger.

After what seemed an eon, the nurse called him back to begin the exam. Height, weight, blood pressure, and temperature were recorded. He followed her back into a tiny and much too bright room. It was impossible not to stare at the doctor's wall charts. They displayed the circulatory system, digestive system, and respiratory system, each one in excruciating detail. Joe wondered whether auto mechanics ever consulted blown up versions of the inner workings of vehicles. *Aren't we just a set of parts working in tandem, like those in a car?*

Ten long minutes later, two knocks on the door of the exam room preceded the low voice of Dr. Simmons.

"Joe! Haven't seen you since we performed that Bach piece in December. What brings you in today?" the tall, balding doctor asked.

"Well, I've been experiencing some odd symptoms; rarely, mind you, but I'm an old dude and thought it best to have the chassis inspected," Joe said, trying to sound flippant.

"Uh, huh. Tell me about these odd symptoms, please."

Joe described the incidents of chest pain, dizziness, and increased pulse rate that he'd experienced. After listening, Dr. Simmons ordered a blood draw and an EKG.

Gown on, electrodes attached, Joe stared at the ceiling panels while the EKG monitor ran the test. All done and dressed, he sat on the table and was newly aware of the human anatomy charts. This caused a fresh wave of anxiety. Dr. Simmons entered with the printout of his heart test. He was smiling benevolently. *At least one of us is in a happy mood.*

"Good news, Mr. Wells. Your electrical rhythms look good, at least as of this moment. I can't know what was going on over the weekend when you felt dizzy. I want to give you a Covid test, however, before moving on to anything else."

Fifteen minutes later, Dr. Simmons returned, and Joe sighed forlornly at his positive Covid test result. Simmons gave him an antiviral to reduce the risks of severe illness and sent him home to rest.

Once home, Joe put himself to bed. He was in a foul mood. He had become much more aware of his own mortality in recent months. Sure, Covid would run its course, but how much longer would it be until other ailments came down the pike? Picturing himself as a bedridden old geezer surrounded by machines buzzing and whirring, he began falling into a well of self-pity. Oh, the horror of it all, the sheer *indignity* of fading away to nothingness with only an imprint of his body on the bedsheets left behind.

Most of all, Joe feared dying alone. He realized, in retrospect, that his relationship with Patricia had been a buffer against being alone. Now that there was a danger of having that relationship exposed, thanks to Franklin, the loneliness had returned with a vengeance. *I hope I can live and love more honestly, in these remaining years. I hope Sally will be a partner I can count on, one who cares for me in all the right ways.*

Joe's dad was a strong, vital person until the day he died, always capable of lending a hand to whomever needed one. His pragmatic streak carried a downside, though. Neighbors convinced him that Joe's dog was killing their cats. He knew that couldn't be true, but the family gave her away to another family, anyway. If that was what actual strength was, Joe had decided that he wanted none of it.

He considered where all of his self-protection and secrecy had landed him, here in lovely Chapel Bay. He had spent years inside his alabaster, eggshell walls. Over time, his inner critic blared so loudly that it had become an outer critic, and not just one that attacked himself alone. The eggshell had cracked just enough to let his critical voice out; now, it was audible to others. This voice was so very different from the gentle one he'd used when working with patients, and, as the years progressed, Joe knew he'd become downright abrasive from time to time.

Joe had developed a desperate need to be right about things, driven by an ugly, fearful force that seemed to have overtaken his entire persona. He'd been trying, of late, to make more friends and curtail his loner tendencies—New Year's Eve notwithstanding. *But was this a case of too little, too late?*

More to the point: How could he make the changes he wanted to make with Franklin's threats hanging over his head?

18

Curled on her couch on Saturday morning, Brenda thought back upon her week. Life's weather patterns had blown a series of storms in her direction. With hurricane-force, prevailing winds had whisked away familiar life patterns, leaving empty spaces in their wake. From the injury to her thigh muscle to her sudden dependence upon others—such as Harriet—to do her job, everything felt very out of control and foreign.

The most troubling ill wind blew in courtesy of an article in the *Chapel Bay Times,* the local newspaper. A former city official had attracted attention by driving around in a vehicle adorned with stickers from a national militia group. Another article in the same edition told of protesters at a library in a nearby county. They burst in during a reading of passages from Toni Morrison's book, *The Bluest Eye.* Burnishing a neo-Nazi flag, they shouted racist slurs and assaulted the event host, who ended up getting stitches in his face. Several of the violent offenders fled the scene before the sheriff could arrive, but they took the guy who hit the librarian into custody.

Brenda was tired of waiting for the Chapel Bay library's IT department to unmask the so-called Lovers of Literature who'd sent her that nasty email. After several hours of computer research, she found something quite interesting. The violent neo-Nazis from the news article had a connection with the militia group advertised on the Chapel Bay city official's bumper. This came courtesy of an anonymous source quoted by the newspaper reporter. The source had rented a cabin at Big River State Park over Memorial Day weekend. They had gone to high school with members in each of the two hate groups and saw them in neighboring cabins.

Her hands were shaking; beads of sweat formed on her forehead. *Having either group within one hundred miles is frightening; knowing that both groups congregate within thirty miles of here is unbelievable! Terrifying.* She placed a call to the local chapter of the NAACP. They took her concerns seriously and promised to do their own quiet investigation into the connection between the groups.

Brenda's stress level was at an all-time high; she was desperate for an escape from her fears. Running was out, for the time being. The piano was and would always be a familiar source of joy, yet her infrequent practice sessions had limited her ability to just sit down and play any old thing that came to mind. At least meditation was a reliable source of strength—or so she hoped.

On this Saturday, per usual, the Dharma Center offered a meditation and talk. Picking herself up off of the slightly worn sofa, Brenda drove up to the small yellow cottage that served as the temple. Even if the session gave her little in the way of solace, she could at least get out of the house for a while.

A bonus: The breakfasts served at the nearby omelet house were crave-worthy. Smiling at the Buddhist idea of working to rid herself of cravings and then giving in to them immediately afterwards, she gathered her belongings and prepared to leave the cottage. As she made her way down the hallway toward the front door, the little white box containing her DNA sample caught her eye. Deciding that she had time for a quick trip to the post office, she snatched it up and headed out to her car.

Package mailed, Brenda drove the mile and a half to the Dharma Center and pulled her black Camry up to the curb. Gray skies threatened to bring rain or perhaps afternoon fog. Rain would be more fitting for her mood. With a sigh, she walked up the brick path and into the small yellow structure.

After shedding her coat and taking a seat on a cushion toward the back of the room, her shoulders relaxed. A sense of relief settled over her. No phone, no computer, no household chores beckoning. Just her own mind, the rinpoche—a Buddhist priest —and the six other people who sat in front of her. Looking at the beautiful, ornate altar with the Buddha statue sitting prominently in its center, Brenda felt herself release negative thoughts and emotions.

After preliminary greetings and blessings, the meditation period began. Eyes closed, Brenda began with a body scan, breathing into the tension in her neck, shoulders, back, and legs. Next, the attendees recited silent compassionate phrases toward themselves and others. Because she knew to include not just friends, such as Jonathon, but those who were "troublemakers," she wished grumpy Joe would be safe, well, at ease, and joyful. She pictured busybody Harriet, repeating the mantra. That felt like quite a stretch but so be it. Satisfied with her level of compassion, she returned to awareness of the breath. Shortly thereafter, the rinpoche sounded the meditation bell.

Today's talk was "Where do suffering and happiness come from?" *Oh, kind of perfect,* Brenda thought. In a nutshell, the rinpoche said that both suffering and happiness came from our own mental states. The three reasons people were unhappy:

1) Not appreciating what they have, no matter how much or how little.

2) Not getting along with others.

3) Jealousy of someone's success.

Because each heartbeat brought people closer to death, it was very important to remedy these ills and live moment by moment. The remedies:

1) Appreciate what we have.

2) Forgive others.

3) Be kind.

Wow, sounds so simple. As the dharma talk ended and she rose from the red velvet cushion, her arm brushed against someone beside her. She turned, surprised to see Scott Muramoto standing just off to her left.

"Scott! I didn't see you when I came in. Not to be cliché, but do you come here often?" Brenda asked, wriggling an arm into a coat sleeve.

"Actually, I started coming here a couple of years ago but haven't been back since last summer. Michaela wanted to go to the reading circle at the library, so I dropped her off and swung by to check out the service here," Scott said.

"Oh, cool! Well, it's nice seeing you in a different setting. I'm going to try to get here more often myself ... it's been a while since I've attended. Give Michaela a hug for me, and say hello to Jenny as well," Brenda said, taking a step toward the door.

"Oh, say, Brenda, is there any chance you could read over some historical information about the Japanese internment I found on the web? I want to cut out extraneous material before the Day of Remembrance, and I figured since you work for the library, maybe you would be a good person to help me choose the most pertinent stories to include on our site." Scott walked outside with her. "Oh, and thanks for volunteering to read at the memorial service," he added.

"Sure, I'm happy to help, Scott. Just send the info to my library email and I should be able to look it over next week," Brenda said with a smile. It felt good to be asked to contribute to the work of the local group, especially considering that she was its newest member.

Once outside, a light drizzle of rain tickled her head and shoulders. She walked the half block back to her car with quick steps, mulling over the dharma talk. Climbing into the vehicle, she drew the seatbelt across her torso. At 53, it was time to take stock of her life in a more measured way. If she was causing her own suffering, then it meant forgiving herself and others.

Such a long list of others came to mind. Her mother, her former girlfriend, Joe, Harriet, Franklin, even former President Roosevelt (because of his signing of Executive Order 9066, which sent Japanese to the camps). Book banning and the anonymous person or people behind the threatening email she'd received flashed like a neon sign in her brain. *Am I supposed to forgive them, too?*

As she turned the corner, she decided those questions were too big to tackle in one morning. Heading toward the library, she realized she was starving. Her thoughts drifted toward a Denver omelet with hash browns, and a small dose of appreciation seemed within reach—if only for a warm breakfast.

BUSTLING out of the rain and through the heavy front door of the library, Brenda saw a group of energetic children headed her way. Boys in khakis and jeans with brightly colored hoodies, girls wearing yoga pants and long-sleeved T-shirts with 'LOVE' and 'PARIS' spelled out in sequins; she marveled at the little style mavens these kids had become. Last, but not least, was Michaela. She was dressed all in black, with her hair pulled back in a pony-tail. *That is one intense kid!*

"Oh, Ms. Brenda! Didn't know I'd see you here today! Do they make you work on the weekends?" Michaela asked.

"Haha! No, no. I just forgot to bring something home when I left yesterday, honey. Are you enjoying the reading circle?" Brenda inquired.

"It's fun! Ms. Harriet is reading *A Wrinkle in Time* out loud to the kids and I'm helping with the group. There's some kind of time machine thingy in it, and a little girl named Meg who meets some goofy old witch-looking women," Michaela said, all smiles.

"That's great! I think I read that one when I was a kid. Good to know it's still around and being shared with your generation," Brenda said, nodding appreciatively.

Michaela jumped into Scott's car. Brenda remembered the comments Scott had made about Michaela's sexuality but couldn't think of a way to help. Her thoughts went to more immediate concerns. *How could I forget Harriet would be at the library today?* Not a minute later, Harriet rounded the corner and gave her a big smile. Her short gray hair was uncombed, and her sweater looked more than a tad bit shabby. *Is she dressed in costume, impersonating Mrs. Whatsit from the book?* Brenda mentally chastised herself for how quickly she could default to snark.

"Brenda! You're working overtime!" Harriet said, loudly enough for other patrons to turn and stare.

"Nope, just retrieving something from my office. I'd forgotten that you read to the kids on Saturday mornings. How's it going?"

"Oh, better than it did last week. The ten-year-olds didn't really get into the book until time travel entered the picture. Now, they think it's going to be like Harry Potter or *Free Birds*, whatever that is. Say, I don't suppose you've read any of my work yet, have you?"

Brenda gulped. "Um, not yet. But I will grab that while I'm here and give it a look. Don't you worry."

Harriet, pleased with that answer, nodded and then sauntered outside. *Would that woman never stop pushing?* Oh well, better to face the music. Chapel Bay was a small town, and she couldn't afford to alienate an eager library volunteer. And besides, she *had* lined up Frances Wong for the February 17 author night, thanks to Harriet. *Compassion, forgiveness. . . .*

Once in her office, Brenda rifled through the pile of things on her desk, finally uncovering the folder of Elsie Star's poetry. She kneeled and opened a file drawer, retrieving a canvas bag to carry the folder along with Harriet's masterpieces. Once she'd securely placed all the writing into the bag, her stomach issued a warning growl: *Feed me soon or face the consequences!*

Just then, her phone buzzed with a text. Pulling it out of her jeans pocket, she saw it was from Jonathon. *Oh, good. A useful distraction.* She read the text:

> Hey, girl. I miss you! Any chance I can come down and take you out tomorrow?

Brenda shot back a text:

> Really?? That would be so good, J. Can you be here late morning? Brunch at the gay-owned place outside of Carmel is pretty good.

He replied:

> Can't wait! Will be at your house by 11.

Yay! Thanks to Jonathon, life's teeter totter was tilting back toward the balancing point. Scurrying out of her office and back to the front entrance, she had a spring in her step despite the dreary weather. *If I'm going out for brunch tomorrow, may as well settle for leftovers today.*

Clutching the bag full of literary jewels, she hopped into the Camry and headed for her cozy cottage. Appreciation, forgiveness, and kindness were peering at her from the back seat, and she aimed to get them home in one piece and possibly invite them in for a cup of tea. As she drove down the street, she couldn't help but wonder whether the trio would accept her invitation.

SUNDAY MORNING ARRIVED, made better by the sunlight wafting through the white wooden shutters next to Brenda's queen-sized bed. Throwing back the sheets and quilt, she sat up and stretched her arms. Letting out a yawn, she remembered Jonathon was coming to town. She noted she had over two hours until her bestie would cross her threshold—time enough for a leisurely cup of coffee and perhaps a walk, if her injured thigh would permit.

Putting on her favorite jeans and sweatshirt, she walked to the kitchen to set up her French press. While she waited for the water to boil, her thoughts drifted back to yesterday's talk about suffering and happiness. *Am I really going to learn to release resentments? Be more accepting of irritating people?*

Brenda supposed it was like the old advice about how to get to Carnegie Hall: practice, practice, practice. *Huh.* Pouring the water into the glass pot, she reflected that once the water hit the ground coffee, everything changed. Maybe she needed some hot water to stir up her own beans.

Brenda drank half of her cup of coffee, then sat down at her piano. After two or three scales to warm up her hands, she stood and opened the piano bench. Selecting a Mozart sonata, she placed it on the music rack and plopped back down on the bench. As she played through the opening allegro, stopping to correct mistakes, the worries that had plagued her just a few minutes earlier faded. In their place, a sense of order and calm flowed back and forth between fingers, mind, and heart.

As she came to the end of the movement, she drew in a cleansing breath and closed her eyes for a moment. In that moment, she sensed things were about to change, that somehow, she would learn to navigate the new territory. Just what the territory was, or how she would cope, was not at all clear.

An hour later, returning from her walk, she saw Jonathon pulling up in front of her house.

"Hey, lady! Know any places a queer can get something to eat around here?" Jonathon said through the open window of his sports car.

"I've heard that there is a place catering to people with your sensibilities, sir. They're pretty liberal, though. Straight people are allowed in every so often," Brenda said, shading her eyes from the sun.

Getting into the car, she directed Jonathon a few miles down the coast. Walking into the brightly lit restaurant, Jonathon grinned as he looked at the colorful artwork that featured LGBTQ heroes such as Harvey Milk, James Baldwin, Phyllis Lyon and Del Martin—the gay and lesbian pioneers and activists from San Francisco.

"Way to make a guy feel at home," he said. "Do we just sit wherever we want?"

Just then, a tall butch woman came toward them, menus in hand. She looked to be about Brenda's age, but several inches taller and fuller around the waist. Her name tag read "Cheryl." After pulling out a chair for Brenda, she gave her a wink.

"Sweetie, I'd recommend either the 'hot to trot eggs' with a side of sweet melons or the 'orange you cute' waffles," Cheryl said.

"What specials do you have for me?" Jonathon asked, not wanting to be left out of the picture.

"Oh, we have wonderful Canadian bacon with 'pretty boy pancakes' as well as our famous 'corned beefcake hash,' served on a very warm plate, of course." Cheryl grinned and walked to another table.

"That woman has a hankering for you, sister. How have you stayed single for this long, lovely as you are?" Jonathon asked, looking over the top of the plastic menu.

"Seriously? She probably does the flirty thing with every woman under ninety who comes through the door. Going for a big tip, most likely." Brenda's cheeks reddened at the mention of female attention, but she kept her eyes firmly on her menu.

"Here's a tip: Stop playing hard to get!" Jonathon quipped.

As they continued their repartee, more patrons came in and their coffee arrived. Brenda looked up and across the small room. There, sitting alone, was the lovely Tara Winslow. Jonathon noticed his friend's distracted state. After they'd placed their breakfast orders (a Greek omelet with sourdough toast for him, bacon and eggs for her) he kicked her under the table.

"Do you see somebody you know?" he asked.

"Um, kind of. The blonde woman over there is the same one I

keep seeing when I'm out running. She was there at the end of the local half-marathon, then again at the end of the marathon. Don't you remember seeing her? And I saw her next to the ocean last week. We ran together for a bit, just before I hurt my quadriceps," Brenda said in a hushed voice. "We exchanged numbers, too."

"My, my. Is she following you? There could be worse fates than having a beautiful woman hanging around your sad little life," Jonathon said with a smirk. "And exchanging numbers? That sounds very promising, Brenda."

"Cut it out, idiot. I don't even know that she's gay," Brenda said, trying to sound businesslike. "We just wanted to run together. But now that I messed my leg up, that seems unlikely."

Just then, a short red-haired woman joined Tara at her table. Before sitting, she leaned over and kissed Tara on the lips.

"Uh-oh. Looks like you're wrong there, Sherlock," Jonathon said, kicking her under the table again. "That wasn't the kiss straight women give one another!" he added with a wink.

"Would you puLEESE stop kicking me? And so what? She doesn't exactly look single," Brenda said bitterly.

"Well, maybe she has a single friend she'll introduce to you," he continued, not letting go of the topic.

Brenda was both sad and relieved that Tara appeared to be dating someone. The attraction she felt, serious as it seemed, could now go back into the box in her head labeled "unavailable women." Too bad. But as she'd told herself, she wouldn't get involved with a lover until she knew she was safe from the threats posed by the book banning people. That, and finding the truth about her father.

Breakfast came, and they moved on to other topics, much to Brenda's relief. As they rose to pay the bill, Brenda left a hefty tip for their server. Heading back to her house, they stopped along the water to watch the mother sea otters with babies on their stomachs swimming in circles. Off in the near distance, a whale spouted exuberantly. The sun glinted off waves, rising and falling in an almost hypnotic rhythm. A perfect view, a perfect day.

Getting back into Jonathon's car, Brenda committed to storing up all the fun she'd had on this day. She would trot out good memories and happy feelings as an antidote to what she felt certain would be rough seas ahead. Life, it seemed, had a way of tossing her into the depths of choppy waters. Usually with very little warning.

IT WAS four o'clock by the time Jonathon dropped Brenda on her doorstep. Jonathon's offbeat sense of humor almost always pulled her out of the darkness and today was no exception. His stupid joke about lesbians (*How can you tell the butchest dyke in the room? She's the one with the kick-start vibrator!*) got her laughing until she cried, and she actually thought his teasing about her being attracted to Tara Winslow was pretty cute.

While walking into the kitchen to fetch a glass of water, her eyes fell upon the book bag containing the folder of poetry and Harriet's writing. She hoisted the green canvas bag from the kitchen table onto her shoulder and brought it back to the living room, along with her water. *Might as well dig in before the good mood goes south,* she decided. Putting on her big girl panties, she pulled out the snippet of Harriet's work in progress. With low expectations, she opened the folder and put on her readers.

Here goes nothing,

Twenty minutes later, Brenda slid her glasses from her face and ran her fingers through her dark hair. *Is this really the work of Harriet Conley? THE Harriet Conley? Busybody extraordinaire, head of Chapel Hill's gossip mill?* The writing was interesting, concise, and lyrical.

> *Three British destroyers descended upon Genoa's harbor in February 1941. It was Sunday, the 9th of February. The Sabatini Family, devout Catholics, were preparing to attend mass at the Cathedral of San Lorenzo, as was their custom. However, once the*

sounds of exploding shells reached their ears, they realized that their religious observances would need to be postponed. Miraculously, they later learned that the fifteen-inch shell that struck their beloved cathedral impacted the roof, but didn't explode. The Holy Grail, housed within its walls, was preserved. Miracle or not, Giuseppe and Maria decided then and there that they must make plans to leave Genoa. The couple considered their available options for escape and they realized they must be prepared to give up the centuries-long ties that rooted them to this land and its customs. The dark cloud of despair that surrounded the family was thick, like the plumes of smoke rising from the bombings.

As the Sabatinis packed just what they could carry into several suitcases, they couldn't help but wonder what would become of their little home. They hoped that the Ricci family across the street could take in Mimi, their little terrier. Most of all, they really hoped they could trust the man who said he could help them gain passage onto a ship that was to leave the port early the next morning. War was disrupting their lives in ways they couldn't have imagined even a month before. Would they ever feel free again? Could Giuseppe find work once they'd found their way to California? So many questions, so few answers.

Although the internment of Japanese Americans differed from this, she could see how, on an emotional level, this Italian family had been impacted similarly to her own. Brenda saw an opportunity to offer acceptance and kindness to Harriet. Summoning up a measure of courage, Brenda grabbed her phone and punched in Harriet's number.

Harriet answered on the second ring.

"Hello, Brenda! It's interesting that you're calling. I was just thinking of calling you."

"Really? I want to let you know how much I'm enjoying your new work. I'm excited to read more about the Sabatini family and their escape from the turmoil in Italy during World War II. Is the novel based upon a real story?" Brenda asked.

"Yes, it's based on my family history. My mother was one of the three Sabatini children who came across the ocean with Giuseppe and Maria, escaping both Mussolini's regime and the bombings afflicted upon Genoa, courtesy of the British," Harriet said.

"Really interesting, Harriet. I'd love to meet face-to-face soon and discuss your project."

"Yes, that would be terrific, Brenda. But the reason I wanted to speak with you has nothing to do with my writing. I just learned that Joe West is very ill with Covid, and I'm looking for volunteers to deliver meals to him until he recovers. Can you help?"

"Oh, my. I guess I kind of thought Covid was in the rear-view mirror these days. That's awful news. Sure, I can help. What do you need, and when do you need it?" Joe wasn't her favorite Chapel Bay resident, but she was sad to know he was sick.

"Between me and several of Joe's neighbors and fellow choir members that are mutual friends, it looks like we're good through Wednesday. How about bringing something over on Thursday?" Harriet asked.

"Okay, Thursday it is. I make a pretty mean pot of ham and bean soup and could throw in some cornbread," Brenda said.

They finished the conversation and agreed to meet the following Tuesday to discuss Harriet's writing. This, Brenda thought, was surely the universe offering her yet another opportunity to tip the suffering-happiness ratio toward happiness.

19

The hard rain this third Tuesday in January was the type that discouraged most people from going on errands. It's a good thing Harriet wasn't "most people." She donned her yellow rubber boots with the ducky logo on their sides, her beige London Fog raincoat, and a green rain hat with a wide brim. Giving herself a once-over in the floor-length mirror that hung on the inside of her coat closet, she nodded and headed out the front door. *Rain be damned.* It was almost ten o'clock. She would get to Brenda's office just in the nick of time.

Inside the library, Harriet passed the circulation desk and sloshed her way down the hallway to Brenda's office. The odor of wet coats and damp carpeting blended in with the aroma of the books in the stacks. Half of the pleasure of being in the library was the earthy, smoky smell that older books exuded. One day, Harriet knew her book would join them.

Brenda's office door was open, and Harriet rapped on the door frame.

"Oh, hey Harriet! I wondered whether you'd really want to come out in the storm. I'm glad you braved it. Come in and sit down!" Brenda said.

Suddenly aware that she was dripping water all over the

braided area rug overlying the office carpeting, Harriet carefully parked her umbrella in the hallway, removed her raincoat, and slipped out of her boots.

"I'm so happy to get to discuss my creative work with you at last, Brenda. I wasn't about to let a touch of weather keep me away this morning," Harriet replied. She gingerly parked herself on the cushioned, straight-back chair to the left of Brenda's desk.

"The pages from the draft of your new work are interesting. Now that I understand that your writing is based upon your own family history, I can see that we have a lot more in common than I thought," Brenda said.

Harriet shifted in her seat. This new, friendly tone was unexpected. She allowed the feeling of acceptance to sink in for a moment before replying.

"Oh, really? That's not why I handed you the pages. I guess I was just wanting some feedback from you, since your finger is on Chapel Bay's literary pulse. Maybe you'll want to read it once the book is finished?" Harriet asked, tilting her head slightly. *Couldn't hurt to ask.*

"Uh-huh. But here's what caught my attention. I'm sure you're aware of the Japanese internment that took place during World War II. My mother and her parents suffered because of warmongering. Your mother and her parents did, too. Our family histories vary, but I never considered how people in other countries had to escape the brutalities."

The fan attached to the central heating kicked on, and Brenda turned in her chair. The movement of air knocked a paper from her desk to the floor. Harriet, ever helpful, picked the paper up. She readjusted her glasses and read what was on the page. *Unbelievable! It's one of Elsie Star's poems.* She read the poem once more, then slowly raised her head until she made eye contact with Brenda.

"My Aunt Elsie wrote this!" Harriet beamed through the tears that were forming in the corners of her eyes. "How ever did you find it?"

Brenda tilted her head, raising an eyebrow. "Wow! Your aunt wrote poetry? I found a folder—of her work, I guess—tucked away in a library alcove. I've been reading and really enjoying them. Here's a question: Would you consider reading the poems at the March author's night?"

"It would be my honor, Brenda. Aunt Elsie would have liked that." Harriet put her hands together in a prayerful gesture.

"Just one thing: How do you imagine the poems got into the library in the first place?" Brenda asked.

"I can't be sure, but here's my guess. After Elsie died, my mother told my father to clean out her room and donate anything that wasn't trash. She was his sister, after all. Elsie was a huge collector—okay, a hoarder—and they decided to divide and conquer. It's likely that he found the poems and dropped them off with whomever was in charge here at the library," Harriet explained, removing her glasses and gently placing them on her lap.

Brenda couldn't keep a smile from forming. "Thanks so much for identifying the poet, Harriet. It's nearly noon. I don't know about you, but I could eat a horse!"

"Well, I'm buying. Just don't order a thoroughbred. I'm not sure my budget can stretch quite that far!" Harriet replied.

The two dodged the raindrops on the way to Harriet's car, laughing as they scooted into the Volvo. As they drove off, they heard car brakes squealing from one or two streets away.

"Must be somebody who needs a brake job; driving with bad brakes in the rain is no fun," Harriet piped up.

Brenda nodded, and they continued toward their destination, giving no more thought to the sound they'd heard moments before.

∾

JOE'S PHONE RANG, waking him from a nap.

"Hello?"

"Hey, pal. Sally here. I'm calling to check up on you and to see if I can fetch you anything from the market."

"Oh, nothing I can think of offhand. I'm still not feeling that great, so I'm not doing much cooking. Oh, wait; maybe some of that good chicken noodle soup they sell there? The already-prepared kind?" Joe asked.

"Yes, of course. And if there's anything else in the deli section that looks good, I'll grab it for you. Harriet tells me that folks have been delivering food to your doorstep," Sally said.

"Right, God bless them. I may be up and at 'em by the middle of next week, though. The people walking my dogs must certainly hope so!" Joe laughed, sending himself into a coughing fit.

"Oh, I know you'll be better soon. Hey, I've been on the Covid merry-go-round three times now. No fun at all! I'll text you when I'm pulling up to your house, Joe. Oh—one more thing. Did you hear about Franklin?"

"Fargo? No, what has he done now?" Joe asked, exhaling loudly, this time without coughing.

"It's not what *he's* done, exactly. Someone did it *to* him! A driver hit him while he crossed the street last week. He didn't make it, unfortunately. My neighbor was downtown when it happened and saw the whole thing. I'm sorry to be the one to tell you," Sally said, her voice dropping.

"Wow. Are you sure it was Franklin?" Joe felt his hands go cold.

"Yes, no doubt about that. The next of kin is thousands of miles away, but his picture had been in the local paper ahead of his book talk. And book jackets had his photo on them too," Sally said. "Poor old fool. Even Franklin didn't deserve an ending like this."

"I didn't like some things he said and did, but I'm sorry that he died like that." Joe couldn't hide the shock in his voice.

Lying prone in his double bed, Joe looked up at the ceiling. *Franklin is dead!* A sigh of relief welled up inside and escaped from his open mouth. *Thank God! Maybe Harriet won't ever have to know about me and Pat. But I shouldn't have such feelings—the man just died!* It was all a lot to take in.

He closed his eyes, grateful to have Sally in his life. As he drifted off, he couldn't help wondering who had killed Franklin. *Was it really an accident?*

$\sim$

IN THE PRODUCE AISLE, Harriet reached to put apples into a bag and felt a jostling from behind. *Why does everyone appear at the grocery right at ten a.m.? Heathens!*

Reflexively spinning around, she found herself face to face with Sally. Wide-eyed, she took two steps back and raised both hands in mock surrender.

"Oh, pardon me, ma'am! They sure don't make aisles as wide as they used to," joked Harriet.

"I'm afraid the aisles are the same width as ever. We, however, have put a few extra minutes on our hourglass figures!" Sally smiled.

"Yes, that's true for me. You? No way. Slim as you ever were. It's great to see you out and about, Sal! Oh, and you'll never guess what's happened!" Harriet turned her cart so that she wasn't blocking the entire berry section. She winced as her finger got momentarily caught in between her cart and Sally's. Two shoppers pushed past her, as oblivious to her pain as she was to their impatience.

"Oh, I probably won't be able to guess. And I've got news of my own, but you go first," Sally said, right hand in a gesture of supplication.

Harriet shook her throbbing finger, trying not to let it distract her from her story.

"Well, you remember how we were talking about my Aunt Elsie a few months ago? How you'd found that political button she'd given to your mother? Get a load of this: Brenda at the library has come across a bunch of poems Elsie wrote! She had no idea Elsie was my aunt!"

"Gee, that's incredible! You must be so happy, H."

"Oh, I'm over the moon! And the best part is that she's asked me to read some of Elsie's work at the March Meet the Author event! Can you believe it?" Harriet wanted to jump up and down but thought better of it.

"I'm so happy for you! Now, can I tell you my bit of news? I have two things to share. One actually has to do with Brenda Kato, also," Sally said, leaning in conspiratorially.

"Oh! What is it?" Harriet asked, just a little too loud.

Sally put her index finger over her lips.

"A few weeks ago, I asked you whether you thought Brenda was a lesbian, remember?" Harriet nodded. "Well, I have it on good authority that she is!" Sally whispered.

"What do you mean, 'good authority'? Did you sleep with her?" Harriet asked, exasperated. Her finger still hurt, making Sally's pettiness even more irritating.

"Oh, c'mon. No. But here's the thing. The sister of one of my book club ladies co-owns the Rainbow Café near Carmel. This sister told her that Brenda showed up at the café with an obviously gay man last week, and she kept ogling all the pretty lesbians in the place," Sally said. A Cheshire Cat smile spread from ear to ear.

"Oh, and she recognized Brenda because she has gone to more than one of Brenda's Meet the Author events," Sally said, finishing her gossip.

"Well, hot damn. Good for Brenda, though. Can't be easy meeting people around here. I mean, look at you and me. We've got a bigger dating pool to choose from, and we still struggle!" Harriet said, adding, "Not that you seem to have as much trouble as me. By the way, any word from Joe? Did you call him?"

"Oh. Yeah, just phoned him on my way over here. That brings me to my second bit of news. Did you hear about Franklin Fargo? He got hit by a car here in Chapel Bay last week and died!"

"What?? How did that happen? I mean, was the driver at fault, or did Franklin career out into the street or trip or something?" Harriet was flustered and didn't even care whether other shoppers overheard her.

"Oh, I'm not sure, H. According to the ex-mayor's wife, he had a drinking problem. I didn't ask how she knew, but there were those rumors about the two of them sneaking around together ...." Sally leaned in toward her friend and grabbed an apple from Harriet's cart.

Harriet frowned. *Gossip makes her boundaries even looser.* "Well ... that's a big shock. I hope they've found his next of kin and so forth." She paused, embarrassed that her first reaction had been relief that the guy was dead. But who could blame her? *At least now, my mom's personal affairs and indiscretions aren't in danger of being spread far and wide. Joe will never mention the affair, and that monster, Franklin, is gone for good.*

"Well, I need to grab one or two things for Joe since he's still bedfast. Great seeing you, Harriet!" And with that, Sally disengaged her cart from Harriet's and wheeled away toward the bread aisle. Picking up her bananas, Harriet made her way to the cashier station, a bit overwhelmed by the exchange with Sally. *Who said life in a small town was boring?*

ON THURSDAY, Brenda dropped the ham soup and fresh cornbread at Joe's doorstep, then called him. He answered right away.

"Hey, Brenda! It really means the world that you brought me food. We've had a bumpy relationship, and I blame myself. I can be pretty socially unaware and even pompous, so I've been told. Of course, I'm not friends with the people who say such unflattering things."

Hearing the weakness in Joe's voice, Brenda's heart softened. She could feel the ice between them melting.

"It hasn't all been your fault. The distance between us, I mean. I overreacted to your dogs on the trail. That triggered me. Truthfully, I have a fear of dogs and can't seem to shake it. But your dogs seem nice. I know we'll see one another on the trail again, and your dogs will be with you. I'll try to curb my knee jerk reaction."

"I want to let you in on a story I rarely share. I had to give my pet dog away when I was young, and it was terribly painful. Dad believed she'd been killing the neighbors' cats. That's what the neighbors told him. Come to find out that it wasn't her after all. It was a coyote that had done the killings," Joe said. "I'm not afraid of dogs, but I am afraid of my sorrow, which seems bottomless. You'd think a psychologist could have worked this out for himself, right?"

"Wow! If you don't mind my asking, how is it you can still have dogs around?" Brenda hoped this didn't sound too intrusive.

"I guess it's just been a matter of working with that sad little boy inside of me, letting go of the hurt a bit. I still blame my father, though, and that marred our relationship forever. I wish it had been otherwise. He died before we came to terms with that situation, and some others also ..." Joe's voice trailed off.

Before signing off, Joe asked Brenda if she knew about Franklin's death. She did—Harriet had called and relayed the news. Privately, Brenda was certain that nobody was as relieved as she was over the news of Franklin's demise.

She walked to the bathroom and looked at herself in the mirror. *Does my appearance give any indication that my walls are coming down, one brick at a time?*

20

It was the afternoon of February 19, the Day of Remembrance. Despite her insecurities, Brenda began addressing the forty assembled guests. To put her story in context—-and because she was the first to speak—she mentioned the bombing of Pearl Harbor, Roosevelt's signing of Executive Order 9066, and the shipping of 120,000 Japanese Americans to unfamiliar places. She then transitioned to more personal stories.

"In March 1942, my mother, Toshi Kato, and her parents had to evacuate their modest home in Sacramento. Mom hardly ever talked about life at Tule Lake, but I know she attended school in the camp. She said she was a bright and eager student."

Five camp survivors in the front row, each in their eighties and nineties, looked up at her expectantly. Several people shifted in their seats. Brenda paused, looked out at the faces before her, and dropped her gaze to the paper in front of her. She talked about her grandfather's time in the stockade, about the things she'd learned from her internet research. Her heart beat like a drum. *What authority do I have to be speaking in front of such an esteemed group?*

She took a sip of water from the tumbler on the podium and continued her speech.

"In 2003, she had a bout with cancer, which she overcame thanks to her strong will. But in 2012, the cancer returned. She died before the year was up. It is my honor to be allowed to speak before this esteemed group today, in her memory. I sincerely hope that America never again imprisons a group of its own people strictly based on their national origin, looks, or beliefs. Thank you for the opportunity to speak today."

Polite applause followed her time on the podium. Brenda thought she had probably blown the talk. Four other speakers, including Scott Muramoto, came to the podium after she'd spoken, but she wasn't able to listen carefully to any of them. She had a hunch Scott would ask for her feedback on his part of the program. She wouldn't be able to offer anything other than the usual generic positive remarks. The hour-long event ended, and Brenda rose from her chair and walked toward the information table at the side of the room.

As she awaited her turn to look at the array of photos and memorabilia that the club had gathered for the event, Brenda felt a tap on her on the shoulder. Turning, she came face-to-face with an older Japanese lady. She was one of the five survivors who'd sat in the front row. The woman wore a nice pink wool suit and carried an expensive name-brand purse. Tears brimmed in her eyes. As Brenda rummaged in her own bag to find a tissue, the woman spoke.

"I, too, spent time at Tule Lake." Accepting the tissue from Brenda, she continued. "What you don't perhaps understand is your mom returned and cobbled together a life. That is a tribute to her real strength. I never married, never had children. Seemed too iffy to me," she said, wiping her eyes.

"Thank you very much, ma'am. Mom didn't end up getting married, either. In fact, I've never known my father ... but you're right about her strength. She was always a fighter," Brenda said, her own eyes beginning to fill. "Do you have a few minutes to talk?"

The older lady nodded her head, and the two walked over

toward a side room. They sat in twin brocade armchairs. Brenda drew in a deep breath before speaking.

"Can you tell me more about life in the camp? Mom never spoke about it much," Brenda said. *This is another opportunity to know Mom better, like when I got to meet Ruby a few weeks ago.*

"I remember it through the eyes of a child, as I was six and a half when we left our rental downtown. After a month in the detention center, it seemed exciting to be going on a bus to somewhere new. When we arrived at Tule Lake, the first thing that struck me was the biting wind and cold. The little stones on the ground were so sharp, hurting our feet through the thin soles of our shoes. Nothing much grew up there, and spiny tumbleweeds constantly blew across the ground and got stuck in the high fence surrounding the camp." The woman paused, a faraway look in her cloudy eyes.

"You understand that, as Japanese people, we had learned to follow rules and not to make trouble. My parents were so proud of living in America, even though they couldn't become citizens because of the laws. When we got to camp, Mom remained very demure and quiet, even through the hardships. The wind blew through the cracks in the walls at night, the walk to the latrine was so long, and the food hurt our stomachs. But she kept up the hope that it would all be over soon and we would go home to the farm."

"Dad, not so much. He rebelled. He refused to sign the paper, refused to say 'yes' to some questions you spoke of in your talk. They put him in the stockade, like your grandfather. That's when Mom panicked, lost faith. And I felt it too, then. Even now, I have nightmares. I hear the men in the stockade screaming when they are getting beatings." She dropped her head and gripped the arms of the chair.

Brenda knew it was time to stop. This topic clearly made the woman relive times she'd rather forget.

"Oh, I'm so sorry. I appreciate your taking the time to talk to me. Perhaps you and Mom were friends. I hope you found some little ways to pass the time . . ."

The woman looked up, smiling.

"The best parts were the movies they showed us in the mess hall after dinner sometimes. They put up a big white sheet at one end and there was a huge black projecting machine at the other ... I saw Charles Laughton in *The Hunchback of Notre Dame* ... and I remember Bette Davis in movies, too!"

Brenda helped the old lady up, and they hugged one another. The conversation covered unpleasant things, yet there was a peace between the two of them. Just hearing another firsthand account from one who'd lived the life her mother endured at Tule Lake helped her accept the painful truths.

Together, they walked out into the main room. A familiar voice came from the left.

Michaela scooted up next to her. "Ms. Brenda! I loved your talk! Since I had to speak about the Japanese internment in front of my social studies class this morning, I already knew some of the history part. But I never knew that your mom was at Tule Lake. My grandpa was from Sacramento, too, just like Dad said. But since he went to Manzanar, maybe he and your mom didn't know each other," the girl rattled on excitedly.

Brenda noticed Michaela wore fancier clothes than usual, a beautiful green sweater over black wool pants. A cute green bow decorated her long black tresses.

"Oh, I'm sure your talk went well, Michaela! I'm so glad you got out of school a bit early this afternoon and came to hear the presentations the adults made. Your dad and the others on the committee sure did a good job setting all of this up," Brenda added, feeling more than a little guilty for not paying attention to Scott's story.

Looking over a display of objects from the camps, Brenda admired the fine quality of carved miniatures of animals and people made from wood or soap. The newspapers produced in various camps were almost professional in appearance, and it seemed the writers were doing their best to remain positive. The hopeful looks on the faces of teenagers posing with Eleanor Roosevelt on the day the camps closed showed just how resilient the human spirit could be.

If people who had survived such extreme and degrading conditions could hold their chins up, surely, she could control her own moods with more grace and adopt a bit of their resilience. And hearing the older lady's story helped put things into perspective, though it brought her no closer to finding her father.

SEVERAL MINUTES LATER, back in the library's main room, Brenda wondered how much good her speech had done. She'd temporarily forgotten the thanks she'd received from several listeners, not to mention the excitement in Michaela's eyes. In retrospect, it would have been nice to have seen a few of her coworkers at the talk, but she realized she'd not told anyone she was speaking. Besides, they all were busy and couldn't take time off in the middle of the day. *Best to leave it alone, let it go.*

February's anemic sunlight streamed through the floor-to-ceiling windows facing the street. A beam struck the ring that graced Brenda's index finger, and it sparkled. Just that morning, she'd put the small round garnet set in a band of white gold on her hand. It had belonged to her mother. She'd never worn it before, had never wanted to wear it. Now, its beauty spoke to her. She imagined wearing it more often. Thinking about her conversation with the older lady in pink, she could almost see the tumbleweeds blowing, hear the gusts of wind as she gazed into the burgundy depths of the stone.

Toshi, through all of her trials and tribulations, persevered and did her best to raise Brenda as a single mother. The many losses—of childhood innocence, freedom, perhaps the chance to marry the man she'd loved—were heavy. The losses sat trapped in the dark red hue of the ring.

As she walked down the carpeted hallway to her office, Brenda thought about Ruby Yamamoto, whom she'd met at the conference in Sacramento. She thought about the nice lady she'd met a few minutes earlier. Just like her mother, they'd survived a brutal and humiliating situation. They ought to have been enjoying the freedoms of recess, riding bikes to their friends' houses, and squabbling with siblings over who got to eat the last piece of cake after dinner. Instead, they worried about how to stay warm at night, how to get to the latrine in time, and how long they would be stuck behind barbed wire.

She sank into her desk chair, the weight of the injustice descending upon her shoulders. How had Mom carried such weight on her thin frame? A niggling thought surfaced, one she had been trying to ignore. The thought refused to stay buried any longer. It bubbled up through her feet and into her torso like a volcano. In her heart of hearts, she truly believed that she had no more right to live a happy life, to be surrounded by a happy family, than her mom or the other camp survivors.

What was I hoping to gain by participating in the Day of Remembrance? It feels like I stirred up terrible memories for those who lived through the internment; how is that helping anyone? How is it helping me?

It seemed like the horror of the camps never really stopped. Generational trauma. That's the term her therapist used ten years ago when she'd sought help after Toshi died.

There was library work to do, and Brenda switched on her computer and found her emails. An unsolicited offer for her to host an author's book signing popped up. She skimmed through the message, then remembered where she'd heard the author's name before. He'd been discredited for falsifying information in his biography of Mark Twain. *Ugh.* Nothing at all from the IT department concerning the Lovers of Literature. Nothing from the NAACP regarding the connection between her anonymous attackers and the outsiders who'd interrupted the reading from Toni Morrison's book. *Am I the only one who cares about this?*

The last email bore the cryptic subject, "March Ahead." It was from her boss, Justin. He'd scheduled a meeting with Harriet Conley for the next morning, and he wanted Brenda to attend. *Why does he need me there? Is he having doubts about the validity of the Elsie Star's work? Does he think Harriet is fabricating her relationship, and thus the identity of the poet?* She'd attend and let him know Harriet was telling the truth. She'd even forward a sample of the poetry so that he could see that it wasn't schlock.

Idle speculation would get her nowhere. Tomorrow morning would come soon enough, and if it turned out that she needed to find a new speaker for the March event, so be it. Maybe having a discredited author like the guy who emailed would bring out the curious members of the community. People loved a scandal, loved anything slightly bizarre. Case in point: Franklin Fargo's obituary came out only last week and now, the bookstore couldn't keep his latest book on the shelves!

It was already after four o'clock, and Brenda's head was pounding. She placed her hands on her black wool pants, pinching the center crease between thumb and forefinger. *If only life's edges were this defined.* Noticing the graceful way in which her dark blue silk blouse draped over her arms and shoulders, she considered the irony of wearing her finest clothes to talk about the worst days of her mother's life.

A LITTLE AFTER eight the next morning, Brenda fumbled for her key to unlock the library's front door. She loved the morning hours before the library was open to the public. Taking a slow turn around the stacks, she ran a finger across the embossed letters on some spines. So many hours of toil, so much sheer imagination infused into every volume on the shelves. Each one was a precious gem, an offspring born under heat and pressure within the soul of someone she would never meet. *Books keep civilization afloat. Books and little else.*

After setting up the Cuisinart coffee maker in the staff lounge and putting packets of sweetener into the Wedgewood dish on the counter, she walked down the carpeted hallway, turning left into her office. The phone in her pocket buzzed. It was a text from Justin, confirming their nine a.m. meeting. With a sigh, she removed her jacket and hung it on the back of her door. *Not much more quiet time—best to make the most of it.*

The radio was tuned to the classical station, and a Chopin piano sonata sparkled over the airwaves. Elsie Star's poetry was next to her computer. Opening the folder, she chose four poems that she wanted Harriet to read. Harriet could select others, but these four she considered the best of the bunch. Placing them on the top of the pile, she closed the folder and switched her computer on.

A door squeaked open, and Harriet's raspy voice broke through the strains of a Bach concerto. *Sorry, Johann Sebastian.* Brenda rose, picked up the folder of poetry, and walked the short distance down to Justin's office.

"... and then, he took the bread knife and cut right into Mama's lasagna! Haha! She was *so angry* with my dad!" said Harriet, obviously in the middle of a windy story. "Oh, hi there Brenda! Justin and I thought it would be really cool to have your help in selecting the right passages to read to our local fans!"

Um, what? Brenda's left eyebrow shot up like a mini-blind. Unmoored, she plopped down in the only other available chair and turned toward Harriet and Justin.

"I'm sorry, but what do you mean, 'the right passages,' Harriet? I've selected four of your Aunt Elsie's poems, which I absolutely think are her best; I want to ask you to choose four or five more. But what are these 'passages' you're talking about?"

"Brenda, let me catch you up," Justin began. "When I read Elsie Star's work, which you kindly forwarded, I called Harriet to get a little more background information about Ms. Star, this hidden gem who had once lived among us. She graciously agreed to have coffee with me." Justin had taken on a formal tone that clearly was meant to impress Harriet. After a brief pause, he continued. "While we were meeting, Harriet gave me a sneak peek at some of her own new work. Well, I flipped! I've asked her if she would please read a bit of it aloud during the March author's evening."

Justin was bubblier than Brenda had seen him ... well, ever, really. Eyes wide, curly hair falling onto his collar, he looked for all the world like an actor who had just delivered his greatest performance. She swallowed, tilted her head to one side, and forced a smile.

In her mind's eye, she could imagine the creepy Lovers of Literature attending the book talk and hearing Harriet's reading. *Her story was about immigrants, for God's sake! How do we know how far these cretins will go with their hatred? Oh no, this can't happen! The threats against me and the library were vague ... 'protests and other things' ... but I don't feel safe doing this kind of reading, not right now ....*

Brenda swallowed hard. "I also looked at Harriet's writing and I agree it's excellent. However, I need to remind you that our general rule is to not present unpublished work until it's been peer reviewed by three outside sources," she said, sure that this little reminder would rein Justin in.

"Brenda, Harriet and I both feel that her new work is really going to resonate with the literary crowd in Chapel Bay. Hers is not the only family of immigrants who settled here. I kind of thought it would be a good build-up to our April theme of Asian American poetry. You know, because it's along the same lines of people from other countries settling here, of producing powerful writing. Regarding the so-called peer review situation, I'm willing to waive that rule if you are."

Brenda felt her stomach clench. Her pulse raced. *For God's sake! Must I endure the double indignity of having Harriet go over my head and Justin's tone-deafness for protocol? The safety of our library is at stake!* This was just too, too much.

"Justin, I really wish you'd come to me privately about this matter so that we could have discussed the pros and cons of stepping outside of the boundaries that have served us so well in the past. You're blindsiding me with this, and frankly, I don't know what to say." Brenda stopped, took a breath, and rose from her chair, shaking her head slowly.

"Wait, hold on! I'm sure neither of us intended to disrespect your position or the author's night formats. Please sit down, Brenda. Let's have an adult conversation about this," Justin pleaded.

"Oh, Brenda, Justin is right! We aren't trying to pull a fast one. I only thought that since you'd shown me how much you enjoyed the little crumbs of my new novel ... well, it would only be natural to see what Justin thought. I value both of your opinions so very much!" Harriet extended a bejeweled hand as if to grab Brenda by the arm.

Shaking with anger, Brenda nodded and walked briskly out of the office. *Why, oh why, did I show enthusiasm over Harriet's writing? What was I thinking?* Slamming the door behind her, she lowered herself into her leather swivel desk chair and gasped for air.

What in the world was happening? Was Justin allowing the new accolade "Best Small Library in California" to go to his head? And how was it that Harriet Conley suddenly had so much power over Justin? Maybe Justin was nursing a faint hope that Harriet would throw big money their way. If so, this was a disgusting way to go about asking for it. *I have to speak with Justin away from Harriet. He needs to understand what's at stake. He needs to remember that there are outsiders who have threatened to protest and who knows what all else ....*

Needing a distraction, Brenda opened her phone and found her personal emails. The newest one was a response from the company she'd contacted regarding her family history.

Subject: Results of your recent DNA submission.

Finger still poised over the email, she asked herself a simple question: *Will the contents of the email actually improve my life? No.* She hit 'delete.' It was bad enough dredging up the past during the Day of Remembrance, seeing the sorrow in people's eyes. She didn't need to dredge up anything else.

There, one more false hope removed from my life.

This was a positive step toward less clinging.

Buddha would approve.

21

A week passed, then ten days. Justin, away at the annual librarian's conference, had still not followed up on his tense conversation with Brenda and Harriet. He hadn't replied to Brenda's email about security issues, either.

As she finished a breakfast of scrambled eggs, toast, and coffee on this Saturday morning, Brenda thought about how good it would be to get to the Dharma Center and have some structured quiet time. In the weekly email, the rinpoche said his topic would be the Three Poisons. Nobody ever truly got enough instruction about avoiding clinging, aversion, and ignorance. Certainly not in these days and times. Considering her recent feelings about Harriet and Justin, Brenda acknowledged that aversion was her number one hit.

Clad in workout clothes, she strode out the front door to the street and unlocked her Camry. Before opening the car door, she took a moment to suck in a lungful of early spring air. Even without the sweet floral scents, which would come with the blossoms in a month or two, there was a sense of expectation, of gladness for new beginnings, which floated on the slight breeze. The anticipation of joy.

Brenda eased her slim body into the driver's seat, started the car, and pulled away from the curb. In just the few seconds needed for that familiar maneuver, a neighbor's cat darted in front of the car. She slammed on the brakes, missing the little black and white feline by inches.

"Shit!"

Grateful to have avoided hitting the creature, she gripped the steering wheel and kept her eyes glued to the road as she drove the short distance to her destination.

Three minutes later she arrived at the Dharma Center, still frazzled. The brief walk up the foliage-lined walkway and into the small yellow house gave her time to let go of tension. As she found her way to a cushion up toward the front of the room, she was glad to have a place such as this to park her worries, if only for a short time.

The rinpoche made a few introductory remarks, greetings, and prayers and then the silent meditation began. Twenty minutes later, the gong sounded. For all the letting go and the single-pointed focus Brenda had experienced, she may just as well have been drinking coffee and scrolling through Facebook.

Brenda tried to control her fidgeting and forced herself to focus on the rinpoche's maroon robe and colorful stole. She studied the image of the wrathful meditational deity Vajrakilaya gracing the altar. Just viewing his three faces—blue, white, and red—gave her an excuse to escape her thoughts. *Scary dude, that one.* She felt the middle face, the blue one, looking straight at her as its hands clasped the *phurba*, or knife, which the rinpoche said cuts through all three poisons.

"While the deity is undoubtedly ferocious, he is also a fully enlightened Buddha and embodies compassion, unlimited love, and *bodhicitta*," the rinpoche was saying. Brenda remembered *bodhicitta* translated to "awakened mind." *Boy, could I use one of those right about now.*

"Because aversion, in particular, is difficult to destroy using the more peaceful contemplative methods, Vajrakilaya, with his sharp sword, is very helpful in cutting through the hatred and negativity that we sometimes carry," the rinpoche continued. His calm tone contrasted with his words, bringing them even more into focus.

Brenda closed her eyes momentarily and pictured the wrathful deity cutting through her anger with his sword. She had trouble keeping Harriet's face out of the picture, and badly wanted to shout, "Leave me alone, you freak!" Inhaling deeply, then exhaling, she exercised self-restraint. But oh, how she wanted to let that woman know how she felt.

The talk ended, and the participants gave a dedication of merit. Glad for the time she'd spent there, Brenda rose and thanked the Rinpoche. She didn't want to stick around and visit with the others, and she put on her jacket and walked out the door to the street. As she hit the sidewalk, keys in hand, she heard someone calling her name.

"Brenda! Brenda! There you are!" said Scott Muramoto, lumbering toward her. He was sweating despite the cool temperature, and Brenda feared something terrible may have happened. *Did I hit that cat earlier? Is it Scott's cat?*

Turning toward her red-faced friend, Brenda dropped her keys in her haste to see what was wrong. Kneeling to pick them up off the sidewalk, she kept her eyes glued to him. "Scott? Is everything okay? What's going on?"

Scott stopped right in front of her and placed his right hand on her left shoulder. He was out of breath. "Whoo, Brenda! Oh my God! I tried calling you, but your phone went to voicemail. I took a chance and came over here, thinking this was probably your destination on a Saturday morning. I'm so glad I've found you ...."

"Well, you've found me. Now, please tell me what's wrong! You've got me rattled." She straightened up without breaking eye contact.

"It's not that there's anything wrong, just the opposite. What I mean is, I'm so happy I opened my email this morning! I kind of can't believe you haven't called ME! Didn't you read your emails yesterday?" Scott was finally breathing at a normal rate but still wasn't making any sense.

"Slow down! I have no idea what you're talking about, Scott! Did the national news pick up the Day of Remembrance memorial? Is that what's got you so excited?" Brenda was losing patience with this guessing game. And the wind was picking up.

"Oh, wow. I guess you really don't know. Listen, do you want to come over to the house for tea? It may be better if we could sit inside and chat."

"Okay, mystery man. Did you drive over, or can I offer you a lift?" Brenda asked, happy to take this show on the road and away from prying eyes and ears that were emerging from the Dharma Center.

Scott nodded and jumped into the passenger seat. As they drove away, five members of the little *sangha* stood watching, puzzled looks on their faces. Shrugging their shoulders, they parted ways. As she looked at the five in her rearview mirror, Brenda quipped, "It seems that in a small town like Chapel Bay, even people on the path to enlightenment need a little drama with the dharma ...."

"Indeed."

THE FOUR BLOCKS between the Dharma Center and the Muramoto home seemed like four miles. No matter how hard she tried, Brenda couldn't get a word out of Scott. He just kept grinning and looking straight ahead. After she parked in front of the white cottage fronted by a neat flower garden, Scott led the way up to the front door. Brenda followed him inside. She had to fight the urge to go into piano teacher mode. It was only natural to want to go through the living room to the family room, where Michaela's lessons took place. But they traipsed past the upright piano and through the door separating the living space from the kitchen.

"Just let me make that tea I promised," Scott said, putting on the kettle to boil, "and I'll lay everything out for you."

Brenda waited. She perched on one of the black leather bar stools. For a person with control issues, this was misery! But she had no other choice. She drummed her fingers on the counter. After the longest three minutes ever, Scott poured the water and added the tea bags.

"Mint or chamomile?" Scott asked.

Would he just get to the point?

"Mint, with a touch of honey, please," she said.

Scott sat next to her at the breakfast bar and swiveled his stool so they were eye-to-eye.

"Brenda, after all this time, coming here to give my daughter her piano lessons, becoming a friend of the family, even joining the local Asian Pacific advocacy group and speaking about your mom at the Day of Remembrance ceremony ... after all of that, I still had no idea. I am absolutely beyond shocked, really and truly. And Jenny and Michaela ... well, let's just say they are as shocked as I was. Maybe more so," Scott was rambling. Sparks shot from his eyes like those of a crazy person.

"For Lord's sake, Scott! Spit it out! What have I done? How have I offended you and your family? Whatever I did, I'm sorry! Please, you're making this beyond painful!" Brenda slammed the ceramic mug down on the counter, spilling some of her tea.

"Oh, no, nothing bad! It's just ... don't you remember sending in a DNA sample to the genealogy website?" Scott began.

"What? How do you know about that? I did, yes, but so what? I decided after I'd sent my saliva away in the tube that I was doing some elaborate dreaming. The past is the past, and I need to live in the here and now. You get it, mindfulness and all of that," Brenda said. She felt heat rising from her chest to her cheeks. Not mindful at all at the moment.

"Brenda, here's how I know about that. I sent my own DNA sample in about a year ago, and every time a distant cousin five times removed joins the site, I get an email. Yesterday, I got another of those notices, and your name popped up," Scott said, eyebrows raised.

"So, we're fifth cousins? That's kind of interesting, I suppose. See, that's the not-so-useful info I decided I could live without. Hence, my decision to delete the email," Brenda said, trying to calm down. She sipped her tea and mopped up the spill on the countertop.

"No, that's not it. We're much closer than distant cousins. You're my half-sister, Brenda. My dad, George Muramoto, is also your father. Can you even imagine?" Scott threw both arms into the air.

The room went silent. Brenda could hardly breathe.

"Say WHAT? Is this a trick? I don't want you to mess with me, Scott. It's been a rough couple of weeks already. How is this possible?" Brenda's tears were bubbling up. Joy, sorrow, or just fatigue? She wasn't sure. Maybe all three.

"No, this is one hundred percent for real. Here, I'll get my Mac and show you," Scott said, jumping down from his stool and hurrying into the primary suite on the other side of the house.

Scott returned in less than a minute. He opened the email and showed Brenda the chart. It revealed that she and Scott did share a parent. Scott was born in 1982, when Brenda was 13. Brenda sat and stared at the information. Jealousy sprang up in her heart. *This is so unfair! Scott grew up knowing Dad! I was a lonely teenager, longing for a father, when baby Scott came into a family of two parents!*

She felt weak and leaned dangerously far to the left. Scott, seeing her unsteadiness on the bar stool, extended an arm and helped her down. Feet firmly on the floor, Brenda swallowed hard and closed her eyes. She took a beat, opened her eyes, and drank a gulp of tea. The essence of peppermint brought her back into her body.

"Wow. Just wow. This is something I've waited for my entire life, Scott. I have so many questions! Could I see a picture of my, er, OUR dad?" Brenda didn't recognize her own voice. She hadn't uttered the words 'my' and 'dad' together out loud in years.

Scott led her back to the living room and asked her to sit on the floral-patterned sofa. He excused himself and went back to the bedroom, returning with a photo album. He took a seat next to her. Brenda fingered the garnet ring, her mother's, that she'd taken to wearing every day. It felt like touching home base. She knew she'd never again need to invent a father. *Is this real?*

Scott opened the album and pulled it closer to her. There before her was a picture of a strong, well-built man. His dark eyes danced. His hair was very short and neatly trimmed. He was wearing a long blue apron and standing in front of a display case. *It was the same man whose photo had hung on the living room wall when she was a kid—the one her mother claimed was a cousin!*

"This was Dad in our grocery store back in Sacramento. He was so proud of that business! My brother George Jr. and I used to help when we were in high school. Junior took over the business when Dad retired. Maybe you've heard of it? Muramoto Market on Sutterville Road?" Scott said.

Reaching over, he took Brenda's hand in his.

"Oh, yes. The name of the store sounds familiar. But Mom never took me there. And I sure didn't know that I had stepbrothers and a father only a few miles away. This is a lot to take in, Scott!" Brenda said, eyes darting to the photo, then away again.

"There will be plenty of time to get into more family history. And I have my own questions, too. When I was a teen, I overheard a conversation between my parents. It was about money being sent to another family, and Dad sounded really sad, but I didn't know why. I never asked since I'd been eavesdropping," Scott said.

"I AM happy, of course! I have a family! Not only that, I like you all. That's pretty amazing." Brenda wiped a tear from her cheek. "Let me ask you, Scott. You knew our dad, and I didn't. What could have motivated him to ignore one family he was part of and start another?" Brenda heard the words she'd said and wished she'd phrased them differently. After all, it wasn't Scott's fault that she'd grown up without George Muramoto, a successful grocer and loving father to some.

Scott raised, then lowered his eyebrows. He turned his palms up toward the ceiling, shrugging his shoulders.

"Brenda, I wish I could answer your question. One thing I can tell you is that Dad had a great deal of pride. He'd grown up in the old Japantown in Sacramento, and he said that in 1957 they tore it down—the entire thing, razed—to make way for the Capitol Mall. He would have been in his late teens then. The family had to start completely from scratch, build a new house, start a new grocery store ...."

He paused and looked Brenda straight in the eye. Suddenly, the haunted feeling she'd had at the finish line of the California International Marathon made sense. Dad's ghost may have been waving at her, after all.

Scott continued talking. "You told me you were born in, what, 1969? That would mean than he and your mom were dating when he was in his early twenties. It's possible that, proud as he was, he didn't feel he could give her much of a life. After all, it wasn't until the late '70s that he took over the store and did well for himself. ...."

That made some sense to Brenda, but it didn't keep her from wishing that her mother had fought for her new family in 1969. She pondered the situation. The PTSD Toshi had carried from the Tule Lake years clearly shaped her ability to stand up for herself. And there was the whole Japanese tradition of blending in, not making waves. *It must have all been too much in the end.*

"Scott, please don't think I blame you for any of this. I'm lucky to find you, lucky to find my roots. This is all just so new and unexpected." Brenda trailed off.

"I know, I know. Take all the time you need, sis ... it feels funny calling you that! We all have quite a lot to get used to," Scott replied.

A KEY TURNED in the door, startling Brenda. In came Jenny and Michaela. When they saw Brenda sitting with Scott on the sofa, big smiles broke out on both faces. Michaela rushed over to Brenda and gave her a hug, but her eyes widened when she realized what she'd done; she backed away for a moment.

"It's okay, Michaela! We've all received the most amazing news, after all! I guess you get to call me Aunt Brenda from now on. That'll take getting used to, right?"

"I kind of love the sound of that, Aunt Brenda! This is so awesome! I would have picked you as a relative even if we weren't already related!" Michaela said, eyes twinkling.

"Welcome to the family, Brenda! When Scott showed me the email from the genealogy website, I said to him, 'This has to be a mistake or something.' But the more I thought about it, the more I realized it had to be true. You and Scott look very much alike, and after Scott told me that your mother was from Sacramento— he heard you say that in your talk the other day—well, it all made sense. Anyhow, I'm really jabbering on. Would you care to join us for some lunch?" Jenny asked.

Brenda, at a loss for words, wiped her eyes on her sleeve and nodded.

Lunch was turkey and cheese sandwiches and tomato soup. After they'd eaten and put away the food, Brenda and Michaela put jackets on and went to hang out in the backyard.

Sitting together on the deck glider, they were quiet for a while. The Steller's jays called their "shook shook shook shook" declarations of ownership across the tops of eucalyptus trees. A few monarch butterflies flitted in the sunlight. Everywhere she looked, Brenda could see that members of the same species related to one another in their own way. *But what is it to be lost for so long, and then found? Do the birds and butterflies know this feeling?* Overly analytical, as always, Brenda guessed no feelings were ever truly unique to humanity.

"Brenda, was it hard not having a dad around? Sorry if I'm asking too hard of a question, or if I'm being rude. Mom says I need to think before I speak," Michaela said, looking out toward the pyracantha bushes that flanked the south side of the yard.

"Oh, Michaela, it's okay to ask questions. I'm not sure I have an answer for you, though. I just know that it's nice knowing who he was. Scott said Dad, your grandfather that is, passed away a few years ago. But I've found a brother, sister-in-law, and the best niece I could have asked for!" She placed her right hand over Michaela's left hand.

"Hey, it's Saturday. Are you still taking part in the book circle at the library?" Brenda asked, attempting to lighten the mood.

"Oh, that. Yes. Ms. Harriet is almost finished with *A Wrinkle in Time*. I suppose it's a good book and all. Lots of interesting science. But it is giving me a funny, kind of left out feeling," Michaela said.

"Left out? In what way, Michaela?" Brenda asked, voice breaking.

"Well, there's a big deal made about the relationship between a girl, Meg, and her little brother, Charles Wallace. And this is going to sound stupid, but since I don't have any brothers or sisters, it just makes me sad. Like, I'd like to know if I would be as protective toward a little brother as Meg is," Michaela said.

"Oh, I think I get that. You know, I didn't have siblings growing up either. It got lonely. I often wondered how it would feel to be part of what seemed like a real family, for sure."

"Yeah, and I guess there's another reason I feel kind of sad about the story. Meg seems to have a special friendship with this Calvin boy. They start out as acquaintances but by the end, they are holding hands and even more. I just feel left out, is all," Michaela said, almost to herself.

"Don't worry, niece. You have lots of time to develop those special friendships. You're what? Ten years old?"

"Yes, but can I tell you something? I think I'm attracted more to girls than to boys—maybe. Can I talk to you about this, Aunt Brenda?" Michaela whispered.

"Sure, honey." Brenda whispered back. "I understand this feeling more than you know."

"Well, it's confusing and it would be great if you didn't talk to Mom and Dad about this, please. We haven't really discussed any of it. I've been talking to a nice man, Mr. West, at school. He's working part time to help kids who are sad or confused. He's helping me sort it all out," Michaela finished.

Wow! This day was turning out to be one for the books. First, she's a member of an actual family in her own community. Then, her brand-new niece comes out to her. Finally, she learns that Joe West is her counselor. And he's actually being of help!

"Well, that's a lot to deal with, I'd say. I also think you'll be just fine. Believe me, life *will* get easier as you grow up. And Michaela, you are not alone. Not in any sense."

Brenda reached over and squeezed Michaela's shoulder.

"Brenda! Michaela! Would either of you like some ice cream and cookies?" came Jenny's voice from the open back door. They both nodded in the affirmative.

Brenda was not sure how she was supposed to feel about anything that had happened to her on this day; Michaela looked equally confused. But maybe, she decided, being unsure was okay for now.

After the dessert treats, Brenda glanced at her watch; it was five o'clock. Gracefully excusing herself and promising to meet the family (her family!) on Sunday for dinner, she gathered her things and walked out to her car.

As she was about to open the car door, her phone pinged with a text. Glancing down, she saw it was from Harriet. *Oh boy; I'm not sure I'm ready to cope with this one today.* Driving home, she considered that maybe this was, in fact, the most surprising day she could remember ever having. The phone pinged a second time. Brenda sighed. Common courtesy meant that she needed to respond. *Yes, yes, Ms. Bossy Pants. Be right with you.*

"Ugh."

BRENDA WAS BACK in her own cottage by five fifteen. She read Harriet's short text (*"please call me when convenient"*) and decided that things between the two of them couldn't go any worse than they had in Justin's office. Besides, she'd already had such an odd day, it surely couldn't get any stranger than it already was. She placed the call.

Harriet was most apologetic. She said she had given some thought to her hasty (Brenda thought *underhanded and secretive)* meeting with Justin, and she regretted going behind Brenda's back and giving him part of her new novel.

Brenda knew it was time to come clean about her fears.

"Harriet, I need to tell you about something that has been worrying me for months. Last October, I received an email from an anonymous source identified only as Lovers of Literature. The sender issued a veiled threat regarding my author events. There was a long list of books and authors deemed controversial, and I was further warned not to schedule any speakers who touched on one of a whole list of themes."

She cleared her throat and went on. "Themes included LGBTQ, religious minorities, people of color, and stories about immigration and Japanese internment. To be blunt, I'm fearful that your reading may stir the hornet's nest. Your immigrant family's story is wonderful. But these crazies might use your story as an excuse to escalate their tactics," Brenda finished. This wasn't easy, and she hoped her methodical approach would let her words penetrate Harriet's stubborn skull.

"What? That's terrible, Brenda! As someone born and raised in Chapel Bay, I refuse to allow book censorship to gain a foothold here! I want to help rid the community of such cowardly fanatics," Harriet said, her anger exploding through the phone line. Harriet's vehement tone made Brenda jump.

"But what can we do? My IT department hasn't been able to identify the sender of the email. Justin feels frustrated, too, but we've wanted to keep this quiet so as not to panic the library patrons," Brenda replied.

"I belong to an organization called PEN America. It's a group that speaks out against book censorship all over the world. I'll contact the organization and make them aware of this scheme. And we can find some big guns to help ferret out these so-called Lovers of Literature; I'm sure of it. I'll put my resources together and hire lawyers if need be. I'll help you find other people who can help, too. This will not stand!" Harriet said.

Amazed by Harriet's energy and indignation, Brenda let out a loud "Wow!" Harriet was saying some of the same things she'd heard at the Writing Wrongs Conference. *I never thought the old busybody would be such a kindred spirit ....*

Harriet added, "By the way, you know that *A Wrinkle in Time* is on the list of banned books, right? I couldn't be happier to be sharing it with the kiddos in the library reading circle!"

Brenda smiled involuntarily. Lightening her tone, she said, "Harriet, you don't know how much I appreciate your support. It sounds like we have a lot of organizing to do, and soon! The library is planning to feature poetry by Asian Americans in April for our national poetry month. The Walk of Remembrance, honoring Chinese immigrants who settled in Chapel Bay, is coming in May. That's Asian American and Pacific Islander Heritage Month. I look forward to having you on board!"

It was as if someone had lifted a giant layer of pain from her shoulders. Suddenly, it didn't feel threatening to have Harriet share her immigrant family's story with the public. Yes, there was the worry of censorship. But there was a new layer of protection, a magic shield around her. Now that she knew who her father was and had blood relations here in the community, she felt more grounded. She had a tribe now. In good times or bad, she would never be completely alone in the world again.

"Let's go ahead with the plans you and Justin have made for

your reading. I'll call him on Monday and let him know we had this conversation. I'll tell him about the advocacy group you mentioned, too. Together, I feel we can tackle this censorship attempt," Brenda said, relieved.

She ended the call with Harriet and thought more about her newfound family. So much to process! So many questions! It would take time to fill in all the gaps. How was it that Toshi Kato and George Muramoto cared enough for one another to make a baby, to create *her,* but somehow couldn't form a family? Scott offered an explanation, yet she couldn't stop wondering. Looking at her cooling cup of tea, she considered that love could be like that: starting hot, cooling over time. Strong but also bitter and poorly blended. The heart, she knew, was a delicate organ.

Not all loves are meant to last. Impermanence, right?

22

"Jonathon! Can you talk? Is this a good time? Sorry, I know I usually text before I call."

"Hello, sweet pea! I can talk for a couple minutes, but I have someone picking me up for brunch soon. What's shakin' bacon?" Jonathon was his usual comedic self.

"I've found my family! I mean, I know who my dad was and I have a brother and a niece and goodness knows what else!" Brenda knew she was speaking too rapidly. She couldn't seem to rein herself in.

"Slow down! I thought I was your only brother. You mean there's another one? Does he look like you?" Jonathon's voice seemed to go up by an octave.

"Oh, JB—it's amazing. I got one of those kits from a genealogy website and sent in my spit. Long story short, my half-brother and his family live here in Chapel Bay! My niece, Michaela, has been studying piano with me for a year now. My half-brother, Scott, is chairperson of a local Asian group that I just joined. I just found out yesterday! I know I'm babbling, but this is like winning the lottery!"

"Brenda, honey, I'm so happy for you! This is what you've always wanted. I'm even a little jealous ... your family sounds way more functional than mine! So, what's your next step?" Jonathon asked.

"I'm still pretty much in shock, but it's a good shock … I guess I'll let these warm feelings soak in for a few days and then figure out whether Scott and Jenny can introduce me to more of the Muramoto family. I know Scott has at least one brother. Oh … and I'm going over to their house for dinner tonight!" Brenda said.

"That sounds great, Bren. Listen, I've gotta go now, but didn't you email me that your next author event is coming up this Friday? Maybe I'll take the afternoon off and drive down and we can celebrate over the weekend," Jonathon said, voice finally back in its normal baritone range.

"Oh, that would be super! Okay, enjoy your brunch date. Be nice to him, JB!"

Brenda couldn't help teasing Jonathon. He was nice to a fault. Most of his boyfriends ended up being cute, vacuous men. He had a difficult time letting them go, even when that was what was best. She could use a little dose of that, she thought. *Maybe a girlfriend, even a casual one, wouldn't be the worst thing.*

…

Brenda noted that Sunday dinner was only half an hour away. She dropped by the local grocery and picked up an apple pie. It was going to take a while before she could honestly feel as if she deserved this family; she still had to get used to the idea. Bringing pie felt like a thing a family member ought to do. It was a place to start, anyway.

Heart pounding, she parked the Camry in front of the Muramoto's house. Stunning beautiful purple wildflowers announced themselves from across the street. She didn't know the name of the plant, but she recalled a quote by Ralph Waldo Emerson:

> *Love is like wildflowers; it's often found in the most unlikely places.*

Indeed. Walking up the short path to the front door, every one of her senses spoke to her. The air seemed gentler than usual, giving her the sensation that the atmosphere was offering her a hug. Bird songs blended in a symphony of song. The red front door appeared to glow in the mid-afternoon sunlight. *Love may not always last, yet this feeling, this heart opening, this groundedness—it's an excellent change for the better.*

Jenny welcomed Brenda in and gratefully accepted the apple pie. As the four of them sat down, Scott offered to say a blessing.

"In gratitude for all the bounty at this table, we promise to be kind and gentle to all living beings. May suffering be transformed into peace, and may all hearts be open to the wisdom that naturally flows when we remember we are all truly one."

Brenda thought that this was the most appropriate blessing she'd ever heard. They passed the platters of steamed vegetables, roasted chicken, rice, and green salad. Once everyone had consumed a few bites, she couldn't hold back any longer.

"So, Scott, we talked about our father the other day. What else can you tell me about his life around the time he would have met Toshi? I mean, they both grew up in the Sacramento area. I would have thought that the Kato and Muramoto families would have crossed paths at some point. There weren't that many Japanese in the area at the time, right?"

Scott put down his fork and wiped his mouth with his napkin.

"Here's what I know. Dad was born in 1935. The family owned a grocery store in the area known as Japantown, close to where the state capitol sits today. In 1942, when the orders came for all Japanese to evacuate, he and his mother, father, brothers, and sisters ended up going to Manzanar in Southern California. When they returned from camp in 1945, the store was a complete wreck. So, they started over. Grandpa found a spot on Sutterville Road. That's when the new Muramoto Market got its start," Scott said, taking another bite as Brenda processed the information.

He tilted his head and chewed his food. "But they may have met at the Buddhist Church in Sacramento as young adults."

This jibed with the information Brenda had received from Ruby Yamamoto at the Writing Wrongs Conference. Ruby remembered Toshi had dated a man she'd met at church. But what she really wanted to know was how it felt to grow up knowing who your dad was. *This* dad, *their* dad. It didn't feel like the right time to ask such a question. Brenda wondered if there would ever be a right time.

"Well, considering that Mom and her parents farmed strawberries south of town and went to Tule Lake Camp, it makes sense that the two kids—our parents—might not have known one another early on. You said that Japantown got torn down in 1956 or 57 in order for the new Capitol Mall to be constructed? I'm glad that your—our—grandpa got a jump on things back in '45. They would have had to move eventually, anyway," Brenda said.

"Yes, I suppose that good comes out of bad sometimes. Dad never talked much about life in camp, except to say how dusty everything was all the time. Life in the desert took a toll. Too hot, too cold, soldiers pointing guns at people. And each Japanese person could only bring whatever they could carry. Can you imagine?" Scott said, eyebrows rising.

"I really can't fully grasp how awful it must have been. Mom didn't want to talk about camp either, at least not very often. The humiliation of it all ... it ground people down." Brenda took another bite of food.

"Dad carried a sense of shame, which surfaced as anger from time to time. In some ways, I'm glad you didn't have to deal with that anger, Brenda. Junior and I had to tiptoe around when Dad went into one of his tirades" Scott said, eyes downcast.

Well, at least he wasn't perfect. I still wish I'd known him, but it seems like he had demons to contend with. Maybe his anger scared Mom, and that was another reason she raised me all by herself. Brenda smiled at Scott, then her face clouded.

"I sometimes wonder how much this country has really

changed since then," she said. "I mean, I read that in the late 1980s the internees received $20,000 in reparations money, which is about $40,000 in today's money. But isn't it really too little, too late? And what about the recent uptick in hate crimes against Asians? There's plenty to make us angry now, too," Brenda said.

She paused and looked at Michaela across the table. This was a lot to unload on a ten-year-old's ears.

Jenny came to the rescue, turning the conversation away from the dark side.

"Today, how about just rejoicing that we've found one another at last? I have always liked you so much, Brenda. To find out that you are a Muramoto is like icing on an already beautiful cake! Or maybe the ice cream with a good pie. Let's dig into the dessert Brenda brought!"

After eating, they played a board game and listened while Michaela played a movement of one of the piano sonatas she'd been learning. Acknowledging that she was becoming quite a fine pianist, Brenda rose to leave.

As she drove home in the fading light of the day, a deep peace settled in her heart. *So, this is what it's like to belong somewhere. But ... what if Scott and Jenny don't accept that I am a lesbian?*

Tabling that for the time being, she allowed herself the simple contentment that had eluded her for so very long.

ONCE BRENDA AGREED Harriet could read from her own work, along with her Aunt Elsie's, it was all systems go. Volunteers materialized, catering orders were placed, and the third Friday in March arrived right on schedule. Now fully healed from Covid, Joe manned one of the refreshment tables. He was pleased (and embarrassed) that neighbors and friends came over to greet him and exchange pleasantries. It delighted him that Sally sat in the very front row. She had promised to save him a seat.

Looking around the audience, Joe saw that several friends

from the local chorus were in attendance. He spotted the woman he'd flirted with after the Christmas concert. Beautiful as always, she sported a dark blue pantsuit with a matching pearl necklace and earrings. His singer friend Cassy, the one who'd led him to his counseling work at the elementary school, walked past him and gave his arm a playful squeeze.

Presently, Brenda walked to the front and faced the audience. Those still standing took seats, and conversations ebbed. The Muramotos sat in the center of the second row, smiling broadly. A smartly dressed man with dark curly hair whom Joe hadn't seen before walked in and took a seat in the back. He sat next to a lovely blonde woman with piercing green eyes.

Brenda took a breath and brought the microphone closer to her mouth.

"Good evening, friends. It gives me great pleasure to feature one of Chapel Bay's own literary talents this month. Many of you already know Harriet Conley, who has lived here most of her life. A few months ago, I discovered a cache of poems in a folder."

"By happenstance, Harriet saw the folder of poems one afternoon when we met in my office. Right away, she identified the work as her Aunt Elsie's. I asked her whether she would be so kind as to read some of them for tonight's event, and she graciously accepted. I hope Harriet will send them in for publication, so that others might have ready access to this fine collection."

Brenda paused and gazed at the assembled crowd. Joe had never seen her this happy.

"As a bonus, Harriet will also read from some of her own new writings. Because her new novel is based upon her own family's story, it seems especially fitting that she is including a sample along with Aunt Elsie's poetry tonight. So, with no further adieu, I give you Ms. Harriet Conley," Brenda finished.

Harriet and Brenda, finally on the same side. And I'm no longer persona non grata ... it's a great day. Joe smiled.

∾

DRESSED in black wool pants and a purple sweater, Harriet came to the mic. She watched as Brenda took her seat in the front row. Once the applause died down, Harriet launched into her reading of Elsie's poetry. After each poem, there were nods of appreciation. After she'd completed reading her aunt's work and acknowledged the audience's appreciation, she said a few words before beginning to share a portion of her own new writing.

"I am deeply indebted to Brenda Kato for helping to bring Elsie Star's work to light. Without her, these poems would have remained unread and unappreciated for who knows how much longer. It was such great good luck that we could connect and collaborate to share some of the work with you all here this evening. "

"Now, I'm honored to get to read a small sample of my own newest work, as yet unpublished."

Adjusting the wire-rimmed glasses on her nose, Harriet regaled the audience with a portion of her tale. Fifteen minutes later, she took her glasses off, put the pages aside, and looked up at the assembled gathering. The applause was loud and long.

The feelings of acceptance, finally being seen by her hometown literary community, were like an elixir. It had taken years for her to be rid of the old "you aren't one of us" tapes, and this reading, this "coming out" to her community was a balm on old wounds. *I belong. Chapel Bay is really my community, my people.* Wiping a tear from her eye, Harriet stepped out to greet her new fans.

∼

AFTER THE READING, people filtered toward the refreshment tables; old friends reconnected. Jonathon stood off to the side and waited patiently while Brenda made her way through the crowd, shaking hands with friends and patrons. Harriet stayed at the front, sharing laughs and hugs.

Jonathon acted as though he had a sudden need for cookies and coffee, and he walked to the refreshment area.

Just then, Brenda saw a familiar presence positioned off to her right. *It's Tara Winslow—and she isn't with anyone!* Tara held her hand up to her face in the universal "call me" sign. Brenda smiled and lifted her index finger, making her way over to Tara's side. They chatted while others continued to mingle. Jonathon beckoned Michaela over to the table of sweets, and Joe smiled at her as she selected several chocolate chip cookies.

Excusing herself from Tara for a moment, Brenda walked up behind Harriet and put a hand on her shoulder. Just then, Joe came out from behind the table of goodies. With tears in her eyes, Brenda enclosed Joe and Harriet in a warm embrace. Scott Muramoto, standing just off to the side, loudly proclaimed the evening a great success.

Thoughts of finding her "new" family, excitement that Jonathon had made the trip from San Francisco, pleasure at the thought of getting to know Tara and perhaps becoming more than friends ... quite a lot for which to be thankful! And, starting next week, it would be time to firm up commitments from poets for the April event.

Chapel Bay, Brenda decided, was not such a bad place to call home. Looking over her shoulder, she was sure she could see her mother smiling at her. Relaxing, she smiled back.

23

A week after Harriet's reading, Brenda sat in her office inspecting the names of poets she'd confirmed for April's Meet the Author event. With Justin's support, she'd invited the most diverse group of poets ever assembled in Chapel Bay. The list included Asian Americans, African Americans, and several members of the Latino community. Two of the poets belonged to the LGBTQ community as well.

Harriet's offer to help uncover the bigots who wanted to ban books and authors from marginalized communities was genuine. So far, ten members of local writing groups had joined forces under her leadership; they'd already placed an editorial in the local paper. The piece informed the public of the threat posed by those who would deny others the right to be represented in print. Harriet also recruited Joe West. He was organizing school librarians and teachers to march in a rally to bring books related to race, gender inclusion, sexuality, and religious freedom into schools and public libraries. Brenda felt truly lucky to have the support of her townspeople.

Brenda's phone rang, bringing her back to the here and now. Joe's name appeared on her screen.

"How did you know I was just thinking about you, Mr. West?" Brenda asked.

Joe told Brenda that Sally had learned from a friend on the Chapel Bay police force that Franklin's death was accidental. "The person who hit Franklin clearly had no idea who Franklin was. The driver was a tourist from Miami, Florida, running late for a wedding reception on the other side of town. She was doing fifty in a fifteen mile-per-hour zone."

"Oh, I see. Just between the two of us, I would venture to guess that some in the community suspect the driver hit him on purpose," Brenda said.

I suppose I will never know if he was the Lover of Literature who sent me the threatening message.

Brenda asked Joe about the driver. "How can the police be *sure* it was an accident? Maybe Franklin had pissed the woman off. He was famous for doing that to people everywhere he went."

Joe hesitated before answering. "Brenda, all I can tell you is this. The woman driving the car was only eighteen years old, and had been out of the country attending boarding school until six weeks ago. This was her first time in California, her first time in Chapel Bay. Authorities will bring her up on charges of involuntary manslaughter. I just honestly can't see how she would have known Fargo."

Brenda agreed that Franklin's demise sounded like the result of an accident, a case of a drunken man struck down by a combination of his own inebriation and a young woman's poor judgement behind the wheel. They ended the conversation with a discussion of Joe's work recruiting people to get involved in Poetry Month. Joe asked for names of poets who might speak with students in the schools.

"Hey, I'm retired," he said, "and I support what you're doing with diversity. Bullies are the worst! I have time on my hands, and I'm ready to take them down!"

After the call, Brenda opened her emails and read one from Justin. An attachment listed his choice of books for the poetry month display. It was a model of inclusiveness. She hoped that the eager groups of anti-censorship crusaders would be loud enough to drown out the voices of any dissenters. She winced at the memory of the article about neo-Nazis attacking a library staffer less than one hundred miles from Chapel Bay.

Expecting book lovers to make lots of noise seems rather oxymoronic. Brenda laughed aloud at her own joke. At least there were two more weeks until April's events rolled around. With any luck, the next fourteen days would find even more folks spreading the word that censorship was NOT welcome in Chapel Bay!

Brenda looked at her watch. Ten minutes until noon. *Crap, I need to get out of here—I'm meeting Tara for lunch!* Adrenaline made her heart race; she grabbed her bag and headed for the door.

It looked like everybody in town was eating lunch at Jack's Diner on this sunlit Friday. Brenda scanned the restaurant crowd and finally spotted Tara sitting at a table facing the bay. She had a moment to admire Tara in profile. *Her good bone structure is a beauty to behold! High cheek bones and a well-formed chin with lush, full lips in between ....* The moment passed, and the women made eye contact across the room. Brenda walked to the table wearing a smile that radiated all the way through her body and down into her well-polished toes.

"Hi there. How long have you been waiting?" she asked.

"Long enough to work up a real hunger," Tara replied.

Brenda felt herself blushing. It had been years since she'd felt this giddy with someone. Desire had trickled through her once or twice when they'd met on runs, but this was different, more exhilarating and freeing. Tara arched an eyebrow and tilted her head to one side, a smile slowly spreading across her perfectly symmetrical face. *I could get lost in those green eyes, and swim there for days.*

It may have been a few minutes or half an hour before they ordered and got their food. Brenda didn't know. She didn't care. Breaking eye contact for a minute, Tara looked at Brenda's leg and asked her how it was healing.

"Oh, that. I've been stretching and doing walk-runs for the past month. I may be ready for a nice run soon," Brenda said.

"I'm glad to hear that! We can finally have the run date I'd hoped for! Running alone isn't nearly as entertaining as being with a partner, particularly when she looks as good in spandex pants as you do, Brenda," Tara said, winking.

"Oh, my. Such a compliment, especially coming from a woman who so clearly knows her glutes from her quads," Brenda replied, relaxing into the banter. "In fact, I have a new pair of shoes I'm dying to try on the trail. Do you think you can keep up with me?" she asked, reaching her hand across the table.

Tara took Brenda's hand and placed it between both of her own. They spent a moment taking in this first expression of intimacy, no words necessary. Between the talking, eating, and hand holding, an hour passed without either of them noticing. As they parted, Brenda headed back to the library. Tara walked back down the street to the marine biology lab, where she worked as a research scientist.

Brenda was sure that they would have many more long lunches in the upcoming days and weeks. *I hope it goes beyond lunch.* She wasn't sure she'd ever stop smiling.

IT WAS A BRIGHT, sunny Saturday morning. Brenda was glad to have time alone. So much had happened this week, this month, this year. Dreams of a future with the Muramotos had replaced the nightmares she'd had about searching for her father. Her many suspicions of other people, especially those she'd once considered peculiar, were nearly gone. Sometimes, she feared her heart would explode, like it had grown three sizes larger.

She'd yet to speak with Scott and Jenny about her identity as a lesbian. *Do they already know?* Even if they knew, she needed to be sure about them. Sure that she was safe, that her whole person was welcome in the family.

"But how can I do that?" she wondered aloud. "What if they don't already know, or they know and are trying to ignore that I'm gay?"

And, of course, there was the question of being able to support Michaela. She wanted to do so without causing tension between herself and Michaela's parents. *This is really complicated! I never considered the "and then what" part of finding my family.*

Brenda saw she had time to walk to the Dharma Center for the weekly talk, and she laced up her shoes and headed out the door. The walk would do her some good, and the meditation would get her mind to focus on something other than the new challenges of family life. She crossed Barnacle Street and made a mental note to stop at Mallory's for a coffee and snack on her way home.

The uphill part of the walk made her wish she had stretched her quad muscles before heading out. *Between the shock of finding my family and having a date with Tara, I'm distracted as heck; it's no wonder I forget little things like stretching.*

Fifteen minutes after leaving the house, she was standing on the front porch of the Dharma Center, removing her shoes. Once she had taken her seat, she saw Scott on a nearby cushion. He was obviously enjoying the peacefulness of the room. She didn't disturb him. The rinpoche appeared from a side room and took his place at the front of the room, next to the large and ornately decorated altar.

A talk on the Paramita of Generosity followed the meditation. Brenda remembered her commitment to help in the local food pantry. Once the service ended, Scott turned and noticed Brenda behind him. He smiled broadly, brown eyes warm and shining. They hugged.

"Brenda! It looks like you and I are both turning into regulars here. Hey, do you want to come for lunch tomorrow?" Scott asked.

"Sure, brother! What should I bring?" Brenda replied.

"Jenny's making pasta, so a green salad would be wonderful.

We'll see you between one and one thirty, okay?" he asked, tilting his head to one side.

"Sounds like a plan! Looking forward!" Brenda said as they walked out the door together.

That evening, she called Tara. They discussed Brenda's coming out dilemma, weighing the options of saying something now or waiting until more time passed. Given everything that she was currently juggling thanks to the upcoming author event, National Poetry Month, and her own personal security concerns, they agreed it was best for her to wait at least a month before addressing her sexuality with her newfound family.

"Besides," said Tara, "you realize people will see the two of us out around town together and tongues will wag. You might let gossip do your job for you!"

Brenda chuckled at this, then allowed the humor to carry her into a more serious question she'd been wanting to ask of Tara.

"Speaking of people seeing others around town, I've been wondering about something. My friend Jonathon and I—you may have met him at Harriet's talk—we were having brunch at The Rainbow Café one morning a couple of months ago. We saw you there, too, and a redhead came to your table. You kissed. Is she an ex-girlfriend?"

"Oh, no! Robin is my oldest pal from my school days. She and I came out at the same time thirty years ago. We've never dated; we're like sisters. I can't wait to tell her you thought she and I were together! She will laugh so hard!" Tara said, giggling.

Brenda laughed, too. This woman had definite possibilities.

～

THE FOLLOWING DAY, Brenda assembled a green salad for lunch at the Muramotos. As she was slicing the carrots, her phone rang. It was Harriet.

"Hello, Brenda? I'm sorry to bother you on a Sunday, but this couldn't wait," she began.

Brenda laid her knife on the cutting board and sat down. *Best not to be holding a sharp object when important news is being shared.*

"Hey, Harriet. What's going on?" Brenda asked.

"I just got off the phone with a district attorney in San Jose. They've identified the source of Lovers of Literature! Their so-called anonymous threats stopped being anonymous when a hacker finally unmasked them," Harriet said, rapid fire as usual.

"Okay, okay ... who ARE these jokers? Don't keep me in suspense, Harriet!"

Harriet sighed. "I was just getting to that, Brenda. Before I say more, you'll be interested to know there was a connection between Franklin Fargo and the hate group, and not in the way you may think. Despite his craziness, his poor behavior, and his reputation for causing others misery—maybe even because of this —he played a role in solving the mystery. Franklin knew about the Lovers of Literature, even knew who the local point of contact was. He tried to stop them."

She went on. "The district attorney I spoke with said that Franklin placed a bug in the home of a local individual, the former mayor, if you can believe that! He got proof of the ex-mayor's involvement with the group. I have my hypothesis about why he was in the house and why he planted the bug. He had a history of blackmailing women with whom he had affairs, and my guess is he was trying to see whether the husband already knew about him and the wife. I'll bet he was trying to see whether it was worthwhile extorting her. The recordings provided evidence for the authorities." Harriet stopped to take a breath.

"Long story short, the police learned the mayor was actually the ringleader! It turns out that he had orchestrated several other anonymous threats to libraries and had hooked at least one other unsavory character, a man with priors for breaking and entering, into his little ring of hate. Police suspect others are involved, and the investigation is ongoing.

"Once they knew the name, they turned it over to the district attorney. From there, it was just a matter of issuing a warrant and confiscating his computer. They've charged him and he's in jail, awaiting next steps. The other individual is being sought even as we speak," Harriet finished.

"Oh, my lord! That is the best news I've heard in months, Harriet! I can't wait to tell the other library staffers in Chapel Bay. So funny that Franklin's nefarious activities produced something good in the end! The folks I met at the Writing Wrongs Conference will be relieved to hear the good news as well. Some of them received threats from this criminal as well. So many of us have suffered!"

"Yes, I was sure you would want to hear the news right away. Of course, that doesn't mean that other similar groups won't keep up their evil doing. But it's a win! I'm taking it!" Harriet's glee was contagious.

"Thank you, Thank you, Harriet! You are a true gem. Let's get together for a celebratory glass of wine sometime this coming week, shall we? My treat!" Brenda said.

"I accept your kind offer, friend. Enjoy the rest of your day!"

Brenda resumed her salad prep, stopping after she had chopped each ingredient to recite a mantra of thanks. *Wait until I tell Tara!*

On the way to the Muramoto's, Brenda made a pit stop at Mallory's Magic Brew. She hoped Mallory had made strawberry scones, hoped that there were four left over after the morning rush. She was in luck; the last four sat in the front pastry case, unclaimed. Grabbing the bag of sinfully delicious goodness, she got back into her Camry and drove the rest of the way up the hill to her family's home. *Family! I can finally say the f-word!*

While parking the car, she saw something new on the front lawn. She got out and stepped closer. It was a sign. There, in front of the charming little house, a house she had come to love more and more over the past month, stood a symbol of inclusiveness.

IN THIS HOME WE KNOW:
WOMEN'S RIGHTS ARE HUMAN RIGHTS
NO PERSON IS ILLEGAL
BLACK LIVES MATTER
SCIENCE IS REAL

AND THERE, in rainbow colors:

LOVE IS LOVE

AS SHE WIPED a tear from her cheek, Brenda knew, felt in her bones, that her many struggles had been worth enduring. Yes, there would be more challenges ahead; that was how life worked. But she'd found out who her father was, found family, and found a possible new love. She looked forward to a brighter future. Chapel Bay had wrapped its arms around her, and she felt safer than she'd imagined was possible.

A familiar voice brought her out of her reverie.

"Hey, Aunt Brenda, stop dawdling! We're starving in here!"

"Coming, Michaela!" Brenda replied.

Maybe I'll eat dessert first today!

THE END

THANK YOU!

Thank you for reading *Chapel Bay Secrets*. I would love it if you'd leave a review of the book on Amazon and Goodreads! Honest reviews help other readers discover my book and help me continue to improve my skills as a writer. If you are part of a book club and would like questions for discussion, visit my website: https://juliesniderauthor.com.

To receive updates on my writing, occasional gifts, and insider information for readers and writers, please subscribe to Julie's Writing Newsletter by scanning the QR code below.

MORE ABOUT THE
JAPANESE INTERNMENT

On February 19, 1942, when President Franklin D. Roosevelt signed Executive Order 9066, Japanese Americans suffered a terrible injustice. The U.S. government incarcerated over 117,000 individuals—both first generation (Issei) and second generation (Nisei)—in one of the 10 prison camps, euphemistically called "Relocation Centers."

I first visited the Tule Lake National Monument a number of years ago. A feeling of shock followed by revulsion crept into my consciousness. As I looked at the primitive barracks, the barbed wire surrounding them, and the watch towers, I wondered: *How could this have happened in the America I love? Why was I never taught about the Japanese American camps as a schoolchild?*

I learned that Camp Tulelake became the temporary home of the so-called "worst of the worst" Japanese Americans in the camps, the ones deemed disloyal as a result of answers to two of the questions on a form given to all detainees. For more information on the Japanese American internment, conditions within the camps, and the present day work being done to bring the injustices to light, please visit https://Densho.org.

ACKNOWLEDGMENTS

This book would not have made it to the final stages without the help of many people. I'm grateful for the guidance and editing of developmental editor Cris Beam. Patiently working through several revisions with me, she helped me keep the weave of characters and themes flowing.

My beta readers—Cirre Emblen, Debra Manion, and JB Maerten—provided critical feedback in the middle stages of writing. Copy editor Amanda Royal went above and beyond in helping shape the final text. I'm so lucky to have found her. Proofreader Luanne Oleas spent hours detecting errors in my final copy when I could no longer see what was on the page versus what I imagined was there.

Karen Phillips made a gorgeous cover design, and I'm beyond thrilled with the results!

The early morning writing group to which I belong has given me a ton of inspiration and support, and the friendships that have arisen from the group enrich my life on a weekly basis. California Writing Club, Sacramento Branch has provided solidarity in the writing trenches. I've learned so much from the members. The six other women with whom I collaborate on Substack have been supportive of the writing I've done while preparing Chapel Bay Secrets for public consumption and several were on my advanced reader team. I'm so grateful!

Finally, I thank my wife, Tina, for her support and love during the creation of this book. Being married to a writer is a difficult path, and I owe her everything for sticking with me.

ABOUT THE AUTHOR

Julie was born and raised in Ohio and always thought she would be a concert violinist. As time went by, her curiosity took her beyond the world of classical music. In her thirties, she received a teaching credential and began teaching science.

Twenty- six years of working with middle and high school students whetted Julie's appetite for writing something other than lesson plans. When she retired in 2021, the call to tell stories grew louder. Julie also writes nonfiction essays, poems, and short humorous works that appear in various places on the internet and on her Substack site.

You can find links to all of Julie's writing at her website: https://juliesniderauthor.com or by scanning the QR code located here: